Leaning
into the
Curves

Leaning into the Curves

A novel by
NANCY ANDERSON and
CARROLL HOFELING MORRIS

DESERET BOOK

Salt Lake City, Utah

This book is a work of fiction. Although there is an organization named Temple Riders Association, the characters, trips, and incidents in the book are the product of the authors' imaginations or are represented fictitiously.

Library of Congress Cataloging-in-Publication Data
Anderson, Nancy, 1950–
   Leaning into the curves / Nancy Anderson and Carroll Hofeling Morris.
     p. cm.
   Summary: When Hank retires, Molly's life is turned upside down. After he buys a motorcycle and joins an LDS motorcycle group, Molly starts making some changes of her own.
   ISBN 978-1-60641-235-0 (paperbound)
   1. Retirees—Fiction. 2. Mormons—Fiction. 3. Temple Riders Association—Fiction. 4. Motorcycle clubs—Fiction. 5. Motorcycle touring—Fiction. 6. Domestic fiction, American. I. Morris, Carroll Hofeling. II. Title.
   PS3601.N5444L43 2010
   813'.6—dc22
                                          2010001648

Printed in the United States of America
Malloy Lithographing Incorporated, Ann Arbor, MI

10 9 8 7 6 5 4 3 2 1

*To men and women everywhere who have discovered
that there's a lot of life to be lived after retirement age.*

*You have reinvented yourselves, enriched your relationships,
served others, and grown spiritually.*

And you have had fun doing it!

Thanks for setting great examples for us to follow.

Acknowledgments

To the Temple Riders Association, a unique and wonderful group that inspired *Leaning into the Curves*; to members Tom and Eileen Kenney, Nancy's neighbors, for the hours they spent talking to us; to Tom for taking Carroll on a ride on their Gold Wing; to Temple Riders members who contributed through e-mail interviews: Drew Hanson, Chris Udall, and especially Cindy Gillman. To Mark Hendricks (not a TRA member) for being an invaluable resource and taking Carroll on an exciting ride to Arivaca, Arizona, where she interviewed other riders. To our brother, Leland Hofeling, whose own story of buying a Gold Wing and whose many pertinent suggestions helped give the motorcycle passages an authentic feel.

To Lael Littke, our coauthor on *The Company of Good Women* series, for her insightful comments during the writing process; to the presenters and participants of the past two LDStorymakers Writers Conferences for the information, inspiration, and community they provided; to Nancy's daughter, Keri, for proofreading the book yet another time. Finally, and most important, our deepest thanks to family and friends who support us in doing what we love to do. Blessings on you all.

Chapter 1

Saturday breakfast on Monday was Molly's first clue that life after her husband's retirement really was going to be different.

She'd gone down to the Stay Out Room that morning to fetch some ribbon and paper to wrap the silly gift she'd bought him, an "I'm Retired" version of a handicapped parking permit.

Too bad I can't levitate, she'd thought as she stood in the doorway. The plastic box holding her wrapping paper and ribbon was in the built-in cupboards on the far wall, and piles of finished, almost finished, and abandoned projects covered the floor between her and the shelves.

She scooped up a mound of the yarn she'd purchased when half the women in her ward had been knitting dressy scarves on fat needles. She tossed the leftover, brick-hard clay from her Native American art project into the trash can by the door. She was trying to figure out where to shove a pile of textbooks from the many classes she'd taken when her favorite weekend smell, frying bacon, wafted down the stairs and tickled her nose.

That could mean only one thing. Hank was at the stove, preparing his cardiac special: eggs, extra-thick bacon, and pancakes with blueberry syrup.

Only it wasn't Saturday, it was Monday. And not just any Monday. It was Labor Day and the first day of Hank's retirement from his job as an environmental engineer at Kennecott Copper—a coincidence she knew he considered a fine irony.

He must be fixing it to celebrate, she thought. She backed carefully out of the room, shut the door, and took the stairs up to the kitchen two at a time.

Hank stood in front of the stove, pancake turner in hand. Except for wearing his Saturday Chef apron, he looked the same as he had every Monday morning for as long as she could remember. He'd showered and shaved—she could smell his citrusy cologne—and combed his still-thick gray hair back from his forehead. He was dressed as if for work in creased chinos and a collared cotton shirt, and he had the stance of a man with something to accomplish.

"Morning." She put her arms around him from behind as he flipped a pancake. "Happy Labor-slash-Retirement Day."

"Thank you, ma'am," he said, tossing her an air kiss over his shoulder.

She rested her cheek against his back and gave him the double squeeze that was her way of saying, "I love you and I'm glad you're here." A wrestler in high school and college, he had a wiry frame she'd always thought was a perfect fit for her petite stature. He'd gotten love handles in middle age that his exercise routine had never fully banished, but she didn't mind. She rather liked them.

He put the last pancake on the platter and turned to face her. "Do you realize this is the first time I haven't been gainfully employed since I was thirteen? That was the year my dad died and the old uncs gave me a job at the Mancuso Auto Shop."

With her index finger Molly calculated the math in the air. "Let's see, sixty-five minus thirteen equals . . . Wow. You've worked for over half a century."

"No wonder it feels strange not to have someplace to be or something to do."

He turned back to the stove and started to make the scrambled eggs. She began setting the table for two. She didn't normally eat much for breakfast during the week, usually a smoothie or yogurt and toast. But since this was a special occasion, she decided to eat what he'd prepared and work it off later.

She put a half gallon of milk on the table, wondering how her husband would handle this abrupt transition. His whole adult life had been focused on work and family. He hadn't developed an interest in any hobbies or connected with a group of buddies to do things with. When she'd asked him what he planned to do next, he'd said, "Maybe I'll make a list of all the things I've wanted to see and do but haven't had time for. Even if I check off one adventure a day, I figure there will be enough on my list to keep me busy the rest of my life."

That had seemed strangely vague, coming from her plan-ahead, live-by-the-numbers husband, but Molly hadn't pushed him to be more specific. Now she wished she had. *Change is coming,* she thought, *and it makes me nervous. Hank may have retired from his everyday schedule, but I haven't.*

As a stay-at-home mom, Molly had centered her life on her children. Laurel, the daughter she still struggled to understand, was their firstborn. After her came Wade, the son Molly knew so well that he once accused her of eavesdropping on his thoughts. Each step the two had made toward independence had been like a highway sign letting Molly know she was getting closer to the day they wouldn't need her mothering the way they had when they were little.

That had allowed her to ease into a new phase of her life. These days, it was structured around her family, friends, church, the classes she loved, and performances at her parents' dinner theater. It hadn't been easy to make the adjustment, but she was in a good place now, and frankly, she didn't want Hank rocking her boat.

They tucked into the big breakfast he'd cooked. While they ate, the conversation centered on the upcoming retirement celebrations: the family dinner Molly had organized for that evening and the open house on Saturday.

"I'm glad you made reservations at Lugano's." Hank poured himself a second glass of milk. "We haven't been there for a while and it's my favorite place to eat."

"I don't know how you're going to make room for a big dinner after this breakfast."

"I can always make room for food that tastes like my mother's cooking. Now, what are we going to do for the rest of the day?"

Here it comes, Molly thought. "Is there something on your adventure list you'd like to do?"

"It's nice weather. We could take that Lake Bonneville hike you've been talking about ever since you had that class on Utah geology."

The hike ran across the foothills of the Wasatch Range along what had been the shoreline of the ancient Lake Bonneville. It offered great views of Salt Lake and opportunities for bird watching. "I'd love to," she said. "I'll bring my camera along." She'd recently signed up for a class on how to use digital cameras, and she was eager to take some photos using what she'd learned.

They spent longer than they'd anticipated on the trail, so they were pressed for time when they returned to their three-bedroom rambler off Creek Road in Sandy to get ready for their evening out. Even with Molly putting on her makeup while Hank drove to Lugano's, they got there with only a few moments to spare.

Laurel was waiting for them when they walked inside. Thirty-eight and single, she was a litigator in a firm focusing on corporate law. "Happy retirement, Dad." She gave Hank a hug and then linked arms with him as he told her how he'd spent his day.

They're a pair, those two, Molly thought. Although Laurel had inherited Molly's blonde, blue-eyed looks, she had inherited her father's careful, thoughtful personality. Her stunning eyes, which were emphasized by her short precision haircut, could be affectionate but were mostly cool and assessing.

Wade and his family arrived right behind them. He was tall like Molly's father but dark like Hank's side of the family. His grin was pure Wade. He held open the door for his pregnant wife, Heather, and their three children. Lisa, the oldest at age eleven, was followed by Hayden, nine, and five-year-old Katie. After a flurry of greetings, the whole group followed the hostess into the dining area.

Molly could tell carrottop Hayden was itching to tell her and Hank something. He bounced on the seat of the family-size booth with barely contained excitement, and he kept looking at his father as if asking for permission.

Finally Wade gave his son a nod. "Go ahead, tell them."

"We got a four-wheeler today! Dad took us for rides on it. It's wicked bad!"

Molly gaped. "Wade! How could you do that? You know how I feel about anything resembling a motorcycle. If it doesn't have—"

"Four wheels and a hardtop, it isn't safe. I know, Mom. You've been telling me that since I was fourteen and wanted a scooter."

"It does have four wheels, Grandma," Lisa said earnestly.

"And we have hard-tops." Hayden's eyes danced. "Our helmets!"

The fact that Wade had discussed her fear with his family and then done the very thing he knew would trigger it left her speechless.

She'd been only six years old when a motorcycle gang had pulled into a rest stop where her family was having lunch after a gig. The throaty rumble of the machines and the rough look of the riders had terrified her. Her fear was exacerbated when, years later, she was the first to arrive on the scene of a bloody motorcycle accident near her and Hank's starter home in Murray. Over time, her fear became part of who she was. Sometimes months or even years went by without her feeling the slightest twinge of it, but then some sound or sight would poke it awake, setting her heart pounding.

"It's a work vehicle, Mom, not a souped-up street cycle," Wade said reassuringly. "I'll only use it around the farm and for going back and forth to the theater." Both Molly's parents and Wade's family lived on the homestead where the Finley Family Theater was located.

Heather patted Molly's hand. "Don't worry. Wade will be careful. Especially when the kids ride with him."

When the kids ride with him? Molly was tempted to launch into all the reasons why that should never, ever happen, but this was Hank's night, and she didn't want to spoil it. Summoning every ounce of her self-control, she nodded and changed the subject.

Hank himself brought it up again on the way home, saying how useful the ATV would be on the farm. When she tried to express her concern about Wade's purchase, he said, "Come on, Molly. That's an old horse. Isn't it time you let it die a natural death?"

Except for dinner out, Monday set the pattern for the rest of the week. First Hank got ready for the day as if he were expected at the office. Then he made a hot breakfast, which grew increasingly more elaborate. When they were finished eating, he asked the question, "What shall we do today?"

By the time Friday dawned, Molly felt as though her life had been preempted. While she'd enjoyed their outings, she'd had to cancel a movie afternoon with her best friend, Micheline Uttley. The laundry was piling up, and she could have written a novel in the dust covering her dining room table.

Hank seemed unaware of the havoc his plans were wreaking on her daily schedule. *Is this going to be the way the rest of my life goes?* Molly wondered. *Stuffing myself with gigantic breakfasts every morning and then doing whatever activity he's come up with? If it is, I might as well sign up for Weight Watchers right now and get a running start.*

The thought made her shudder. Hank's adventure-a-day plan was not working for her, and sooner rather than later she was going to have to tell him. Could she do it without hurting his feelings? Perhaps. Early in their marriage, she'd learned that if she used a light tone and kept her expression pleasant, he would be more likely to listen to what she needed to say.

She was contemplating how to approach him when he called, "Molly, breakfast's ready."

She joined him in the kitchen. After a week he was still dressing as if he were on his way to work. Somehow she'd had the idea he might switch to jeans and a T-shirt and maybe go without shaving once in a while.

Guess not.

He'd outdone himself making breakfast this time. In the middle of the table was a platter of bull's eyes—eggs over pork and beans over toast, a dish he'd learned to like on his mission to England. He pulled out a chair for her and then took his own seat while revealing his plans for the day. "The Mt. Nebo loop should be beautiful this time of year. If we leave by nine, we can be back by suppertime."

Another whole day lost sent Molly's plan for the light approach out the window. "Honestly, Hank. Retirement isn't six Saturdays followed by a Sunday."

"No? That's exactly how it feels."

"I hope you're not thinking we're going to do the same thing next week. And the week after that."

"Why not? The kids are grown and on their own. The house practically takes care of itself."

Molly didn't know whether she should make a scene or make an appointment to have his cognitive skills evaluated.

"The children may be grown, but the house does *not* run itself," she said with exaggerated sweetness. "Meals do not spontaneously generate, and the laundry does not show up clean and folded in your drawers by magic. You may have retired, but I haven't. I still have a schedule, and I need to get back to it. And to my normal breakfast."

Hank looked from her to the platter and back again. "I take it you don't want to eat this."

She laughed in spite of herself. "I'll eat it if you promise not to cook breakfast tomorrow."

"But tomorrow's Saturday."

"Hank!"

"Just kidding."

Molly enjoyed the bull's eyes, though she ate only part of what was on her plate and felt like a stuffed toad afterward. She also enjoyed the drive over the Mt. Nebo loop Hank had planned for them. But their unfinished conversation niggled at her. They had to come to an understanding about their life post-retirement, and soon.

Heavens to Murgatroyd, Molly thought, using one of her father's favorite phrases. *What am I going to do with that man?*

Chapter 2

There was no time for a reprise of the "Retirement and What It Means to Me" discussion the next morning. There was too much to do to get ready for Hank's open house. "From 1:00 to 3:00 P.M.," the invitation read. "Roast and Toasts at 2:00."

Hank had requested the open house after having attended one for a colleague, Dallin Sager. Molly's mind had immediately gone into planning mode. She loved to entertain, and her parties were lively affairs like those her entire family was known for.

Hank's response to everything she proposed was "No."

No to the fancy decorations. No to the party favors. No to Wade doing a roast, and a polite but double no to a performance by the Finley Family Fiddlers. Molly belonged to a family of professional musicians who were always delighted to perform at each other's events.

"Just food, family, and friends," he'd said.

Feeling rebuffed, she'd scratched out all her ideas but one. "Okay, if that's the way you want it. But the roast stays in."

Neighbors began arriving midmorning with the outdoor furniture Molly had asked to borrow, and they stayed to help with the setup. She was directing the placement of the tent that was to shelter the buffet tables when Laurel arrived with deli trays of spinach rollups and mini ham sandwiches from Harmon's grocery store.

Micheline followed close on her heels with dessert trays from the bakery. She'd been friends with Molly ever since she'd introduced herself at church, explaining that no, she wasn't named after the tire company. "Micheline is the female version of Michael in French. My mother picked it out of a book of baby names."

When Micheline put her load of trays on the counter, Laurel started laughing. "Look at you two. You're wearing matching outfits. *Again.*"

Molly looked at her friend and giggled. They were both wearing khakis and a red shirt.

It wasn't the first time they'd dressed alike without prior consultation. With the same taste in clothes and chin-length frosted hair, they were often taken for sisters even though their facial features weren't all that similar. Molly's round eyes and button nose were more Kewpie doll, while Micheline's almond eyes and straight nose were Barbie doll.

Time was running short when Molly put Laurel in charge so she could shower and dress. While applying her makeup, she talked to God. It was an informal conversation like those she'd been having with Him since she was a little girl. *Thank you for helping me pull this together. Hank's worked hard his whole life, and his retirement should be celebrated. Bless everyone who comes. If it pleases Thee, keep the sun shining and the wind low.*

Wade and his family were the first to arrive, along with Molly's parents, Roy and Bess Finley. Roy, ruddy and bald, wore his usual plaid sport shirt and jeans, the latter held up with suspenders. He towered over Bess, whose pure white hair was coiled atop her head for extra height.

"Well," he boomed, his hug lifting Molly's toes off the ground. "Today's the big day."

After them came Molly's two sisters and their husbands. The sisters were frosted blonde like Molly, but that's where the similarity ended. Hope was formal in demeanor and dress, and June, tall like their father, was a plaid-shirt Mother Earth type. They were both more serious than Molly, who'd been tagged as The Giggler from the time she was little. And the one with the fastest fingers on a fiddle.

The steady stream of guests that followed—neighbors, ward members, and Hank's business associates—kept Molly and Hank occupied. They were standing together when Bruce Aldridge, a younger colleague who lived in their stake, arrived with his wife, Lori. Bruce had always struck Molly as being self-absorbed and a bit vain, and it took all her self-control to stifle a snicker at the new hair plugs that poked out of his scalp like clumps of grass.

Bruce shook Hank's hand, and then Lori handed him an African violet in a glazed purple pot. "Happy retirement."

"Uh, thanks for the thought." Hank gingerly accepted the gift.

Lori chuckled at his reaction. "It's symbolic. My dad took up raising African violets on a whim after he retired. Now it's his passion. This is one of his cuttings."

"Are you sure you want to give it to me? I'll probably kill it."

"I'll see that he takes care of it, Lori," Molly said. She was putting it on the table where cards and gifts for Hank were piling up when the Sagers approached her.

"Where is the man of the hour?" Dallin asked. "I guess congratulations are in order."

Molly sent him in Hank's direction, thinking his tone of voice sounded anything but congratulatory.

"I hope for your sake Hank handles retirement better than he has," Dallin's wife said. "He's having a hard time getting off the fast track. He's always trailing me around, wanting me to find something for him to do." She looked to where Dallin had Hank cornered in conversation. "I'd better get over there before he convinces your husband his life is over."

At two o'clock, guests started filling the chairs that had been clustered around a makeshift podium for the roast. When everyone was seated, Wade stood to welcome them. "As you know, my father retired a week ago after working more than thirty years at Kennecott Copper. There are two things he's going to have to figure out now. Who the boss is, and what a day off is."

Molly looked at Hank, holding her breath. She relaxed when he chuckled.

"Who is the boss in your family, Hank?" called Micheline's husband, Cal.

"Who do you think?" Hank shot back to appreciative laughter.

I was right to keep the roast in, Molly thought. The afternoon was turning out to be a great success, even without the frills and fiddlers.

Only the presence of Hank's family would have made the celebration better.

Not that she'd expected any of them to make the trip. His mother and step-father lived with Hank's sister, Helena, in Cucamonga, inland from Los Angeles, and age and infirmity kept them close to home. They hadn't forgotten the occasion, however. The night before, Hank had enjoyed a long talk with them. And that morning, a huge bouquet of flowers and a package of silly retirement gifts from Hank's old uncs had arrived after breakfast.

By three o'clock the crowd had cleared out except for a few guests and family members. They sat in a circle of chairs enjoying a quiet conversation and nibbling on the remains of the deli platters in the lull before cleanup began.

"What plans have you made for your retirement, Hank?" asked June's husband, Matt.

"None, really, except to make a list of the local destinations I've never been to. Molly and I already checked off some last week."

Molly saw an odd look cross Laurel's face.

"Aren't you going to volunteer at a hospital or be a mentor at a school?" Laurel asked. "Habitat for Humanity would love having you work on their houses."

Wade answered before Hank could. "Maybe Dad doesn't want to go from one set of obligations to another, Sis."

"I for sure didn't." Cal stretched his legs out in front of him and crossed his ankles.

"That's the truth," Micheline said. "I remember asking him what he was going to do with his time. He said, 'Whatever I want.'"

"I can't imagine Dad ever saying something like that," Laurel said.

"I can't either," said Scott, Hank's ex-boss. "I'd wager that in all the years Hank and I worked together he never even took the fifteen-minute breaks he was entitled to by law. You wait and see. He'll be back in the saddle before you know it."

"Hear, hear. Retirement isn't all it's cracked up to be." Dallin's voice was sour. "Enjoy today, Hank. It's all downhill from here."

Put a sock in it, Dallin, Molly thought. *Hank doesn't need to hear something like that when we're supposed to be celebrating a new phase of life. I don't either.*

~

The morning after the open house, Molly didn't feel her usual Sunday contentment. The get-together had been a great success, but echoes of the dire predictions made by Dallin and Scott had made for a restless night. Was it possible that instead of entering the clichéd golden years, life after work for Hank would go steadily downhill?

Judging from her parents' active life, it didn't have to be that way. But then, they'd never completely retired. Even after Wade had taken over the management of the Finley Family Theater in Lehi, her parents were still involved in both planning and performances. Hank's old uncs, Leo and Phil, were also enjoying life as octogenarians, but they hadn't hung up their working hats for good either. They still checked in on the Mancuso Auto Shops periodically and held court at the Cucamonga shop most Saturdays.

Maybe Scott is right, Molly thought. *Maybe for Hank to be happy, he'll have to be doing some kind of work. It's like what Cesar Millan says about dogs.* (Watching reruns of *The Dog Whisperer* was one of Molly's feet-up, diet-soda indulgences that Hank's adventure-a-day had been getting in the way of.) *They've got to have a purpose.*

What she needed to be happy was some time to herself. She told Hank as much after their lunch of leftovers when he laid out his plans for Monday—a full day at Temple Square.

"Can't we skip a day? I've got a ton of things to catch up on. Besides, tomorrow's Bean Night at the farm, and we're singing, remember?"

Bean Night was a monthly family gathering at the farm that included potluck and a family home evening presentation. This month Wade and Heather's family was responsible for the program, and their kids had requested that Molly and Hank sing "Tell Me the Stories of Jesus."

"How is that supposed to work?" Hank had grumbled when she

told him. "You're going to sing and I'm going to . . . what? Clap to the rhythm? Shake one of the kids' tambourines?"

"You take the melody and I'll sing the harmony. You can do it. You used to sing with me when we were courting," Molly reminded him. "You impressed Dad when you said music in the home was on your must-have list."

He grinned. "I married you so you'd take care of it, and I'd never have to."

He'd practiced reluctantly with her several times before preparations for the open house had taken precedence, but she had the feeling now that he was looking for a way out.

As if on cue, he said, "Do I *have* to do this? Why can't it be a sing-along?"

She played her trump card. "I cut out having the Finley Fiddlers at your open house because you asked me to. You can sing with me on Bean Night because the kids asked us to."

When he grumbled, she added, "You sing tomorrow night and I'll go with you to Temple Square on Tuesday. In fact, how about I keep my Tuesdays and Thursdays free for whatever adventure you plan?"

They left for the farm at five thirty the next evening. When Hank took the Lehi exit and headed west through a new housing development bordering the farm, she leaned forward as if she were trying to move him along faster. "I love Bean Night."

With an exaggerated western twang, she started singing the silly words her mother had put to Annie's refrain from the Irving Berlin song "Old Fashioned Wedding," her fingers tapping out the rhythm on the dashboard of the car.

"It doesn't matter if it's *kid*ney beans or *li*ma beans or *pin*to beans. It doesn't matter if there's *ham* hock or *on*ions or *home*made bread. It doesn't matter if there's *ice* cream or *ap*ple pie. As long as we're together, what's for dinner doesn't matter at all."

"Beans for dinner," Hank muttered when she finished. "How do you Finleys turn privation into a party?"

It was a question Molly had heard repeatedly over the years, and she'd given up trying to answer it. No matter what she'd said, Hank had never understood how the hearty navy bean soup Molly's mother made during hard times had become a favorite that her family associated with togetherness and fun. The dishes his mother had made with the cannellini or cranberry beans used in Italian recipes were associated in his mind with the grim year after his father's death when he'd felt it was up to him to keep the family afloat.

Nor had Hank been able to understand the casual attitude Molly's parents had toward money. He'd been appalled when he had learned her father's system for managing theater funds. Roy stuffed bills due in the right-hand drawer of his desk. In the left-hand drawer he put theater profits, paychecks from odd jobs, and the occasional windfall donation from someone interested in promoting the arts. At the end of the month he applied whatever funds were in the left drawer to the expenses in the right. When he ran out of funds, he simply shut both drawers and turned his attention to something else.

It drove Hank nuts. Thinking he was being helpful, he set up an accounts receivable system for his father-in-law, complete with ledgers, file folders, and charts showing when bills were due. Roy was grateful for his interest and praised his ingenuity. But after three months of struggling with the paperwork the new arrangement required, he'd given up and gone back to the two-drawer tally. "If it ain't broke, don't fix it."

"No wonder your parents do country songs so well," Hank had said in exasperation. "They live the lyrics."

Molly knew Hank appreciated the fine qualities her parents had, but he had always kept a distance, as though he feared their chaotic lifestyle might be contagious. She was secretly hoping the performance tonight might make him feel more a part of the family. The thought made her smile as he drove through the gate over which hung a painted wood sign proclaiming "Finley Family Theater."

At the end of the lane stood the barn Roy and Bess had turned into a venue for the popular country music evenings that showcased members of their talented family. A younger generation of Finleys and other cast members now commanded the stage, but Molly, her sisters, and their parents were always part of the Christmas and Independence Day programs.

To the left of the theater stood the family home, a rambling one-story log cabin with porches all the way around and a river-rock chimney. The private parking area between the cabin and the barn was full of cars.

"Looks like the family's out in force," Molly said.

She was reaching in the back for her casserole when she heard the *rummm-rummm* of a revving motor. Looking in the direction of the sound, she saw a camouflage-painted ATV coming toward them on the lane that went to Wade's house. She gasped as it flew over a bump and the child in front of the driver shrieked with delight.

Molly's involuntary shriek came almost at the same time. She put her hand over her wildly thumping heart when the ATV pulled to a stop in front of her and Hayden pumped the air. "Rad!" he said.

Wade turned off the engine and removed his helmet. "Hi, Mom. Dad."

"What are you *doing* on that thing?" Molly cried.

"Heather sent me home to get ground sage for the soup. Hayden wanted to come along."

"I meant the way you hit that bump."

"I wasn't going fast enough for it to be dangerous." Wade dismounted and sent Hayden to the kitchen with the sage. "Wanna give this baby a try, Mom? It won't bite."

"Don't tease your mother, Wade," Hank said. "You know she's never going to do that."

Molly appreciated Hank's support. Her fear of motorcycles and anything similar had become a family joke, but it wasn't funny to her.

Then he ruined it by saying, "But I wouldn't mind going up the lane once."

He reached for the handlebar, and Molly grabbed at his sleeve. "No way. Everybody's waiting for us inside."

The long great room of the cabin was full of people, conversation, and activity—a happy chaos Molly loved but Hank found wearing. She put her casserole on the serving table and then went into the kitchen where her mother and Heather were adjusting the flavor of the soup. The aroma that wafted from the large pot made her mouth water.

"I heard you met the latest member of the family," Heather said.

Molly's eyelid twitched. "I suppose there's no chance you can send it back where it came from."

"My sentiments exactly," Bess said. "Soup's on. Ask your dad to call people to the tables."

The meal was a noisy affair, with numerous interruptions as the children took turns calling the family to attention by clanking their silverware against their glasses and then telling jokes. Wade had started doing that when he was in seventh grade, and it had become a regular part of the evening. Molly would have enjoyed it had it not been for the continual references to the ATV parked outside. She was glad when Roy made his usual announcement. "Cleanup first, and then family home evening."

"Aw, Pops," the children complained, but even the youngest helped clear tables and load the dishwasher while the adults put away folding tables and pulled chairs into a loose circle in front of the fireplace. After a song and a prayer, it was time for Wade's family to give the lesson.

Now that the focus was off the ATV, Molly settled back to enjoy watching her grandchildren take the stage. But Hank's increasing nervousness kept diverting her attention. When she squeezed his hand, she found it slick with sweat. *He really does hate doing this.*

"Now comes the best part," announced Hayden, whose innate showmanship made him a natural as the MC. "My sisters and I asked our grandpa to sing with our grandma—*and he's going to do it.* Come on, everybody. Give it up for Hank and Molly Mancuso." With a flourish, he waved them up to the front of the room.

Molly kept hold of Hank's hand as they sang, hoping he would know from her touch how much she appreciated him doing it. She was delighted when the song went off without a hitch and was about to tell him how proud she was of him when he held up his hand to quiet the applause.

"In case you think this is the beginning of something," he said,

"I want you to write the following down in your journals: Tonight, Hank Mancuso sang, and then announced it was his last performance."

Molly was caught between surprise and grudging admiration at how neatly her husband had squashed any further plans to get him to perform.

"You mean you're not going to start a new career as a singer?" Roy kidded. "You've got to do something now that you're retired."

"Anything but that," Hank said.

After the closing prayer, Roy draped his arms around Hank's and Molly's shoulders. "That was a great party on Saturday. Mother and I especially enjoyed hearing about those jaunts you two have gone on. I don't think she and I ever went anyplace that wasn't hitched to a paying gig."

"Maybe you should try it," Molly said.

"It sounds fun," Bess replied, "but I wouldn't want to do it every day."

Laurel spoke from across the room. "That is a bit much, isn't it? All work and no play may make Jack a dull boy, but all play isn't such a good idea, either."

Molly slipped her arm through Hank's and gave him a little hip bump to show she was on his side. "Maybe not, Laurel," she said, looking at her daughter. "But a couple of play days a week can't hurt."

To start, she amended mentally. *Then maybe I can get it down to one.*

Chapter 3

The trips Hank planned for their adventure days were to places he knew Molly would enjoy visiting. She appreciated him trying to please her, and it was fun to see the historical and geological sites she'd only heard about in her classes. She also got a kick out of impressing him with odd bits of information she'd learned, frequently prefacing them with "I took a class . . ." But there was always something niggling in the back of her mind: Church sisters she needed to visit, class assignments to finish, e-mails to catch up on, a special day she'd promised to spend with Lisa.

Sometimes they invited Cal and Micheline to go along with them. Together they climbed to Timpanogos Cave, enjoyed a sunset cruise on the Great Salt Lake, and took a tour of Antelope Island. In preparation for that trip, Molly looked at her notes from a class on Utah history and printed out the most interesting information.

"Did you know the causeway was originally built in 1969?" she asked as they drove over it, "and that the park service reintroduced antelope in 1993?"

The scenic loop on the island took them through a landscape of wild beauty, inhabited by more plants, wildlife, and birds than she'd thought possible. When they caught sight of the resident buffalo herd, she said, "Did you know that the buffalo were brought here way back in 1893? And that the island is an important stop for migrating birds? I took a—"

The rest of her sentence had been blotted out by laughter.

Molly had given up resisting the changes in her life and was finally settling into their new schedule when Hank threw her a curve ball.

Instead of presenting the itinerary he'd designed, he said, "If you don't mind, I'd like to stay home tomorrow. Enjoy a lazy day."

Hank enjoying a lazy day was such a foreign concept that Molly laid the back of her hand against his forehead to check his temperature. "You're not coming down with something, are you?"

"I'm not sick; I'm just ready to do something different."

"What about the rest of the week? Should I keep Thursday cleared?"

"Hmm. No, I don't think so."

Molly was dumbfounded. "Wait a minute. I've reordered my life to go on your jaunts Tuesdays and Thursdays. And now you announce you're 'ready to do something different'?"

"What can I say? I'm reordering my life too."

The next day he retreated to his office, where he spent hours with his feet on his desk and his nose in a current trade journal or a book. That's the way the whole week went, with Hank seemingly bent on moving everything from his to-read pile over to his have-read pile as quickly as possible.

"It's too weird. After weeks of adventuring, he's holed up in his cave," Molly told her sister, Hope.

"You're complaining? It wasn't that long ago you were frustrated because he was dragging you from one place to another."

"But at least I knew the drill. Now I have no idea what to expect. Who knows when he'll poke his head out of his lair or what he'll want to do then. It's like I'm in limbo, and I hate it."

"Well, don't think you have to stay home just in case he gets a burr under his saddle. You have a life, too."

"It doesn't seem like it. I'm always wondering how he's feeling and what he's going to do next."

A few days later, Hank emerged from his office.

Molly thought he would go back to his adventure list, but instead he took to following her around all day, questioning everything she did. "Why are you doing it that way? Wouldn't it be better if . . . ?"

She'd been amused when Dallin's wife expressed her frustration at the way her husband hovered around her all day long. But she wasn't amused in the least when Hank hung over her shoulder while she used

Photoshop to alter an old picture of Micheline she'd scanned into the computer.

"Isn't it cheating to remove the tree coming out of Micheline's head?" he asked.

She spun her chair around, eyebrows pulled together in exasperation. "If you're so interested in this, why don't you take a class?" She picked up the latest course catalog and thrust it toward him.

Hank glanced at it briefly before putting it back on her desk. "Classes aren't the answer to everything, Molly."

Maybe not to you. Classes had been Molly's lifeline, providing the knowledge she'd missed by not getting a college education and helping her learn the skills she needed to be a good wife and mother. She was surprised Hank didn't realize that.

"Then what do you want to do?" she asked with exaggerated politeness.

He perched on the edge of her desk. "Try new things. Only I don't need a class, just the materials and the instructions. You've got plenty of both in the Stay Out Room."

Molly had claimed the downstairs room when she and Hank had first moved into the house. She'd been thrilled to have a place for her sewing machine, paints, and craft supplies. A place where she could leave a project out until she was finished working on it—all she had to do was shut the door. The Stay Out! sign had been added years later when Molly caught Lisa and Hayden in her room squeezing paint from tubes onto pieces of expensive watercolor paper.

Hank's request felt like an invasion of her space. "It's called the Stay Out Room for a reason," she said. "Nobody goes in there without supervision."

"Aw, come on, Moll," he wheedled. "I'm not going to tangle up your yarn or eat something toxic."

She was about to give him a big no when she realized that giving him a yes would get him out of her hair. "Tell me what you're interested in doing, and I'll set you up."

"How about letting me look around until something catches my eye."

The thought made her clench her teeth, but she led him down the stairs and opened the door to her room. "Put things back where you find them, okay?"

He grinned slightly, and she realized how silly that must have sounded to him, given the piles and stacks on the tables and floor.

It took great determination not to shadow him the way he'd been shadowing her, and an extra dose of it not to check the room when he came upstairs later in the day. *What is he up to?* she wondered. *Which of my supplies is he using? Has he left things where they were?*

She learned the answer to the last question several days later when he called her down to the Stay Out Room to see what he'd created. He sat in front of her craft table, the floor around him so clean she could see what color the carpet was.

"What did you want to show me?"

He slid his chair to one side to reveal his creation. It was a sculpture made of bright yellow Play-Doh from the grandchildren's art box. "What do you think?"

It wasn't vegetable or mineral, that much was clear, which left animal.

"It's pretty good for a—" The sculpture had a head, four legs, and what was either a fifth leg or a tail. She took a guess, crossing her fingers, "—horse."

"It's not a horse." Hank sounded offended. "It's a dog."

She swallowed a laugh. "Oh, I see it now. Not bad for a first try."

He began picking up the bits of Play-Doh from the table. "This is a waste of time. I don't have any hidden talents. I'm not going to start a second career unless it's as a greeter at Walmart."

Molly patted his back fondly. "Hank, dear, how did you think you'd fill your time when you retired?"

"I don't know." His shoulders slumped. "I didn't realize until now how important work was to me. I miss it, Moll. I liked having challenges—tackling a hard problem and solving it. I felt useful. Needed. And maybe even a little important."

Molly had always thought of Hank as the most self-assured person in the world. *I don't understand*, she thought. *How can it be that he doesn't feel useful or needed?*

"Maybe you need a change of scene," she said. "How about visiting your mom? You always said you would spend more time with her after you retired."

He brightened. "That's a great idea. When do you think we should go?"

She hadn't intended to go with him, but it had been some time since she'd visited the folks in Cucamonga. "How about over a weekend? That way I wouldn't miss any of my classes."

Molly's reluctance to go to Cucamonga had nothing to do with Hank's immediate family. She'd always felt comfortable around his mother, Ruth, and his stepfather, Joseph, in no small measure because they were longtime Church members. The rest of the Mancuso clan was another story.

A small-town Utah Latter-day Saint girl, she'd had virtually no experience with people not of her faith when she was first introduced to the old uncs, who enjoyed their cigars, wine, and beer. To say nothing of colorful language. She'd tried to emulate the acceptance shown by Hank's parents and his sister, Helena, but she always felt out of place and uncomfortable when she and Hank visited. So she was a tad anxious when she and Hank arrived at the Ontario airport two Fridays later.

They'd entered the baggage claim area when a wide-shouldered man with dark, slicked-back hair hailed them. He held a gray chauffeur's hat in one hand and a sign with the name Mancuso in the other.

It was Helena's son, Freddy.

Freddy greeted Hank with a handshake and a clap on the shoulder. Then he kissed Molly on both cheeks. "Man, it's great to see you two."

"What's with the hat? And the sign?" Molly asked.

"As long as I'm driving you, I thought I might as well act the part." He tipped his chauffeur's hat and bowed slightly. "Uncle Leo sent me in his 1941 Lincoln Continental. Shows how much he thinks of you."

Molly saw the resigned look in Hank's smile at the reference to the very tall pedestal Uncle Leo and Uncle Phil had put him on. It dated from the time of his father's death, when he'd taken on being the man of the family. After that, a line of family firsts had kept him there. He'd won scholarships for undergraduate work at UCLA and grad work at BYU, notable achievements for a boy from the steel mill town of Fontana. He'd been the first Mancuso since the family had arrived in America to land an upper-echelon, white-collar job.

Although many of his cousins and their children had achieved successes of their own, Hank's position on that pedestal was a matter of family lore. *There's no way he'll ever get off it*, Molly thought.

After they'd claimed their luggage, Freddy led them to a deep green convertible with a heavy grill, flying-woman hood ornament, and white sidewalls.

Molly laughed at the sight. "Do you provide bulletproof vests for passengers? This car looks like you swiped it from the set of *The Godfather.*"

"Uncle Leo loves it when people say that." Freddy stowed their luggage and opened the passenger door. "Who gets the front seat?"

"You take it, Hank," Molly said. "That way you two can catch up while I enjoy the drive to Cucamonga."

Molly had gotten up very early that morning, so she leaned back on the sun-warmed cushions and closed her eyes while listening to the men talk. She liked the way Hank's voice sounded when they visited his family. It was warmer, and he laughed more.

"How are the Mancuso Auto Shops doing these days?" Hank asked.

"Purring right along. Your cousin Lennie and I are running the old Fontana shop. Uncle Phil handed the Cucamonga shop over to Chester and his boys. But the uncs still make surprise visits every so often, and they spend Saturday afternoons in the back room in Cucamonga."

The mention of the back room brought back memories to Molly. She'd seen the original in the old Fontana shop, a '50s-style gas station on what had been Route 66. Even knowing how much time they spent in it, she'd still been surprised to see it had been completely recreated in the sleek, modern Cucamonga shop, with battered table, old leather chairs, out-of-date calendars on the wall, and an ancient coffeemaker. There were always some Mancuso men from all four generations gathered there on Saturday afternoons, while the old uncs drank bad coffee and talked about classic cars and NASCAR races.

She hadn't intended to fall asleep, but the motion of the car lulled her into napping. When she opened her eyes, Freddy was parking in the driveway of Helena's trilevel house. A moment later, Helena and Russell came out to greet them. It was easy to see that Helena and Hank were related. They both had the dark Mancuso eyes, strong chin, and, much to Helena's oft-stated dismay, wide shoulders.

Helena gave Hank a hug and then pulled Molly into a squishy embrace. "I don't know how you stay looking so young. What's your secret?"

"I'll tell you, if you tell me the secret to living with a retiree," Molly said.

"Nothing to it." Helena flashed a grin at Russ. "Give him something to do that gets him out of the house for hours at a time."

"So that's why you've been sending me on wild-goose chases." Russ turned to Hank. "Sometimes I think she has me looking for items that don't actually exist."

Laughing, everyone followed Helena into the house. When they entered the living room, Ruth rose from her favorite chair, holding onto a walker for stability. Molly could see the effort she'd made to look her best for them. Her cheeks and lips had a hint of pink, and her wispy white hair was curled becomingly. Joseph, who stood protectively at her side, had a fringe of equally white hair that made Molly think of the man behind the curtain in *The Wizard of Oz*.

"Henry dear." Ruth rested her fragile hands on Hank's shoulders and held her face up to receive his kiss. Then she gave Molly a hug that was as light as a whisper. "Molly dear."

Molly smiled, knowing that she and Hank would be called "dear" more in the next few days than in the last half year.

When greetings had been given all around and everyone was comfortably seated, Helena said, "I hope you don't mind, but I told the family to give us some time alone today. We'll see them all at Lennie's barbecue tomorrow, so they forgave me."

"Is there anything planned for Sunday?" Hank asked.

"The old uncs wanted to take you to the classic car show in San Bernardino," Freddy said, "but Grandma Ruth reminded them that we Mormons don't do that sort of thing on Sunday. So they came up with an alternative."

Hank's cocked his head. "What might that be?"

"They've invited everyone to go on an afternoon ride," Freddy said. "I'll be driving the car I picked you up in today, Chester's got the 1938 Cadillac, and Lennie the 1962 Austin Healey." His eyes shone with glee. "They figured you wouldn't mind if we drove by the show. Slowly. Veeerrryyy slowly."

Ruth shook her head with an indulgent smile. "The old show-offs."

Shortly before noon the next day, Lennie and his wife, Sue, met Hank and Molly at the door of their Mediterranean-style home and led them through to the lushly planted outdoor living area where other guests were gathered. They were all making small talk when Molly heard the sound of old men's voices and hoarse laughter ending in alarming coughs. It was punctuated by high, wavery female admonitions. Uncles Phil and Leo and their wives had arrived.

Molly used her fist to stifle a hoot when they shuffled onto the lanai. They were both bent and bald, and the plaid pants and cardigans they were wearing looked like they were from the '70s. After shaking Hank's hand, they kissed Molly's cheeks. The wives, coiffed and ruffled, with daubs of rouge that drew attention to their pleated cheeks, fluttered around her with expressions of delight.

While Hank and Molly answered the questions fired at them by the uncs, Sue and a granddaughter made the rounds offering wine coolers and beer to adults, and soda and lemonade to the minors and the Latter-day Saints. This was one part of their visits that always made Molly uncomfortable. She tried not to look disapproving, but she was afraid it showed in the line of her mouth, because everyone seemed careful and even a little apologetic around her.

They treat me like a guest, not like a member of the family. I wonder if that's the reason why. It's not just because I'm a Latter-day Saint. Ruth and the rest of Hank's immediate family are too.

Lunch was a leisurely affair that lasted until nearly two o'clock.

Then Uncle Phil stood and said, "It's time for the *signori* to adjourn to the office."

"And for the *signore* to head to the living room for Mexican Train," Sue said. "The kids are going to take care of cleanup."

Mexican Train was a domino game that could be played while chatting, which is why the older women liked it. Molly had learned it could also be played while thinking about something else. While she tried to come up with a strategy to rid herself of her dominoes, she mused on the ways that the Mancuso uncles were like her father. They were committed to family, loved a good party, and had never stopped working.

Poor Hank, she thought. One day he'd been gainfully employed, the next day he wasn't. One day he'd been putting money into his retirement funds, the next day he was taking it out. No wonder he felt like he had the bends.

When the men returned for cake and ice cream at four, Lennie was bursting with news. "Guess what? We got Hank on a motorcycle."

Molly swallowed a gasp. "He wouldn't do that. He promised."

He'd made the promise after the motorcycle accident in front of their Murray, Utah, home. Hearing a dreadful crashing sound, Molly had hurried out into the street to see the next-door-neighbor boy crumpled underneath his motorcycle, a delivery truck almost on top of him. She screamed "Call 911!" to another neighbor, and then swept up Laurel, who had toddled after her.

When the EMTs arrived, Molly retreated to the steps of her house, not wanting to see or hear what was happening. She was horrified to think that if she hadn't asked Hank to stop for milk on the way home, he could have been the one lying senseless in the street.

Hank and his Suzuki street bike had come as a package. When he was just starting his career, he rode it to work during good weather even though she didn't want him to. "Look at it this way," he said. "It's me on a motorcycle or you without a car."

She'd worked hard to suppress the panic every time he left for work on it, but by the time the ambulance pulled away with the neighbor boy, lights flashing and sirens blaring, it had full rein. When Hank turned into their driveway a few minutes later, she flung herself into his arms, pouring out the gruesome details.

"That could have been you. We have two small children. They need their father. I need you. Promise me you'll never get on a motor-cycle again," she'd cried. "Never, ever, cross your heart." She'd stopped short of saying, "and hope to die."

A promise is a promise no matter how many years have passed.

Freddy broke into her thoughts. "You want proof?" he asked, hold-ing up his cell phone. "I took a photo."

She pulled it closer so she could get a better look at the image, and sure enough, there was her husband astride a Harley. "Hank?"

He looked abashed. "Sorry. I had the chance and—"

"All of us Mancusos have our bikes over at the shop for their yearly tune-up," Lennie explained. "There were—how many would you say, Freddy?"

"At least seven."

"Well, the minute Hank saw them, all he wanted to do was talk motorcycles. Who owned which bike, what trips we'd taken lately. You should have seen his face when I told him he could take my custom Fat Boy for a spin."

Freddy gave Hank a slap on the back. "I think you better watch out, Molly. He looked like a man in love."

Hank put his arm around her. "I'm sorry, Moll. I only went around the block, and I was wearing a helmet."

It didn't sound like a big deal, but for Molly, Hank getting on a motorcycle was worse than Wade buying the ATV. She was about to tell him so in no uncertain terms when she realized that all the Mancusos were watching her with eager eyes. *If I say what I want to, they'll think I'm a nut case. Or they'll joke about it the way Hank and Wade do.*

So she decided to make light of it. "Far be it from me to stand in the way of true love."

Chapter 4

After they returned home from Cucamonga, Molly expected Hank to go back down to the Stay Out Room. Instead, he organized his toolbox and began a hunt for things to repair.

"Does he really fix things?" Micheline asked when she came to pick up Molly for a walk. "Or make such a mess you have to call a repairman?"

"Oh, he fixes them. Yesterday he adjusted the lawn mower, and he won't even be using it for the next six months."

Just then Hank came in from the garage, toolbox in hand. Molly gave Micheline a knowing grin. "What are you up to?" she asked him.

"There are a few things I need to take care of downstairs."

"Come to my place when you finish," Micheline kidded.

All through their walk, Molly kept wondering what Hank was working on. He'd had something in mind, she was sure of that, but he hadn't wanted to say what, and that made her nervous. Coming home to a quiet house didn't do anything to allay her concerns.

"Hank?" she called. When he didn't answer, she clattered down the steps into the old playroom, hoping to see him working on the treadmill. He wasn't there. He wasn't in the laundry room, either. Full of trepidation, she opened the door to the Stay Out Room.

Hank was sitting in front of her tipped-over sewing machine. Her expensive, computerized, repaired-only-by-the-Sewing-Machine-Doctor sewing machine. The one she'd mentioned in passing needed to have the bobbin timing adjusted. His repair kit was open on the table beside him, and one hand was holding a screwdriver poised over the bottom plate.

"Henry David Mancuso!" she shrieked. "What are you doing?"

His hand froze. "You said the bobbin timing needed fixing. I watched what the Sewing Machine Doctor did when he was here last. It didn't look that hard. "

He moved the screwdriver ever so slightly and she reacted without thinking. "Stop right now! Keep that screwdriver where I can see it and move away from the machine."

Startled by her vehemence, he scooted his chair back, hands held high. The sight of him looking like a suspect in an episode of *Law and Order* was so bizarre, a giggle escaped Molly's lips.

He stared at her like she was certifiable, but then she saw a glint of humor in his eyes. "Am I under arrest?"

"No. But if you'd ruined my sewing machine, I would've had to take you in."

"On what charge?"

"Felony fiddling, I think. I know you were trying to help, Hank, but fixing the bobbin timing is tricky. I prefer to leave it to the pro."

He dropped his hands. "Guess I'll have to find something else to work on."

Hank wandering around the house with his toolbox was the definition of dangerous. Molly checked her watch. "It's close to lunchtime. I was going to take some photos up Big Cottonwood Canyon for my photography class. Fall colors, water shots. Why don't you come with me? We could have lunch at Silver Fork Lodge."

"Sounds good. I love their Reubens."

⌒

The ride up Big Cottonwood Canyon was one of Molly's favorites, especially in the fall when the red and yellow of fall leaves stood out in sharp contrast to the deep green of the pine trees. She loved the rugged mountains, the lively creek, and the biting mountain air that made her glad for her jacket.

Hank drove, which allowed Molly to scan for possible photos. "Pull over, quick!" she said whenever something dramatic or unusual caught her eye.

"You sure you wouldn't be better off walking up the canyon?" Hank asked when she asked him to stop for the fifth time.

"I know I'm being a pain, but I like the way the creek meanders through the willows here. I'll make it fast, and then we'll go eat."

She was looking for the most artistic frame when she heard the roar of motorcycles coming up the canyon. Without thinking she swung her camera around, turning the setting to action as she did, and began taking photos. The riders were moving too fast for her to notice details, but the impression she got was of older riders, mostly couples. A bearded man on a "tricycle"-type vehicle. A woman on a bright red machine. At least she thought it was a woman, but the long gray braid could have belonged to a man as well.

When the last of the group (*gang* was how she thought of them) rounded the curve, she turned back to the creek. After the excitement of the action shots, the landscape before her seemed flat, and she climbed back into the car.

"Did I see you taking pictures of those riders?" Hank asked. "I'm surprised, knowing how you feel about motorcycles."

"We're supposed to shoot whatever looks interesting, not just what we like."

A few minutes later they rounded a corner and Silver Fork Lodge came into view. Molly squinted as reflected sunlight hit her eyes. It was glinting off a row of motorcycles parked in front of the café. "Oh no. That's all we need, a bunch of gray-haired juvenile delinquents messing up our peaceful lunch."

"Not all motorcyclists are Hell's Angels, Moll." Hank found a parking spot east of the café. They had to walk back past the motorcycles to get to the front door, and Hank slowed his pace to admire them. "Those are some nice machines." Then he stopped short. "Who would paint pink flames on a Harley? That's bad and wrong."

"I think a woman was riding that one."

"Of course. It's a chick bike."

They walked through the entry area of the rustic lodge into the dining room, where a low-burning fire filled the room with the smell of pine. The riders sat at several tables pulled together in front of the fireplace.

"Rats," Molly said. "They not only took our parking space, they stole our table."

"We can sit over here." Hank pointed to a table by the windows with a view of the mountains.

Molly sat with her back to the riders. She tried to ignore them while she and Hank waited for their Reubens, but their loud voices and laughter irritated her. "I wish that bunch would hold it down."

"Don't mind them," Hank said pleasantly. "They're no different from us—just nice people enjoying a ride up the canyon for lunch."

"If you say so." She glanced over her shoulder. The jackets that hung over the chair backs caught her eye. They all had the same logo in the center back with the letters TRA.

Hank noticed it too. "I wonder what TRA stands for?"

"Totally Raunchy Adults?"

Hank chortled. "I don't think so."

"Terminally Regressed Adolescents?"

"That's not nice," he said, but he was smiling. "Look, here come our sandwiches."

For a while the group at the other end of the dining room took second place to lunch and the beautiful mountain view. Then Hank said, "I think I've figured out who rides the red Harley with the pink flames. That woman at the end of the table. The one with the long braid."

Molly cranked her neck around. "What makes you think so?"

"Look at her nails."

Even from where Molly sat, she could see that the long, red nails had pink detailing on the tips. "I bet you're right. They look like they're painted to match that bike."

"Why do women like those claws, anyway? How do they manage everyday tasks with them?"

"Couldn't tell you." Molly looked at her own nails, kept short for violin playing. "What kind of a woman do you suppose she is?"

"Probably somebody's grandmother."

"It's possible. Theoretically." She gave the woman with the gray braid an appraising glance. "I bet she's a dog groomer. Think of the mats she could untangle with those things."

"Think of the nits she could pick."

"Are you referring to primate grooming practices? Yuck. Maybe she's a flower child who never made her way out of the '60s."

"That's a lot of years to be locked in a time warp. Whoever she is, I doubt she's bored." Hank lifted his water glass. "Here's to Nails, who's clearly found a way of life that floats her boat and a group of congenial friends to enjoy it with."

"Nails. That's good."

Molly raised her glass to clink his, but her thoughts had snagged on what he'd said and how he'd said it. "Are you bored, Hank?"

"Sometimes, but I'll be fine. Don't worry about me."

As if that were possible.

~

As it turned out, Molly didn't have to worry about him. Not long after their lunch at Silver Fork Lodge, he two-stepped into the kitchen to tell her he'd had a call from Scott, his old boss.

"He needs me to come in on a contract basis to redesign a tailings pond and work on a couple of other projects. I'll start tomorrow."

"That's one way to solve the problem of what to do when you're retired," she said. "Go back to work."

"You won't miss me. You'll be too busy now that you're gearing up for the holiday show."

Their whole married life the holiday season had been about the Finley Family Theater rather than her and Hank's personal celebration. From late October through Christmas, Molly was either rehearsing for or performing in the show that ran Wednesday through Saturday from the day after Thanksgiving until Christmas Eve. This year, she and her sisters would be playing "My Favorite Things" with the "grands" and "great-grands" who fiddled, as well as accompanying various singing groups. She'd also been asked to do solo spots on a set of Western holiday songs.

Molly and Hank slipped easily back to their usual winter schedule.

He left early in the morning to miss rush-hour traffic on the way to work. She put something in the Crock-Pot on rehearsal days and headed out for the theater before he came home. He was often in bed by the time she returned.

Thanksgiving at the theater didn't offer a break. Bean Night on adrenaline, it was the jumping-off point for the holiday show. With the help of kitchen staff and volunteers, a turkey dinner was served to everyone who had anything to do with the show, as well as anyone the Finleys knew who didn't have a place to go. Those not performing were the audience for the dress rehearsal that started shortly after the traditional pumpkin pie and whipped cream.

"Nice show," Hank commented when they finally started for home late that night. "The audience loves you. And your fingers are as fast as ever."

"You're sweet to say so," Molly said, eyelids drooping.

They didn't see each other much for the next two weeks. Then one day Hank came into the kitchen as Molly was putting supper in the Crock-Pot. "What are you doing home?" she asked. "I didn't think I would see you until I got back from the performance tonight."

Hank put his briefcase on the countertop and took off his coat. "I had a meeting with Scott after lunch to go over what I've done for him. Seems I've worked myself out of a job."

"Oh. I'm sorry, Hank. I know you've enjoyed being back at work."

"It was good while it lasted." Hank flipped through the mail, sorting out the bills. "The money was good too. I won't be getting my final check for a month or so, but it will be a nice chunk."

"Just in time to pay off the Christmas credit card bills," Molly joked. She saw the expression on his face before he turned to get milk from the refrigerator, and she hurriedly added, "Better yet, you could use it for something for yourself."

"I don't need anything."

And I don't want anything, either, Molly thought in perfect time with him saying it. She'd heard it often enough that she'd known it was coming. He was nearly impossible to shop for on Christmas, birthdays, and Father's Day.

"I've been doing some Christmas shopping whenever I have a spare moment, and I've got everyone taken care of but you. Give me some help here. What would you like to find under the tree?"

"A motorcycle?"

"Pffft. Don't let those Totally Raunchy Adults put ideas into your head. Give me a real answer, or I'll have to guess. Like always."

He didn't, so she got him a subscription to *Scientific American* and the DVD of *Planet Earth*. He seemed genuinely pleased by her choices when he opened his presents on a quiet Christmas morning, just as she was pleased with the gift she'd purchased and wrapped for herself. Years earlier, after he'd bought her yet another present that was almost but not quite what she wanted, he'd suggested she should buy her own gift. That way he wouldn't have to shop, and she wouldn't have to return.

But the best present she received was the safe arrival of Junie, the cute baby girl Heather and Wade named for Molly's sister. The second best was having the holiday program over. She didn't like to think she was getting older, but the demanding schedule, plus the time she'd spent with Heather and Junie, made her uncomfortably aware that it was true. She was glad she had a chance to rest before she and Hank spent New Year's Eve with the Uttleys.

Micheline had made the plans that year. After watching *The Bucket List*, a movie they'd talked about viewing together ever since it came out on DVD, they were going to go downtown to take in some of the New Year's Eve celebration. Then they would enjoy a late supper at The Roof, a premier buffet restaurant atop the Joseph Smith Memorial Building.

Everything Molly had heard or read about *The Bucket List* had led her to believe it was a comedy, so she was surprised at how teary she got at the sad parts and its tender message. The way Hank squeezed her hand during the scenes of last wishes and final good deeds told her he was feeling it too. She wanted to talk about it, but conversation went a different direction when Micheline hurried them into their coats and gloves for the drive into the city.

The atmosphere downtown was festive, and holiday lights and falling snow added to the beauty of the scene. Molly enjoyed walking arm in arm with Hank as they jostled their way through the growing crowd along South Temple Street. She could see her breath as she walked, and her cheeks were tingling by the time they took the elevator up to the restaurant.

When the hostess at The Roof called for their party, Molly followed slowly behind Micheline, craning her neck to get a look at the sumptuous buffet. She caught a glimpse of a whole poached salmon and a tempting presentation of giant shrimp before they were led to an oversize semicircular booth with a view of the lights in Temple Square glittering through the snow.

They spent the next part of the evening sampling and critiquing as many of the amazing variety of dishes as possible. After they'd had dessert and were enjoying the music being played at the grand piano, Molly finally got them talking about the movie.

"Have any of you ever thought about writing a bucket list?" Hank asked.

Micheline made a desultory gesture. "I'm too young for that."

"I don't need one," Cal said. "I'm already doing what I want to do. But I'm surprised someone hasn't made the idea into a parlor game. You know, where players try to guess the top thing each person wants to do before they die."

"I know what you'd put on your list," Micheline said. "Play in the Master's Tournament."

"Aren't we supposed to pick something that's actually possible?" Hank gibed.

"Gee, thanks, pal. What's on your list?"

"You're talking to the man who always says he doesn't want anything," Molly said.

That didn't keep them from tossing out suggestions both serious and silly, but Hank kept shooting them down. Finally they gave up.

"Okay, amaze us," Cal asked. "What is it?"

"Buy a motorcycle and ride the Coast Road."

There was a sliver of silence, a moment when Molly might have taken what he said seriously. But then Cal and Micheline burst out laughing, and suddenly it seemed as funny to her as it did to them.

"I can see it now, Mr. Conservative starring in an LDS version of

Wild Hogs." Cal gasped, running his index finger below one eye to wipe away tears of laughter. "I guess you'll be getting a tattoo next."

"And spanky leathers from a Harley-Davidson store," Micheline added with a chortle. "You'd look good in those."

"Especially if you grow a beard and wear a do-rag," Cal sputtered.

Molly held her aching sides. "Like that would ever happen."

Chapter 5

Hank and Molly spent New Year's Day at home, resting and eating pizza while they watched football. He was quieter than usual, but she figured he was absorbed in the games. When that behavior continued for several days, she became concerned, so she sought him out in his office and asked if there was something on his mind.

He glanced her way. "No, I'm good."

But there was something bothering him, and she knew it. She racked her brain trying to think what could be the cause of his withdrawal. "You can't be mad that we laughed so hard at you New Year's Eve."

"It was no big deal, but I didn't intend it to be funny."

"You were serious?"

He shook his head as if he couldn't believe she had to ask. Then he turned back to his computer.

A few days later he launched himself into a flurry of activity. He started getting up earlier than usual to study the scriptures and read. He went to the gym every day. He volunteered twice a week at the bishop's storehouse on Seventh South. He even went bowling with Cal, who'd offered to teach him how.

"Did you have fun?" she asked when he came home.

He shrugged. "It was okay. But I wish someone had told me Cal was a 300 bowler. I felt pretty stupid when I threw some gutter balls."

"Are you going to go again?"

"Probably. I'm not about to let a ball and ten pins defeat me."

Listening to him, Molly thought he seemed more determined than entertained. Like he was still trying to find his way, without much luck.

She did what she could to perk him up, but when days and weeks passed without him returning to his normal self, she began to think he was depressed or there was something seriously wrong with their relationship. Or both.

She was in a glum mood when she and Micheline walked into the Relief Society room in February for a weeknight Relief Society workshop, the subject of which was being a good partner. She slumped in her chair, paying little attention to what was being said until the speaker began talking about the way she and her husband shared tasks.

Molly had been looking for a clue as to what might be off in her and Hank's relationship, and she had just been handed a big one. By the speaker's definition, she was a long way from being a good partner to Hank. In fact, she was more like a childish dependent. Fix a broken sprinkler pipe? Get the car serviced? Make financial decisions? She wouldn't know where to start.

Why did I leave those tasks for Hank to do? Molly wondered. *Because he could and would?*

She was so deep in contemplation that Micheline had to give her a little shake to get her attention after the meeting was over.

"You're thinking too much. You need some Marie Callender pie therapy."

"Thanks, but no thanks. I need to talk to Hank."

"That speaker rattled your cage, didn't she?"

"She made me think I've either been lazy, complacent, or incompetent. I've never given a second thought to some of the things Hank routinely does."

"Come on, friend. I'm sure there are things you do that he takes for granted. Has he ever sewn a button on? Mucked out the toilet?"

Molly giggled at the thought of Hank on his knees scrubbing around the base of the toilet bowl. "Not that I know of. But is that the way marriages should work? Get in a routine and keep going without ever considering whether there might be a better way?"

Hank was in the family room reading a bestselling crime novel when Molly got home. "Are you at a place where you can put that down for a moment?" she asked. "I'd like to talk to you about something."

"Sounds serious." He closed the book and put it on the side table.

She sat where she was knee to knee with him. "Hank, have I been a good wife?"

"What kind of a question is that? Of course you have."

"I'm not so sure. I've left certain things for you to do all these years without ever once asking if that was the way you wanted it."

Hank's lips twitched. "Are you talking about the 'man things'?"

He was referring to the way she'd labeled tasks in the early days of their marriage: man things and woman things. She nodded. "I'm thinking it's time I tried doing some things outside my comfort zone. Like paying the bills and balancing the checkbook."

"Something for the bucket list?" He laughed as if she'd told a great joke. "Pay the bills once before you die?"

Heat flooded her cheeks. "Not just once. I'm serious, Hank. You shouldn't have to carry the responsibility for our finances by yourself. Besides, I need to know what you do and how you do it. If something happened and I was left on my own, I wouldn't even know where to begin."

Hank's expression turned sober. "I wouldn't want you to be in that position."

"Show me how you do things," Molly said eagerly. "And then let me try it myself. Of course, you'd need to check my work until I'm totally comfortable with it. Then we could share the responsibility. Maybe set a date to do the finances together once a week."

"Hold on, now. Don't get too far ahead of the game."

She perched on his knee and batted her eyelashes shamelessly. "Will you teach me? Pretty please?"

He smiled as his resistance crumbled. "On one condition. If I take the time to teach you, you have to stick with it. I don't want you sliding into the two-drawer Roy Finley method."

"I won't. I promise." She stood up, excited to get started.

"So what's the exchange rate? If you're going to take over something I usually do, I should take over something you usually do."

Molly was surprised and delighted at the thought. She couldn't think of any single task she did that was equal to balancing the checkbook, but she said the first thing that came to mind. "How about doing the laundry?"

"It's a deal. How long are we talking about?"

"A week to start?"

"That's doable. I was going to pay some bills tomorrow. I can show you my process while I'm at it."

Molly had her first tutoring session with Hank at his desk the next day. She scribbled furiously as he talked, trying to keep track of everything. Which bills were to be paid the first half of the month, which the second half. Which were paid via automatic withdrawal, which by check. How to access account information online. How to reconcile the checkbook with the online statement.

She was mentally and emotionally exhausted by the time she'd written checks for the bills Hank had handed her and muddled her way through reconciling the checkbook.

She felt better when Hank gave her a squeeze. "I'm impressed by how you hung in there, Moll," he said. "I know you don't like numbers."

"Thanks. Do you want me to give you a tutorial on how to do the laundry?"

"Not necessary. I know the basic drill. Besides, there are instructions on the bottles, aren't there?"

I should have traded for something he'd find harder to do, she thought. Then her eyes fell on the photos of his family she'd hung artfully on his office wall. He loved his family and was interested in their welfare, but he'd always left it up to her to write them long, newsy letters (now e-mails), send cards for birthdays and holidays, and get the Christmas package in the mail. What would happen if he took over that responsibility?

"Uh, Hank? What would you think about you taking over communicating with your family instead of doing the laundry?"

"Really?" He grinned. "That hardly seems fair."

"That's what I'd like," she said. *You'll be surprised. There's more to it than you think.*

It snowed off and on the next couple of weeks, light snows that melted in the afternoon sun, clearing walks, driveways, and streets. Then in late February they woke to eight inches of heavy snow.

"Guess I have to get the shovel out," Hank said after breakfast. He put on his coat and gloves and then came back into the kitchen. "Are you sure there isn't something you'd like to swap for clearing the driveway?"

"Let's talk about it in April," she said, smiling sweetly.

The job swap had helped Molly understand the family finances, but it hadn't improved her relationship with Hank to the extent she'd hoped for. They were talking more, but their conversations rarely went beyond the task at hand. *Maybe it's true that the way to a man's heart is through his stomach*, she thought, and she began assembling the ingredients to make brownies, his favorite treat.

She'd just pulled the pan out of the oven when she heard a knock on the front door. She was expecting Micheline, so she called, "Come in."

Micheline walked into the kitchen, shedding her coat and sniffing the air. "Are those brownies I smell?"

"Hank's out there in the cold shoveling the drive and the sidewalk, so I decided to make him a treat." She put a plate of brownies and two glasses of milk on the table. "Try one."

"Mmm. These are fabulous." After taking another bite, Micheline asked, "Now tell me the real reason you're plying your man with these goodies."

Molly sat down with a sigh. "I'm trying to warm him up, if you have to know. I'm sure something's wrong, but I can't get him to talk about it."

"I'm not surprised. Ask men about football or machinery, and they'll talk for an hour. Ask them about feelings or relationships, and they act like you're speaking a foreign language."

"Maybe we are. Men are from Mars, you know."

Molly was topping off their glasses of milk when the front door opened and a happy "Yoo-hoo!" echoed down the hall.

"Oh no. It's Jan," Micheline whispered.

A dog sitter and part-time groomer, Jan Peterson had a slobbery, but well-behaved boxer named Bozo and a passel of not-so-well-behaved children. She was known in the neighborhood for opening doors without knocking and giving her signature yodel. And for her voracious appetite for gossip.

Covering her irritation, Molly called, "In here."

"Hank said to come on in." Jan walked stocking-footed into the kitchen and took a seat at the table.

"You're here in time for a treat." Molly put a brownie and glass of milk in front of her.

Jan took a pinch of brownie. "So, have you heard about the Aldridges? Bruce moved out and asked Lori for a divorce."

"Who are the Aldridges?" Micheline asked.

"Bruce was a colleague of Hank's," Molly said. "The African violet Hank got at his open house? Bruce's wife, Lori, gave it to him." She turned to Jan. "How do you know they're getting a divorce?"

"A friend of my mother's has a daughter, Tana, who plays tennis with Lori at an indoor court. She heard all about it."

"Bruce was the one with the hair plugs!" Micheline crowed as she attached the name to the right face.

"He bought a fancy sports car to go with his new look," Jan said. "Poor Lori. I guess Bruce told her he was bored with his life and wanted something different."

"More like some*one* different," Micheline said.

"I'd bet on it." Her gossip delivered, Jan ate the brownie and then wiped her fingers on the napkin Molly had given her. "If Lori's situation has something to teach us, it's that we'd better pay attention to our men. That sort of thing can happen even to Latter-day Saints."

Molly felt Jan looking at her, wanting her reaction, but she wasn't about to share what she was thinking. *Am I as blind as Lori?*

Chapter 6

By the time February rolled into March, Molly was at her wits' end. She'd tried hard to make up for whatever fault or omission had come between her and Hank, but she still had the sense he wanted something more from her. She had no idea what. The only option left was to ask him straight out—when the time was right.

He presented her with the opportunity when he suggested they go for a walk one mild afternoon. The sun was shining, crocus and daffodils were poking their heads up where the snow had all but melted, and he seemed to be in a better mood. *Perfect*, she thought.

They'd gone several blocks when Molly put her hand in his. "Thanks for suggesting this. We haven't taken a walk together for a long time. It's nice."

He pressed her hand. "Sure is."

"Hank? I may be imagining this, but I keep feeling like there's something I should be doing but I'm not. For you, I mean."

"What are you talking about?"

"I don't know. That's why I'm asking. Is there something you need? Or want?"

"Nope."

"Really? Because it seems like something's bothering you."

"I've got things on my mind, that's all."

Translation: "I'm not ready to talk about it."

Molly blew out her frustration. With the luck she was having, it was pointless to ask what he wanted for his birthday, which was two weeks away. He would no doubt shoot off a glib response like he'd made during the bucket list game on New Year's. *Buy a motorcycle. Ride the Coast*

Road. But this year it seemed more important than ever that he have what he wanted, not what she thought he wanted.

When the solution came to mind, she smiled. "Your birthday's coming up," she said. "I've figured out how to make sure you get exactly what you want."

His response was automatic. "I don't need a present."

"You always say that, but there has to be something you want. So this year you're going to do what I do at Christmas—shop for yourself. I want you to take the money from your contract job and buy something you've wanted forever but would never admit to."

"All $12.72 of it, huh? That's about what's left after being tithed and taxed and tapped to pay the January credit card bills."

She tugged on his hand. "Hold on. I've been doing the finances, so I know that's an exaggeration. But even if that money were all gone, you could always use what's in the rainy-day account. I mean it. I want you to have what *you want* this year."

A strange expression came over Hank's face. "You sure, Moll?"

She nodded.

"Absolutely?"

"Absolutely."

I wish I knew what switch I flipped, Molly thought, watching her husband in the days before his birthday. His step was livelier. He smiled more. And he talked to her more, although not about what he was thinking of buying for himself.

The morning of his birthday, Molly left after breakfast to shop for the ingredients to make the stuffed pork chops he'd requested for dinner. When she got back an hour later, she saw she would be carrying the grocery bags into the house herself, because his car wasn't in the garage.

It took three trips for her to lug in the sacks and put them on the center island. She was emptying the cool bag of refrigerator items when she noticed an old issue of the AARP magazine on the table. It was opened to an article with a handwritten note from Hank: "Read this."

Uh-oh, Molly thought. *That sounds suspiciously like the note Alice found in* Alice's Adventures in Wonderland: *"Drink me."*

Looking at the article and the note, she had the strange feeling that she was entering dangerous territory. *It can wait,* she decided. *I've got work to do.* She put away the groceries and started preparations for Hank's dinner. When she stopped for a drink of water, she reread the note. She walked around the table twice and looked at it again.

The magazine was opened to an article entitled, "A Father's Gift to His Son." At the bottom was a photo of a man by a red Corvette with the caption: "Ken and the Corvette he bought after his last conversation with his father."

Her stomach churning, Molly sat down and read the article accompanying the photo. Ken had wanted to buy a Corvette after he got his first job. He'd even figured out how to manage the purchase, but his father was against it, saying it was an irresponsible indulgence. Not wanting to disappoint his father, Ken bought a more serviceable car and went about living his life. However, the dream never went away, despite other satisfactions he'd enjoyed while building his career and raising his family. Many years later, when the father was on his deathbed, he told Ken he'd changed his mind about the Corvette. "Life's short, son. Buy that car. Now, while you can enjoy it."

Molly felt as though she'd tumbled down the rabbit hole. *A Corvette? Was that what Hank had been secretly longing for? Was he buying one this very moment?*

She grabbed the phone and punched in the number of Hank's cell, hoping he would answer, but it went directly to voice mail.

"Hey, birthday boy," she said. "I read that article you left out for me. Give me a call and let me know what's going on in that handsome head of yours, okay?"

Molly was far more concerned than her lighthearted message revealed. Driven by her nervous energy, she got everything ready for the birthday dinner in record time. She paced around the kitchen looking for things to do. She walked out to the front porch, hoping to see him coming home. Then she started cleaning.

Everyone in the family knew that when Molly was worried, she cleaned. The way she'd reorganized every cupboard in the kitchen when Laurel was taking the bar exam was a favorite family story. She still got teased about how she'd positioned the spices in alphabetical order and the cereal boxes according to types of grain: corn, wheat, and rice.

By four that afternoon, she'd straightened the silverware and utensil drawers and purged the freezer of some outdated items, muttering to herself as she worked. In half an hour Laurel would be arriving with the special marzipan cake she'd ordered from Schmidt's Bakery, and Wade and his family would show up.

And Hank was still missing.

The phone ringing made her jump. She snatched it up and said, "Hank?"

"No, it's me, Micheline. I called to see what Hank bought himself for his birthday."

"I don't know. He left early, and I haven't heard from him since."

"What's he doing?"

When Molly told her about the article and her suspicions, Micheline chuckled. "I wonder if Bruce Aldridge read that before he bought his convertible."

"That's a charming thought. I have to get off the phone, in case Hank calls."

But Hank didn't call, and as the clock ticked closer to the hour, Molly went beyond irritation to worry. This was so unlike him. Something terrible must have happened. She was beside herself by the time the rest of the family arrived.

"Your father's been gone for hours," she said, pulling Laurel into the kitchen. "I have no idea where he went or what he's doing. Or even if he's all right. He left this on the table."

Laurel picked up the article with the note still stuck on it, "Read this." "He wouldn't," she said firmly when she finished scanning it.

Wade's response was much the same as Laurel's. "Not possible. It's Henry David Mancuso we're talking about here." Then he got a huge smile on his face. "But if he did, more power to him!"

"Wade!" Heather chided.

"What?" He picked up Katie and twirled her around. "Wouldn't you like to see Grandpa in a shiny red sports car, Katie, my love?"

"Grandpa's getting a Corvette," Hayden chanted, running around the kitchen.

"No, he's not," Laurel snapped. "Hayden, stop that."

The clamor ceased at the sound of a vehicle pulling into the driveway. It wasn't the sound Molly expected. It sounded like . . . but no, that couldn't be. Her breath quickened as she heard an engine rev a couple of times and then shut down.

"That's not a Corvette," Wade said. "That's a—"

"Motorcycle!" Molly howled as she opened the garage door.

The entire family spilled through the garage and stopped short. Hank stood beside a huge silver motorcycle in the driveway, helmet in hand, looking inordinately proud of himself.

"Hank Mancuso," Molly croaked. "What have you done?"

"Grandpa, you bought a motorcycle!" Hayden jumped up and down with excitement.

"Dude, that rocks." Wade gave his father a knuckle bump. "It's one of those touring bikes, isn't it?"

"A Honda Gold Wing. I've been looking at bikes ever since I rode Lennie's Fat Boy, and I got a great deal on this one."

Molly nostrils flared. "You never told me."

"Yes, I did. I said I wanted a motorcycle when you asked what I wanted for Christmas. And when we played the bucket game New Year's Eve."

"You were joking!"

"Have I ever joked when it came to motorcycles?" Hank said. "When I rode the Fat Boy at Lennie's, you said, 'Far be it from me to stand in the way of true love.' And then you told me to buy what I really wanted for my birthday."

She was floored at the horrible miscommunication that had led to this moment. "I did say those things," she said slowly, "but I didn't mean them the way you took them."

Hank looked as shocked as she felt, but he covered it well when Lisa said, "This is way bigger than Daddy's four-wheeler. Can I sit on it, Grandpa? Please?"

"Sure," he said and swung her up onto the saddle.

Hayden tugged on Hank's hand. "I want to go for a ride."

"Sorry, buddy. We'll have to do that another time when you bring your helmet."

"Can we come tomorrow, Dad?" Hayden wheedled.

"Maybe not tomorrow," Wade said, "but soon. Right now, I think we should all go inside. Your grandpa's birthday dinner is waiting for him."

Hank's birthday dinner was not the festive event Molly had planned. Everything about it was awkward. Laurel brooded silently at her end of the table. Heather was preoccupied with a squalling Junie. Wade was overly enthusiastic about his father's new toy, as if trying to make up for Molly's and Laurel's lack of enthusiasm. The grandkids' rendition of "Happy Birthday" when Molly brought out the lighted cake bordered on hectic, and their voices were too loud when they asked Hank if he liked the presents they'd brought him.

She wasn't surprised when the party ended early.

"I've got to go," Laurel said after they'd had cake and ice cream. "Happy birthday, Dad." She gave her father a brief hug. "I hope you have fun with your present."

The words were right but the tone wasn't. *Finally, something Laurel and I agree on,* Molly thought.

After getting his brood headed for the van, Wade hung back to give her a supportive hug. "I know you're shell-shocked, Mom, but give it a day before you rain any more on Dad's parade."

Finally, something Wade and Hank agree on. "I'll try," she said.

She tackled the kitchen with a vengeance, muttering as she cleared the table, loaded the plates into the dishwasher, and threw away crumpled wrapping paper.

Hank tried to help, but he kept getting in her way. Finally he stopped trying. "I suppose we ought to talk."

"I suppose. This wasn't how I wanted your birthday dinner to go."

"Me either."

Molly snapped the lid on the cake container and shoved it into the fridge. "What did you think would happen when you came home with that *thing*?"

"That you'd say how glad you were that I'd gotten something I wanted. I'd brag about how I saw an ad in the paper for the bike at a great price and snapped it up before someone else did. Then I'd point out the snazzy aftermarket passenger seat and armrests I knew would make you feel safe and comfortable when riding. You'd try on your helmet, I'd show you how the mic works, and we'd take our first ride together back to the seller's house to pick up the car."

Molly ran her hands through her hair in frustration. "Remember me? I'm your wife, the woman who is afraid of motorcycles. There isn't any known world where I'd be happy that you bought one. There isn't any known universe where I'd get on one. Just thinking about it makes me short of breath."

Hank stared at her for a long moment. "I honestly thought you knew I would buy a cycle when you told me to get what I wanted for my birthday. I thought that was your way of telling me that it was okay. I asked you if you were sure. You said you were. Absolutely."

They looked at each other over the gulf that yawned between them. Finally Molly said, "What about your car?"

"I'll get Cal to take me over in the morning to pick it up." He opened the door.

She felt a sudden panic. "Where are you going?"

"To put the Gold Wing in the garage."

Molly sat down at the empty table. She heard the garage door open, then the sound of the motorcycle engine starting. Hank let it purr a moment, and then he revved it a couple of times before driving it inside the garage.

The revving of the engine pushed Molly into action. Fueled by fear no longer old but fresh and growing, she hurried to her office and powered up her computer. She keyed "motorcycle deaths/injuries" into her browser, thinking, *I refuse to lose my husband to a senseless accident because he's having a midlife crisis.* Fifteen minutes later she printed out a page of statistics to put in front of Hank, with the parts she wanted him to pay the most attention to marked in bold. He might ignore her feelings, but there was no way he could ignore the statistics from the National Highway Transportation Safety Administration.

She hurried out into the garage where he was squatting to one side of the motorcycle, owner's manual open on the floor beside him, talking to himself.

No. Not to himself. To that thing! Steaming, she marched into the garage and shoved the paper in front of his face.

"Read this!"

Chapter 7

That night, Molly's sleep was haunted by faces. Her neighbor's face as it had looked the day he came home from the hospital, neck brace partially covering a wide scar that was still red and tracked with the holes from the stitches. Hank's face when he came home with the Gold Wing, an expression of childlike joy in his eyes.

When she woke up, Hank's side of the bed was empty. She dressed, grabbed a sweater, and walked through the quiet house out into the garage. The Gold Wing was bathed in the light coming through the open garage door. Hank was standing next to it, owner's manual in hand. It was almost as if he hadn't moved since she'd delivered her missive the night before.

"Good morning," she said.

His expression was guarded. "Hi."

"How long have you been out here?"

"An hour or so. You didn't have a very good night, did you?"

"No. Sorry if I kept you awake." She sat on the steps to the kitchen. "You know that famous line from the movie *Cool Hand Luke?*"

He nodded. "'What we have here is a failure to communicate.'"

"It describes our situation pretty well, don't you think? I'll take my part of the blame. I know I was giving mixed messages. But you don't tell me what's going on in that head of yours, and I'm not very good at guessing. Obviously."

Hank tapped the owner's manual against his leg. "I guess we have some work to do."

"No kidding." Molly stared at the cycle. "Are you still happy with this thing?"

"It's a motorcycle, Molly. And yes, I'm more than happy with it." Some enthusiasm crept back into his voice. "Gold Wings are wonderful machines. They're stable and amazingly comfortable for long trips. The guy I bought this one from said riding it was like going down the road sitting in a Barcalounger."

Molly had to smile at the image that description conjured up.

"I'd be even happier if I knew it wasn't going to cause trouble between us," he added.

"I wish I could say it won't," Molly said slowly. "The thought of you on it makes me physically ill. I still can't believe you bought it. This is so not like you."

"Actually, I feel more like myself than I have for a long time."

"Then I guess I don't know you as well as I thought I did."

"Sure you do," Hank said. "It's only that you haven't seen this side of me since I sold my Suzuki."

"This is too much to think about on an empty stomach. Can I fix you something for breakfast?"

"I've already had mine, but thanks."

She had her hand on the doorknob when a "Yoo-hoo" from down the street turned her around. She knew before she looked that it was Jan.

"Blast it. The minute Jan sees your motorcycle the whole neighborhood will know about it."

Not that they wouldn't eventually, but there was always a subtext to Jan's gossip. She was tone-deaf when it came to personal interactions, but she had a radar that picked up on others' emotions. Molly knew Jan would zero in on her ambivalence and pass it on with as much verve as the news of the Gold Wing itself.

"Shut the garage door if you don't want to talk to her," Hank said.

"Too late."

Bozo was already pulling Jan and a pair of collies into the garage, straining and panting in his eagerness for a visit.

"Hi, there." Jan's eyes were bright with curiosity at the sight of the Gold Wing. "Now, this is new, isn't it?"

"Yep. It's my birthday present." Hank stooped to give the boxer an ear scratch.

"Molly bought you this?"

"I bought it for myself."

"That's quite the present, I'd say." Jan looked at Molly. "You weren't in on it, not even a little bit?"

"It's Hank's baby."

"Have you gone on a ride with him?"

"Not yet." Molly meant to smile but it felt like she was baring her teeth.

Jan wasn't the only one who was drawn to the motorcycle that morning. Whenever Hank revved up the engine or rode it around the block to check something out, someone else showed up to see the new occupant of the Mancuso garage.

Molly was cleaning the inside of her SUV when Alex Alvarez, a teenager from the neighborhood, trotted up. Molly knew the handsome boy with the flashing smile from seeing him in church. And from hearing him argue with his father. The Alvarez property was on the other side of the Mancusos' back fence, and everything Alex and his father said in the heat of the moment was clearly audible to anyone in the yard.

Alex acknowledged Molly with a wave, but his focus was on the Gold Wing. "Sweet," he said to Hank, walking around the motorcycle. Within moments the two were shoulder to shoulder as Hank pointed out special features of the machine.

Curious, Molly worked more slowly so she would have an excuse for being where she could hear what Hank was saying. She needed to know what was so compelling about a motorcycle. But most of what the two talked about had to do with the machine itself rather than what drew them to it.

Alex reluctantly left a half hour later when Hank said he had to get ready to help with a priests quorum project. "Wait 'til I tell my dad about this. He goes ballistic whenever I try to talk to him about getting a motorcycle to ride to school and work."

Hank drove off in his sedan not long afterward. The minute he was gone, Molly called Micheline and invited her to come see what Hank had bought for his birthday. Her friend arrived in record time, and Molly led her through the kitchen to the garage. "Behold The Beast."

"Wow." Micheline walked around the silver behemoth, her fingers stroking the glossy surfaces. "This is a touring bike, top of the line from the looks of it."

"How do you know that?"

Micheline looked up from checking out the instrument panel. "When I was in high school I worked in the front office of a big motorcycle repair shop, ordering parts, setting up appointments, that sort of thing. The guys who worked there called the Gold Wing 'half a car,' it's so comfortable on the road. Look at these fancy aftermarket seats. You could cross the country on this without getting saddle sore."

"Wait a minute. You're supposed to think this is terrible."

"Is it?" Understanding flashed in Micheline's eyes. "Oh, I get it. You're afraid that Hank buying this cycle means the same thing as Bruce buying his sports car. A big red flag saying Midlife Crisis."

"Having it parked in my garage feels like a crisis to me."

"What are you going to do about it?"

"What *can* I do? I already gave Hank some statistics about how dangerous these things are, but they didn't faze him a bit. He's even talking about taking Wade's kids for a ride on it."

"Sounds to me like you're stuck with it, unless you intend to take some drastic step. Like have it hauled away when he's not at home."

Molly brightened. "Hey, I could do that right now."

"Why don't you try something a little less extreme first? Like what my mother used to do when my dad did something that turned her world upside down."

"What might that be?"

There was a mischievous glint in Micheline's eyes. "How much time do we have before Hank gets home?"

"A couple of hours. He's helping out with the service project the priests are doing."

"Then we'd better get started. It takes some time to pull off my mom's upside-down dinner."

With Micheline's help, Molly had everything ready when the sound of a car door closing alerted her that Hank was home. She positioned herself where she could see him when he came through the kitchen door and waited. And waited some more. Seconds passed before it dawned on her that he was in the garage communing with The Beast.

Sure enough, when she looked in the garage he was washing the windshield. "Dinner's ready."

He gave the windshield one last swipe with a soft cloth. "I had to check for myself to see if I'd actually bought this. And here it is."

"Been there all day."

He followed her into the kitchen. When he saw the unusual arrangement he stopped and said, "Molly, the table's—"

"Upside down. I know."

"And you've got plates on it."

"Uh-huh."

He looked perplexed and a bit irritated. "I hope this doesn't mean you expect me to eat standing on my head."

"That's the idea." She giggled at his reaction. "No, I'm kidding. All you have to do is get your body down on one of those pillows."

"It's your party."

He washed and dried his hands, then lowered himself down with a grunt. "It was easier getting down on the floor when the kids were little."

She put the casserole dish on a trivet. "I made your favorite. Shepherd's pie. It looks different because the mashed potatoes are on the bottom."

"As in upside down."

"And for dessert, we have upside-down cake served downside-up. Which makes it—"

"Ah." He held up an index finger. "I get it. This is your way of telling me I turned everything upside down yesterday."

"Hank Mancuso wins points for the right answer." She dished him up some of the casserole, and they ate their meal in silence. When they were almost finished, Molly asked the question that had been on her mind. "Hank, are we going to be all right?"

He put his napkin on the upside-down table. "I bought a motorcycle, Molly. I didn't ask for a divorce."

"The fact that you did something you knew would upset me seems like an early warning signal."

"The only thing it's a signal of is that lack of communication we talked about this morning."

"What do you expect me to do?"

"You could decide to get over your negative feelings about it."

Quick anger made her voice sharp. "You could decide to give it up."

"I already did that once, remember?"

Chapter 8

The next day was a blustery, rainy Sunday. Molly got up determined to go about her day as if nothing had changed. That wasn't easy with thoughts of her man and his motorcycle filling her head. When it was time to leave for church, she had to slip by the huge machine in order to get into the car. There was no getting away from it.

Hank was backing the car out of the garage when Molly cried, "Stop! Alex is behind you."

Hank stomped on the brakes. "What's he doing here?"

"Darned if I know. He doesn't look too happy."

Alex stepped up to the car and tapped on Hank's window. He wore a windbreaker with the hood pulled over his head, and his shoulders were hunched up against the rain. The cheerful smile of yesterday was nowhere in sight.

Hank rolled down the window. "What's up?"

"I made a mess of things, Brother Mancuso. I told my dad about your Gold Wing."

"I don't have any problem with that."

"But then I said if I got a motorcycle myself, I would be following your example. He's pretty ticked off. Not at me, at you."

Hank grinned slightly. "Tell your dad he doesn't need to worry. If you follow my example, you won't be buying a motorcycle for another fifty years."

It took a second before Alex said, "Oh, got it. I didn't think of that." His shoulders relaxed. "Neither did Dad. He'll probably corner you sometime during church, Brother Mancuso. If he does, ignore him. He's loud, but he's harmless."

"Thanks for the warning. Do you want a ride to church?"

"No. I told my mom I'd be back in a minute." He gave them a wave and jogged off in the rain.

"I'd forgotten what it was like to have a teenage boy in the house," Hank said. "I'd hate to be in Del Alvarez's shoes."

"I'd hate to be in yours if Del does corner you." *But I hope he and a whole lot of other people do. Maybe then you'll see the error of your ways and get rid of The Beast.*

Although their sacrament meeting wouldn't start for another fifteen minutes, other early-comers were in the church foyer when they walked in. Kyle Duprey, the second counselor in the bishopric, was headed for the hallway with a sheaf of papers in his hand and a purposeful expression on his face. When he saw them, he changed direction.

He greeted them with a pleasant "Morning, folks" and a handshake. Then he turned serious. "I heard about that motorcycle, Hank. I hope you don't let riding get in the way of your Church calling."

"I—" Hank began, flustered.

Laughing, Kyle clapped a hand on Hank's shoulder. "Just kidding. More power to ya, brother. " He hurried on down the hall.

"Looks like the word's out," Hank said.

She nodded, wishing Brother Dupree had stopped with his admonition.

Next they were hailed by one of the thirty-something men in their ward. "I heard about your new set of wheels," he said excitedly. "Man, you're lucky to have Sister Mancuso for a wife. Mine would have a fit if I brought home a motorcycle." He turned to Molly. "Good going, Sister Mancuso."

"Don't give *me* any credit. I would be inclined to side with your wife."

Looking embarrassed for all of them, the man beat a hasty retreat.

Ronald Bixby, who had been standing nearby, paused briefly on his way to the chapel to say something in a low voice to Hank. Hank looked after him, eyebrows raised.

"What was that about?" Molly asked.

"He said I wasn't the only one in the ward with a motorcycle."

"Who do you suppose he was talking about? Not himself, surely."

Molly thought of Ronald as a salt-of-the-earth type of man, one of those ward members who could be counted on to quietly do whatever was needed without requiring acknowledgment. Pleasant and self-effacing, the only thing about him that drew attention was his gangly height and the quirky bow ties he wore on special occasions.

"Who knows?" Hank said. "Before this week, would anyone have guessed that I'd have a motorcycle in my garage?"

"Not me, that's for certain. It doesn't have to stay there, you know."

Hank ignored that comment. When they took their usual places in the chapel, they sat farther apart than normal. Molly was uncomfortably aware of the distance between them, and she longed for the peace she usually had when in church. Looking at Hank's Roman profile, she wondered if he was thinking the same.

The Uttleys came in shortly before the meeting was to start. Cal, who was ward clerk, hurried by on his way to the stand, and Micheline slipped in beside Molly.

"Boy, are you two ever the topic of conversation," she whispered.

"I know. Hank and I couldn't have caused any more fuss if we'd shown up pregnant at our age."

Micheline choked on a laugh. "At our age, I'd take the motorcycle any day. How did Hank like his upside-down dinner?"

"He likes shepherd's pie any way he can get it, and we talked some, but nothing much came of it. All evening long he was itching to be out in the garage."

"Be careful, friend. When I worked at that motorcycle shop, I was always hearing guys complain about how their wives threw hissy fits over the time they spent with their cycles. A couple of them even broke up over it."

That thought hung like a cloud over Molly throughout the meetings. When she found Hank waiting for her by the entrance, he looked none too happy either. Taking her arm he hurried her out of the building.

"What's the rush?"

"Del cornered me after priesthood meeting. He dumped every

reason in the book on me about why motorcycles are dangerous. Then he dressed me down for being a bad example. I'm not in the mood to talk to anyone else."

"Don't pay attention to him." Molly gave his arm a squeeze. "I may agree with him about the dangerous part, but he was totally out of line about you being a bad example."

"I'm glad you think so."

They'd walked out to where their car was parked when someone called out to them. It was Ronald.

The Bixbys were older than Molly and Hank. They were fixtures in the ward, known for their strong testimonies of the gospel and their many progeny who lived in the area. Molly and Hank had worked with them on various assignments over the years, especially when Wade was in Scouting. Ronald was a favorite with the boys because of his sleight of hand and coin tricks. Sharon was a retired nurse who liked to pedal her bike around her neighborhood on sunny afternoons.

"Welcome to the club, Hank." Ronald shook Hank's hand as if they'd not seen each other for months. "In case you didn't guess, I'm the one with a motorcycle."

"You're kidding," Hank said.

Molly was as astonished as he was.

"I was what you might call a *biker* in my early years. Chains, leather, bandana, bad attitude." Ronald smiled, enjoying their surprise. "That was before I joined the Church."

"And met me," Sharon said.

"I call myself a *motorcycle enthusiast* now. Sharon says it sounds more genteel."

Molly could see their affection in the look they exchanged.

"What kind of motorcycle do you have?" Hank asked.

"A new Gold Wing with everything, even an airbag. Would you like to see it sometime?"

"Very much."

"Come for dinner Thursday night," Sharon said, "if you don't have anything going on."

It seemed to Molly that fate was conspiring to make it impossible for her to separate Hank from The Beast. But there was no graceful way to decline the invitation. Hank knew as well as she did that there was nothing on their calendar for Thursday night.

"When should we be there?" she asked.

"Let's say six. I'm not much of a cook, but I'm great with a can opener. I was thinking of making The Best Chili You'll Ever Taste." Sharon laughed at Molly's look. "I'm not bragging. That's the name of the recipe."

"Oh. Can I bring something? Homemade rolls maybe?"

"That would be great. Ronald thinks any bread that doesn't come out of a plastic bag is manna from heaven."

The Bixby home was on the opposite side of the ward from where the Mancusos lived, in an area where some older, rural homes had survived the coming of suburban development. "You won't have any trouble finding it," Sharon told Molly. "It's the farmhouse with all the additions."

She was right about that, Molly thought as Hank pulled into the driveway of a house with a hodgepodge of rectangles attached to the sides and back. It and the detached garage were painted white. The windows of both had blue shutters with heart cutouts. Molly found the effect quite charming.

Ronald was at the door before Hank had time to ring the bell. "Welcome, welcome." He fairly pulled Molly into the house with his huge hand. "Here, let me take those rolls. Hank, you can hang your coats up on that rack. Share, our company's here!"

Sharon came out of the kitchen wiping her hands on a cotton towel. "I'm so glad you came. This is a treat for both of us." She gave Hank and Molly a handshake followed by a cheek to cheek, and then suggested Ronald show them his clock collection while she put the food on the table.

For the first time, Molly noticed the room she was standing in. It was so stuffed full of odd pieces of furniture that it had the appearance of a clearance outlet. But what caught her attention most was the collection of odd clocks on the fireplace mantel. Ranging from light and metallic to deep and resonant, their out-of-sync tones struck the half hour as Sharon and Ron brought in the food.

After the blessing Molly dug into her bowl of chili. She made little noises of appreciation as she savored the sweet chunks of green peppers and mixed beans in rich red sauce. "This chili has the right name. It *is* the best ever."

They were passing their bowls to Sharon for seconds when Hank addressed Ronald. "You could have knocked me over with a feather when you said you had a cycle."

"I'm not surprised. Sharon and I get some interesting reactions when we tell people we like riding. It isn't the first hobby folks connect with a pair of seventy-two-year-olds."

"The nurses I used to work with in the emergency ward were the worst." Sharon pulled a face. "They called motorcycles 'coffins on wheels' and helmets 'brain buckets.' Euw!"

"You worked in emergency and you still ride a motorcycle?" Molly was astonished.

"It wasn't a casual decision. I thought about it for a long time before I went on my first ride with Ronald."

"Speaking of rides," Ronald said, pushing his chair back from the table.

Sharon laughed. "Ron has been dying to show off his bike ever since you got here. You two go with him and I'll dish up the cobbler."

Ronald fetched the jackets and led Molly and Hank out the front door. "Sharon always makes it sound like I'm the only motorcycle aficionado in the family, but it's not true. She's always ready for a ride."

When Ronald turned the lights on in his garage, they illuminated the pearl brown Gold Wing parked as if on display. Next to it stood a low, aerodynamically shaped trailer in the same pearl brown.

Hank moved toward them as if being reeled in.

"That's some bike," he said, running his hand over the gas tank and the driver's seat. "It's an 1800, right?"

Ronald nodded. "The oh-eight model."

"Mine's a 1500. How many miles have you put on this baby?"

"Seven thousand." Ronald pointed to a brass plaque attached to the body of the cycle. It showed a map of the United States with faceted, colored rhinestones scattered across it. "Each one of these jewels represents a trip Sharon and I have taken."

Molly had been keeping her distance, but when Hank started asking questions about how the Gold Wing handled, she moved in so she could see the plaque better. The glittering bits were scattered from the East Coast to the West and from Southern California to as far north as the Canadian border.

Sharon's gone on all those trips, she thought. *How does she do it?*

Ronald and Hank had moved on to the trailer. "I bought the Tag-a-long at the same time," Ronald said. "Best thing ever for long trips. We don't have to pack so light or fiddle with our gear so much. We can tie a cooler on the hitch in front of it for snacks and pop and lunch fixings."

Hank made an admiring sound. "You two know how to do it the easy way."

"Easy is best when you're our age."

They were getting ready to go back into the house when Molly noticed that the back fender of the motorcycle sported a set of unique swirls and curlicues, in the center of which were two sets of letters, CTR and TRA. She'd seen the latter initials before, on the jackets of the Terminally Regressed Adolescents at Silver Fork Lodge.

"I know CTR stands for Choose the Right." Molly pointed to the logo. "But what does TRA stand for?"

"Temple Riders Association. It's a Mormon motorcycle club." Ronald doubled over laughing at their reaction. "It's not an oxymoron. Come on. I'll tell you all about it over dessert."

Ronald placed an oversized scrapbook in the middle of the dining room table where Molly and Hank could both see it. An 8 x 10 photo filled the center of the first page. It showed six couples of various ages in their Sunday best standing in front of a row of motorcycles, with the Jordan River temple in the background. The TRA logo arched across the space above it. Below it were the words, "Welcome to the Temple Riders Association of Utah."

"A motorcycle gang called the Temple Riders," Molly said. "That's a new one."

"A motorcycle *club*," Ronald corrected.

Sharon clarified while she served the cobbler and ice cream. "It's made up of Latter-day Saints and others wanting to ride with folks who have the same standards. It's called Temple Riders because our trips always have a temple town as a destination. Everyone who has a current recommend attends a session. The rest do some kind of service."

Molly saw the light in Hank's eyes when he said, "Riding motorcycles for fun and spiritual growth? I like it."

Molly turned to the next page.

"See this photo?" Sharon pointed to a picture of a large group of people scrunched together around the end of a banquet table laden with platters of ribs and fries. "That's the first TRA meeting we attended. It was in January 1995 at Tony Roma's in Provo. I think there were twelve other couples besides us that evening."

"You rode your motorcycles in January?" Molly was imagining icicles hanging from helmets and handlebars.

"We're dedicated, but we're not dumb," Ronald said. "We drive our cars when the weather's bad." He pointed out another photo. "Here's a picture of our first ride with the group. It was April first of 1995, a conference Saturday. A bunch of us decided to take a ride while we listened to the speakers."

He handed the story off to Sharon. "We were listening to the solemn assembly over our CB radios while we rode. When it came time to raise our hands to sustain the Church authorities, we all did. Right hands to the square as we rolled down the road.

"Some folks in the car behind us were listening to conference too. When they raised their hands, they noticed a whole line of motorcycle riders doing the same thing! They found it so touching, they wrote about it and sent it in to the *Ensign*. When did it get published, Ron?"

"March of '96, I believe, right before the April conference. Our claim to fame." Ronald said it jokingly, but Molly could see how the memory moved both him and Sharon. It unexpectedly touched her too.

Hank turned the page to a picture of a long, staggered row of cycles that had to have been taken from a passing vehicle. Each cycle was driven by a man with a woman sitting behind.

"Are most of your members married?" Molly asked.

"Except for Dorothy. She rides her own cycle, a Harley, no less."

"The only Harley in our club," Sharon said. "She sure gets attention."

"She even tunes it up and does her own repairs." Ronald's tone was admiring.

"What about her husband?" Molly asked.

"Husbands. She's had two, and they've both passed on. She has bad luck when it comes to men."

Molly touched the photo. "Do all of the wives ride behind their husbands?"

"Most of them." Sharon started gathering the dessert dishes. "The ones who don't follow along in cars."

The evening ended with a round of Rummikub and a promise to get together again soon. At the door Ronald said, "We're having a TRA meeting next Saturday in a banquet room at the uptown Chuck-A-Rama. We'd love it if you joined us."

Molly glanced at Hank and then back to Sharon. "Is it all right if we let you know later?"

"No sweat, no pressure. If you decide to come, let us know, and we'll watch for you."

Chapter 9

To go or not to go, that is the question.

If they went to the TRA meeting, Molly worried that Hank would take it as a sign she was softening to the presence of the Gold Wing in the garage. If she didn't go, she was certain he would attend without her. Who could tell where that might lead?

Molly laid it all out to Micheline while the two of them walked their route on Flatiron Mesa, a nearby hilltop park with walking paths and playing fields. The day was sunny but cold, and both of them were wearing mittens and ear protectors.

"I hate being in this position," Molly said as they followed the trail around the massive twin water tanks. Painted a bright sky blue, the tanks marked the eastern boundary of the park.

"You're between a rock and a hard place, that's for sure. But Hank has the right to make a choice without being held hostage to your paranoia."

Molly stopped in the middle of the path. "What do you mean, 'held hostage to my paranoia'?"

"Don't get me wrong." Micheline made a cool-down gesture. "I understand your side of the story, I really do. But as long as I've known you, you've been playing hopscotch through every class in the continuing education catalog and jumping from one hobby to another, and Hank's supported you without a word of criticism. This is the first time I've ever seen him choose anything for himself. Couldn't you do the same for him?"

Molly didn't know what to say, so she started walking again. *Am I really holding Hank's choices hostage to an unreasonable fear? Am I being selfish?*

She was plagued by those and similar thoughts the rest of the walk. By the time she got home, Micheline's accusation, combined with her worry about Hank going to the TRA meeting alone, had tipped the verdict in his favor.

"I'll come on one condition," she said when he asked what she'd decided. He waited with the look of a man expecting the other shoe to drop. "We take the car."

He laughed with relief. "I never thought of going any other way. We'll have fun, Molly. We might even see some of those bikers who were up at Silver Fork Lodge."

She was doubtful about the fun part. She went into her office, turned on her computer, and googled Temple Riders Association. The group could be full of kooks, and she wanted to know what she was getting into.

When the search results came up, she first clicked on the link to the official Web site. That the group had a Web site didn't impress her. *It only means they're organized. So was the Gambino crime family.*

But she scribbled some facts on a piece of paper as she went through the site.

Officially organized in 1988 by Frank Reese
700 members and climbing
Mostly retirees who can ride weekdays
Mostly Latter-day Saints, mostly couples, but not all
Gold Wings not mandatory
Usual ride, 250-300 miles a day!

It was late by then, and she'd begun yawning, extravagant yawns that stretched her cheeks. But there was one more link she wanted to check out before she went to bed.

That link took her to an article written by a TRA member. It was obvious from the first paragraphs that the writer was as enthusiastic about the TRA as Ronald was. She would have stopped reading right then—she'd had enough enthusiasm for one night—except for the fun he was having with acronyms, the way she and Hank had at Silver Fork Lodge.

Only his were nicer than Totally Raunchy Adults. *Togetherness, Religion, and Adventure. Traveling with Reverent Associates.*

The article ended with moving journal entries written on a trip through Church historical sites and a closing statement that sounded like it came from a sacrament meeting talk. *We're here to be faithful. But while we're at it, we're allowed to explore. As President Hinckley once suggested, "The trick is to thank God for letting you have the ride."*

She looked up at the author's name and frowned. *Where have I seen the name Wayne Brickey before?* she wondered. Something tickled the back of her mind. She went into the living room and scanned the shelf of Church-related reading material until she found the inspirational book her parents had given her for Christmas. The name on the jacket was the same as the name above the article.

She turned to the author information and started to read. When she came across the name of the author's wife, she sat down. Unless there were two men of the same name married to women with the same name, the writer of the TRA article was a respected LDS educator and author.

When she read the last line, her mouth gaped open. *Twelve children? They have* twelve children *to worry about, and they ride?*

Molly put the book back with a huff. *These TRA members might not be kooks, but they are definitely crazy.*

⌒

When Hank told the hostess at Chuck-A-Rama that they were there for the TRA meeting, the hostess's smile widened. "Part of the Mormon motorcycle gang, are you? Come with me."

She led them through a set of double glass doors opening into a private dining room already filled with a lively group of people. Molly caught bits of conversation as they stood at the open doors, not quite knowing what to do next.

"I haven't seen you since the ride to Mexico . . ."

"Did I hear right? They're considering a tricycle?"

"Bright yellow might catch motorists' attention, but I wouldn't bet on it."

Then Ronald and Sharon descended on them. "Hank, Molly! You came!"

Ronald took Hank off in one direction and Sharon linked arms with Molly. "I'm so glad to see you. We saved some places at our table in case you came. But first let me introduce you to our chapter president and his wife. Jeri and Doyle Connelly are two of our younger members. He's still working, poor man."

L. L. Bean meets Disney, Molly thought, taking in Doyle's blue oxford shirt and Jeri's Winnie the Pooh sweatshirt and oversized Mickey Mouse watch. They had chatted only a few minutes before Sharon directed Molly toward a plump, much older woman with apricot-colored hair. "Thi is Enid Carter, the matriarch of the group. Her husband's Merrill."

"Welcome," Enid said. "What category do you fit in? Drive your own, ride behind, or follow?"

"Definitely follow."

"You're not the only one. See the woman in green over there?" Enid pointed toward a stately blonde with perfectly coiffed hair, dressed in a suit that was, Molly thought, Sunday best and then some. One manicured hand rested on the shoulder of a man who looked younger—and was noticeably shorter—than she.

"That's Trina. Only a written edict from heaven would get her on a motorcycle. The helmet's too hard on her hair." Enid lowered her voice confidentially. "Second marriage and all that."

It's like the first day in a new ward, Molly thought as Sharon continued introductions. *I'll never keep these names and faces straight.* She was glad when they finally reached the chairs the Bixbys had marked as taken.

"I can't wait for you to meet Dorothy," Sharon said as they settled in. "She's the one we told you about who rides her own motorcycle. Such a character."

"Is she here?"

"Not yet, but she will be. See that man Hank and Ronald are talking to?"

Molly looked in the direction Sharon was pointing. "The one who looks spit polished?"

"Good description. That's Howard Norton, our other singleton. Retired, widowed, and well-off. I think he and Dorothy might have a thing going."

"Romance on the road?"

"It happens. We've also had married couples say that riding with us saved their marriage."

"Any who broke up over riding?"

"Not that I know of."

I hope we're not the first, Molly thought.

A bit later Hank and Ronald joined them, and after an opening prayer, everyone in the group served themselves from the buffet. They'd gone from soup to nuts when Doyle stood and tapped his knife against the side of his glass to get everyone's attention. "We've got visitors with us tonight." He asked Molly and Hank to stand as he introduced them to the group. "We hope you'll be official members next time we meet."

He went on to report the success of the previous month's ride and to announce that the April trip would be to the Provo temple via Heber City. Then he shifted gears. "The Forrest family has asked me to pass along a big thank you to all who took the time to call or send cards to Fricka. She's doing much better and with any luck will be back in her Port-a-Pet and riding along with Barney and RaNae soon."

Fricka? Port-a-Pet?

"Now comes the part of the meeting you've all been waiting for—the safety review, led by our one-of-a-kind Dorothy. But before she does her part, she wanted me to remind you to update your emergency information form. Don't be afraid to put down whether or not you wear dentures. In case of an accident, nobody's going to be teasing you if you don't have your own teeth."

More laughter.

Molly folded her arms across her chest. *What's funny about an emergency card and false teeth?* If she could have left without it being obvious, she would have.

Doyle waved to the double doors at the front of the room. "Now, heeeeere's Dorothy!"

The doors opened and in stepped a thin woman in black leathers carrying pom-poms. Molly couldn't see the face behind the pom-pom flurry, but the vibrant alto voice was compelling.

"Give me a T!"

"T!" shouted the group.

"Give me a C!"

"C!" came the response.

"Give me an L-O-C-K. What does it spell?"

"T-CLOCK!"

"What does it mean?"

"Safety on the road," everyone cheered.

Dorothy dropped her pom-poms on the table, and Molly saw that her face was as animated as her voice, with snapping dark eyes and a mobile mouth. She pushed back a lock of her silver hair, which was pulled up becomingly in a soft bun, and pointed at Ronald Bixby. "What does the T in T-CLOCK stand for?"

"Checking the condition of tires and wheels," Ronald shot back in rhythm.

Dorothy moved on quickly to the next question. Molly stared at her as she led the members through bits about checking controls, lights, oil, chassis, and kickstands. *I've seen her before, but where?*

After the meeting, Sharon took Molly and Hank to the front of the room for introductions. Sharon had barely begun speaking when Molly noticed the bright red nails on Dorothy's hands, nails with pink flames. The clues fell into place all at once. Motorcycles. Gray hair. Silver Fork Lodge.

Nails!

"I know you," she blurted out. "I have photos of you pinned to my office wall. I took them when you and some others rode by me on the way up Big Cottonwood Canyon. We saw you again in the dining room of Silver Fork Lodge."

"Well, I'll be." Dorothy shook first Molly's hand and then Hank's. "I'd love to see them. We're always looking for good action shots for our scrapbook."

"I'll be glad to show them to you." Molly handed her one of the cards she'd had printed with her and Hank's names on it.

Dorothy took the card. "Splendid. I hope you'll be joining our group."

Hank glanced toward Molly before saying, "We're thinking about it."

They were among the last to leave the restaurant, because Sharon and Ronald kept introducing them to someone new. Molly was sure some of them had been at the lodge with Nails that day, and their warmth and good will made her embarrassed at how catty she'd been.

Finally they made it out to the parking lot. "Did you enjoy yourself?" Ronald asked.

"It was fantastic." Hank's enthusiasm was unrestrained. "I can't wait to go on a road trip with this bunch."

"The Provo temple trip is coming up, but you don't have to wait until then. Why don't I give you a call, and we can set up a ride for later in the week?"

"It's a deal." Hank took Molly's hand and started for the car.

Molly pulled back. "Wait a minute! Who's Fricka? And what's a Port-a-Pet?"

Ronald laughed. "Fricka is the Forrests' ferret. They've attached a cage to the passenger armrest on their Gold Wing so she can go with them on all their trips."

"Okay, now I've heard it all," Molly said.

She was glad that Hank was quiet on the way home. Nails leading safety cheers, motorcycle-riding ferrets, emergency information forms. . . . If he had asked how she was feeling at that moment, she wouldn't have known what to say.

Chapter 10

Monday morning, Scott called to see if Hank was available for a short stint at the office. Hank was dressed and on his way before ten.

A whole day without having to hear the word motorcycle, Molly thought, two-stepping around the kitchen.

She didn't feel a bit guilty at how glad she was that Hank had been called in to work. It had been motorcycle this and motorcycle that ever since the TRA luncheon on Saturday. Hank's delight at being asked to join the Temple Riders on their April trip was tangible. He talked about it as if his going—*their* going—was a given. She'd had enough of it.

But fate, or at least members of the TRA, had other plans. The phone began to ring as soon as Hank left for the office.

"Good morning. It's Enid, from TRA."

Apricot hair, Molly thought. "Yes, I remember you."

"I know it's early, but I wanted to get to you before Trina calls. You remember Trina, the newlywed who won't get on a motorcycle for love nor money? I mentioned to her that you were a follower, not a rider, and she said you should join her on the Provo temple trip. I wanted to let you know that you'll be hearing from her this morning. I hope that's all right with you."

Before Molly could protest that she wasn't sure she was going, Enid rattled on about the ride she and Merrill were taking that morning in search of a good greasy-spoon breakfast. She ended with a bright, "Got to go now."

Molly stared at the abruptly dead handset. *Okay, that was interesting.*

She replaced it and carried the laundry basket downstairs. She was separating the laundry by colors and hand wash when the phone rang again. She loped into the family room to answer it.

This time, the voice on the other end of the line belonged to Jeri Connelly. When she identified herself as being married to Doyle, the chapter president, Molly thought, *L. L. Bean and Winnie.*

"I wanted to welcome you again to our group," Jeri said. "We're always delighted when a new couple joins."

"Thanks." Molly didn't bother to point out that she and Hank hadn't actually joined yet.

"Now, about the Provo temple trip, I understand you won't be riding behind your husband. But don't you worry about that one bit. Trina Johansen doesn't either, and she's looking forward to having you join her on the trip. She said she'd be calling you to get logistics worked out."

"Thanks for letting me know."

I wonder how many other TRA women will call to tell me Trina will be calling, Molly thought as she hung up. *Ten to one I'll never hear from the elusive Trina herself.*

The phone rang yet again as Molly was getting ready to hand-wash her delicates. This time it was Trina. She introduced herself in a voice that sounded more like a girl than a woman in her sixties and immediately invited Molly to ride with her on the Provo temple trip.

"Thanks for the offer," Molly said. "I hope you don't mind me asking, but why do you drive instead of riding behind your husband?"

Trina's laughter bubbled over the line. "I haven't been married to Gabe long enough to let him see me with helmet head. And there is that occasional bug-in-the-teeth thing. Anyway, he's much happier without me behind him making hand gestures or giving him little taps to focus his attention on something I think is important."

Molly had to laugh at that.

"Besides, I like to keep my temple clothes in a dress bag, and there's no easy way to pack that on a motorcycle. So, should I count on you going with me?"

"Is it all right if I talk to Hank and get back to you?"

"Don't think too hard or talk too long. It'll be great fun. You never know what adventures we car bunnies will get into ourselves."

Molly hung up feeling like she was in an even deeper predicament than before. *If I go with Trina, I can be a part of what Hank wants to do without ever having to ride The Beast. That would make him happy, but it won't make me worry less. And it won't make him any safer.*

After she finished with her hand wash, she went back to the kitchen, exasperated that the day was not turning out as motorcycle-free as she'd hoped. She pulled out her mop, floor cleaner, and a bucket and was attacking the kitchen floor when the doorbell rang.

The front door opened a second later, and a voice called, "Molly? Are you here?"

"Micheline? Oh no!" Molly dropped the mop and dashed to the entryway. Micheline was dressed for a walk in sweats, a jacket, and a fleece band over her ears. "You were waiting for me at the park, weren't you?"

"For the last half hour. What happened?"

"The phone was ringing all morning, and I got distracted and thinking and mopping . . . I'm so sorry."

Micheline pulled off her headband. "It's okay. It's not like I've never stood you up." She followed Molly into the kitchen.

"Do you want something warm to drink? Hot chocolate? Herbal tea?"

"No, I'm fine." Micheline sat on a stool at the center island. "So who was doing all the calling?"

"The ladies from the TRA, inviting me to go on the Provo temple trip."

"And?"

Molly picked up her mop from where she'd dropped it when the doorbell rang. "I said I'd think about it."

"And work yourself into a dither fixating on all the reasons you have for saying no."

Molly's voice was testy. "I have good reasons to feel the way I do."

"I know. But you should accept that invitation from the TRA lady unless you want to be left behind. Hank's going on this Provo trip, with or without you."

"How do you know that?"

Micheline looked embarrassed. "He said as much when he called to ask Cal for some coaching on how to pick up the number seven and ten spares in bowling. "

Molly splashed her mop into the bucket, wrung it out, and attacked a spot.

"You're going to wear out your floor, friend," Micheline said gently. "What we need is some fresh air. How about a walk around the block?"

"I can't. I'm mopping."

"Moping is more like it. Hey, don't look at me like that. I'm doing what we promised we would do for each other—say what needed to be said even if the other person didn't want to listen."

"You do think I'm in the wrong, don't you?"

Something flickered in Micheline's eyes. "All I can say is if Cal came home with a motorcycle and invited me to ride with him, I'd be on it as soon as I could get my helmet fastened." She paused. "Listen, Hank's inviting you to be a part of something that's important to him. That isn't so very awful."

Molly stopped mopping. "You're right, it's not."

After her friend left, Molly sat at the kitchen table thinking, and for the first time, she put herself in Hank's shoes.

Being there wasn't comfortable. Nothing about Hank's retirement was turning out the way he'd hoped it would. Not the adventure-a-day plan. Not his dreams of the two of us riding into the sunset together on The Beast. No wonder he was so glad when Scott called up with more work.

Is that what I want for him? Molly asked herself. *That he get back into his rut, so I can get back into mine?*

She remembered the definition she'd read in *Reader's Digest:* The difference between a rut and a grave is how deep it is and how long you're in it.

She didn't want him back in his rut, she realized. Nor did she want to get stuck in hers. She had a photography class that afternoon, but if she hurried home there would be time for her to make Hank a nice supper for family home evening. Maybe they could find common ground over his favorite dessert, which was anything made of chocolate.

Tonight, she would try something new.

~

Hank wasn't in the mood to talk when he came home. Molly had to pry information out of him all through dinner, asking questions about his day and how he felt being back to work. It wasn't a happy process, and soon she stopped talking too. She hoped the decadent dessert she'd made for him would break the ice.

When Molly put the triple chocolate mousse cheesecake for two in front of him, Hank's mood lifted for the first time that night. "What's this for?"

"To let you know I love you. I haven't said it for a while." She bent to kiss him. "Also, I figured that if we both had a sugar buzz, we'd be mellower when we talk about the Gold Wing and the TRA."

"That might take seconds," he said with the barest hint of a smile. But he enjoyed every bit of his dessert, wiping the last of the chocolate mousse from the plate with his index finger and licking it clean. "That was excellent. Now, what do you want me to tell you about the Gold Wing?"

"Actually, I wanted to talk to you about the Provo trip. I heard from Micheline that you're going whether I do or not."

"Darn that Cal," Hal muttered. "What I said, Molly, was that I was *thinking* of going. I want to, but it wouldn't be much fun if I knew you were at home worrying about me. I was hoping I could help you feel less anxious about me riding, but you didn't want to hear anything I had to say."

"I'm listening now."

"For one thing, I'd be going with the Temple Riders, not a bunch of middle-aged, wannabe show-offs. They have a very good safety record. They prepare carefully, and they always start out with prayer. That puts them in a different statistical category, I'd say."

Molly knew he was referring to her printout of the National Highway Safety stats. "That is something," she conceded.

"For another, I've gone through the basic Utah Rider Education course to refresh my skills."

"You didn't tell me that."

"I decided I should after reading that almost all motorcycle accidents involve riders who never took any training. I've also signed up for the experienced rider course."

He slid his fingers under hers and clasped her hand. "I'm doing it for you, Moll, so you'll feel better about me being on the road. The helmet I bought has the latest safety technology, and I always wear it, even though Utah doesn't have a helmet law. I promise I won't ride when I'm tired or when the weather or traffic conditions are iffy. And I'll get full protective gear before the trip."

She returned the pressure of his hand. "You're bonkers about that machine, aren't you?"

"It's not the machine, it's the ride." He looked into the distance as if seeing something she couldn't. "It's doing something that demands my complete attention precisely because it is risky. It's being hunkered down on the road, seeing things you don't see from a car. It's—"

He kept on talking, but Molly barely heard what he said, she was so mesmerized by what he was revealing. He'd been happy over the years, yes. Also contented, loving, steady, honorable, satisfied. She could think of a dozen more adjectives to describe him, but *exhilarated* was something new.

"Molly? Are you listening?"

She nodded, but she was caught in the light of a terrible possibility: it might be easier for her to confront her long-held fear, the very thought of which made her sick to her stomach, than to live with the consequences of forcing Hank to give up a second motorcycle.

Chapter 11

The next day Molly called Trina and accepted her invitation.

"I'm so glad you're coming," Trina said. "We'll have a lot of fun."

But Molly still had grave reservations about the Provo trip. She aired all of them in a phone conversation with her mother.

"You might feel better if you remember where you're headed," Bess said. "You receive blessings for doing the Lord's work in His holy house."

"Does that include protecting riders from mechanical failure or the stupidity of drivers sharing the road?"

"You know I can't answer that," Bess said after a moment's pause. "But I can tell you one thing. If you can't go without dragging a cloud of doubt and worry behind you, stay home."

"I'm not staying home."

In an effort to dispel the cloud, Molly spent the following days acting as if she'd put her worries behind her, all the while hoping she would eventually feel the emotion she was faking. But her laughter was spontaneous and genuine the morning of the trip when she saw the unlikely pairing of clothing that Hank had laid out on the bed.

At one end were his freshly laundered temple clothes waiting to be packed into the fabric bag that fit into the hard-sided Gold Wing saddlebag. In the middle of the bed was a pair of dress pants, plus a white shirt and his favorite blue-on-blue tie. On the far end, his leather pants and jacket were placed with the same precision his temple clothes had been. A sleek pair of black motorcycle boots with thick soles sat on the floor.

Was there ever an odder combination of clothes than that? she wondered. She was still chuckling when she knocked on the bathroom door and then passed Hank the stack of fluffy towels she'd fetched for him from the laundry room.

She'd already showered and put on a flowered dress and blue twill blazer. Her own suitcase of temple clothes sat by the front door. All she had yet to do was give her hair a final spray and put on some lipstick.

"So you and Sister Johansen are going to be bringing up the rear in her Excursion?" Hank asked as he came out of the bathroom.

"Along with Ada Davis. She's Nails's younger sister."

"Nails's sister, huh?" Hank began pulling on his dress clothes. "You'd think she'd have her own set of wheels."

"All I know is that she often rides with Trina on local trips." Molly wiped the steam from the bathroom mirror. By the time she'd sprayed her hair and put on the long-lasting coral lipstick that was her current favorite, Hank had finished dressing and packing his temple clothes. He stood contemplating the protective gear, a frown line between his eyebrows.

"Are you missing something?" Molly asked.

"No. I'm trying to figure out how to put these—" he patted the leg of his dress pants, "into those—" he pointed to the leather pants on the bed, "without ending up looking like I slept in them when I get to the temple."

"There's probably a trick to it. Call Brother Bixby. He could help you get dressed."

"Cute." Hank started pulling on the leather pants.

There's one plus for riding with Trina, she thought. *I don't have to stuff my skirt down some chaps.* She'd been told some of the ladies who rode behind their husbands did that. Others pulled their motorcycle pants on under their skirts. Either way, it was hard to picture. The whole concept of the trip seemed full of incongruities.

Hank left first. He was meeting up with the Bixbys so they could ride their cycles to the gathering point together. Molly was watching him ride down the street when Trina arrived in her blue Excursion, right on time. She was as elegant as Molly had remembered, and her perfectly styled hair was a subtle blonde that at her age could only be achieved by visits to an expensive salon. *No wonder she doesn't want to wear a helmet,* Molly thought.

"I'm glad you decided to come," Trina said after Molly had buckled herself into the backseat. "This is Ada Davis, Dorothy's sister. You remember Dorothy; she's the one that did the skit on safety."

Molly couldn't have been more surprised by the woman occupying the passenger seat. Where Nails was tall, thin, and strong, Ada was short, round, and as delicate as a watercolor painting. Molly couldn't imagine them being sisters.

Ada seemed to have read Molly's reaction to her looks and her almost boneless handshake. "Yes, I really am Dorothy's sister. I used to be taller and stronger, like she is, but MS changed that. I couldn't ride a motorcycle even if I wanted to."

"Oh, I'm sorry."

"Thanks, but I don't miss out on any fun. I love being a car bunny. And when I go on short rides in Dorothy's sidecar, I get to wear leathers and my cool helmet."

It didn't take long to get to Smith's Food and Drug Center on Bengal Boulevard. Trina pulled into the parking lot and headed for a far corner that was empty but for a dozen or so big touring bikes parked in a circle. Molly scanned the group for Hank's bike. She found Nails's red Harley—it was hard to miss—but couldn't see Hank or the Bixbys.

Panic was threatening to grip her when the Bixbys finally arrived, Hank right on their tail. She let out a long sigh of relief.

"Save the sighing for later," Trina said with an encouraging smile. "We haven't even gotten on the freeway yet."

"You'll feel better after the travel prayer," Ada added.

When they joined the riders who stood in a circle, helmets in hand, Molly slid in next to Hank. She said her own silent prayer while Doyle Connelly asked for a blessing on their travels and for the presence of the Spirit to be with them during their temple session.

After the prayer, Nails approached Molly. "Ada said you were coming along. Welcome."

Molly glanced down at the hand that firmly grasped hers, surprised to see short, nicely rounded, unpainted nails. "What happened to your fancy nails?"

Nails responded with ready humor. "You noticed those, did you? They're stick-on. I never wear them on a temple ride."

She turned to Ada. "Take a nap on the way down if you can, Sis."

Wishing Hank a good ride, Nails went back to where a nice-looking gentleman waited—Howard, if Molly remembered correctly—and swung her leather-clad leg over her Harley.

"That's my sister," Ada said proudly. "The way she clucks over me you'd think she was my mother."

When Trina joined them after her private moment with Gabe, Molly gave Hank a quick hug. "See you in Provo."

To her surprise, he escorted her and the other women back to Trina's vehicle. He helped Ada into the front seat and then opened the back door for Molly. "Thanks for doing this." He gave her a brief kiss, saluted Trina and Ada, and walked back to his bike.

Swaggered back, was Molly's thought.

"My, oh my." Ada fanned her face with one hand. "I wouldn't let that man out of my sight if I could help it."

Molly grinned. "I'm here, aren't I?"

The first of the bikes pulled out of the parking lot and headed down the road. When others didn't follow, Molly asked, "What are they waiting for?"

"We always keep at least a thirty-second lag between sets of riders. After the last set leaves, we'll count down the same amount of time and then follow."

"There are more rules of the road than I realized," Molly said.

"And every one of them is important," Ada said. "Ask Dorothy."

Molly thought of the rousing safety cheer Nails had led at the TRA meeting.

"I see Howard Norton's riding with Dorothy again," Trina's tone was suggestive.

"He's determined; I have to give him that," Ada said.

"Sharon pointed him out to me at the meeting," Molly said. "It sounds like he's lined up to be Dorothy's next husband."

Ada made an unladylike sound. "She likes him well enough, but I think she's done with husbands."

"That can change in a second," Trina said. "I'd known Gabe half a year without giving him a second thought. Then one day he smiled at me, and that was that."

"Trina here is our champion of romance and marriage," Ada teased.

The second group of riders, Hank included, began to leave the lot. Molly leaned forward so she could keep him in sight. Time crawled before Trina finally pulled out into the traffic.

"This is a big club," Molly said. "I'm never going to keep all these people straight."

"What you need is an interesting tidbit to attach to each name," Trina said. "You met the Connellys at the meeting."

"I have no problem remembering the Connellys," Molly said. This morning she'd noticed Eeyore's refrain on the back of Jeri's TRA jacket: "Thank You for Noticing Me."

She's onto something there, Molly had thought. *It should be the group's motto.*

"I know you've visited with Enid Carter," Trina continued. "She and Merrill are our most senior seniors. They're right in front of us."

"Apricot hair," Molly said, getting a laugh from the other two.

"The Forrests are on the brown and black cycle staggered to their right. They weren't at the meeting because Fricka was sick."

"Oh, they're the ferret people," Molly said.

Ada turned to smile at Molly. "I don't know why you're worried about keeping everyone straight. You're doing great."

Molly wasn't sure about that when Trina gave her yet more to remember. "You probably can't see them from the backseat, but the folks on the big black bike are Sam and Rose Hess. Think of them as ferret-sitters. They sometimes take Fricka for visits to adult day-care centers while we're at a temple."

"They don't attend sessions?"

"They don't belong to the Church, but they like to ride with us." Ada tossed another smile to Molly. "Because we're so nice."

She and Trina paired more names with clever descriptions until

Molly put up her hand. "Hold on! That's already more than I can re-member."

By then, they'd reached Parley's Canyon. The grade was steep and the lanes were full of cars and 18-wheelers. Seeing huge rigs box in the line of riders ahead was the stuff of Molly's worst nightmares, and she began to fidget in her seat.

She was embarrassed when Trina gave her a questioning glance, but Ada only asked, "Is there anything else you'd like to know about the group?"

"Yes, actually." Glad to have something to take her mind off what she was seeing, she asked the question she and Hank had been wonder-ing about: "How do matrons react when a bunch of motorcycle riders pull into a temple parking lot?"

"No problem, because we give them fair warning," Trina said. "We don't want to be responsible for any panic attacks or coronary episodes."

"Like what almost happened that time in St. George," Ada said.

"You tell it," Trina said. "I need to concentrate on driving."

Molly earnestly hoped she would. They were approaching the sum-mit of Parley's Canyon with a big rig in front of them and several others in the slow lane to the right of them. She strained forward against her seat belt, trying to catch a glimpse of Hank's group of riders.

"They've headed down the other side of the hill, Molly. Everything's all right," Trina reassured her. "Go on, Ada. Tell her the story."

"The first time the TRA went to the St. George temple, the infor-mation about what kind of group would be coming never made it to the matrons at the door. When one of them heard the sound of the motor-cycles turning onto temple property she called the police."

"Oh no," Molly said, giggling.

"The next thing the group knew, the police had surrounded them, sirens blaring, lights flashing. The temple president had to come down and straighten it all out before the police would let the TRA riders go and the workers at the door would allow them into the temple!"

"What a great story. I can't wait to tell Hank," Molly said.

"No one we know can verify it," Trina warned. "That's why we relegate it to triple M status—Mormon Motorcycle Mythology. But we always make certain the president of whatever temple we're headed for knows we're coming so we don't have a replay."

They were approaching the Heber exit now, and Molly was relieved to have a clear view of both groups of cycles up ahead. She picked out Hank's silver beast as he moved smoothly from the interstate onto the exit ramp.

"It's a straight shot from here to Heber," Trina said. "We'll stop for a break at The Hub when we get there."

Twenty minutes later, Trina pulled into the crowded parking lot of the long, generic diner. As she looked for a space wide enough to park the Excursion, she and Ada tossed descriptions back and forth to Molly's amusement.

"It's quaint," Trina said. "Pine paneling and redneck plaques."

"It's understaffed," Ada countered. "The service is slow."

"But that gives us more time to visit."

"Actually, it's all about the scones." Ada licked her lips. "Not dry English scones, mind you. These are big and hot and greasy, and they're served with whipped butter and honey and lots of napkins."

After parking, Trina helped Ada out of the Excursion and took one of her arms. "It's always hard to get going after I've been sitting for a while," Ada said apologetically.

Noticing how shaky Ada was, Molly took her other arm. Linked together, they walked up the steps and into the café. Immediately Molly noticed the metal signs posted on the wall behind the lunch counter. She read the words of one out loud. "'Sexual harassment won't be reported here, but it will be graded.'"

"How's that for redneck?" Ada said, laughing richly.

The TRA group had taken over the north dining room. Molly found Hank standing by the Bixbys and another couple. "There you are," he said happily. "Meet Sam and Rose Hess."

The nonmembers, Molly remembered. They were younger than the rest of the group and very alike in their appearance. They were the same height, had slight frames, and brown hair, but Rose's skin was paler than Sam's and sprinkled with freckles.

Everyone ordered the scones with extra butter and honey, so Molly and Hank followed suit. For the next while Molly's attention was divided between keeping the grease and honey from dripping onto her clothing and keeping up with the conversations that flowed around her. She felt like she was finally settling into the rhythm of the experience when it was time to go.

"You two enjoy the scenery," Ada said as she buckled her seat belt. "Provo Canyon is beautiful, but I'm napping." She bundled a car blanket into a pillow, leaned into the window, and was soon fast asleep.

Traffic was sparse on this leg of the drive, so Molly had a clear view of the line of motorcycles eating up the wide road ahead. She relaxed a little and let herself enjoy the mountain landscape they were passing through.

She was amazed at the ease with which Hank had moved among the group at The Hub, chatting as though he were among lifelong friends. There'd been a kind of openhearted accessibility in him that she associated more with her side of the family. *It's as though he's found his community. Tribe, even.*

"What an odd group of people," she murmured.

"We are a strange bunch of ducks," Trina agreed, "but we make a sturdy flock."

Community. Tribe. Flock, Molly mused as she watched the riders ahead.

But all thought vanished when she saw the first riders lean into a sharp curve and disappear out of sight behind a steep rise that bordered Deer Creek Reservoir. She held her breath as the Bixbys and then Hank approached the same spot. As though pulled by a giant magnet, the motorcycles slanted farther and farther to the right until Molly was certain they could never recover. She gripped the back of Ada's seat until Trina had negotiated the curve and she could see Hank still upright and safe on The Beast.

After that, all Molly's enthusiasm for the ride was gone. She sat with hands tightly clasped, willing The Beast to stay vertical as the highway snaked down the mountain. With each curve and each rise and fall of the road her anxiety increased. By the time they reached the mouth of the canyon, she was terrified. Neither Trina nor Ada, who had awakened from her nap, commented on her state of mind, but they kept up a litany of casual and calming statements until they reached the temple parking lot.

When she got out of the car, Molly was embarrassed to discover she was nearly as shaky as Ada. She welcomed joining arms with the two women as they crossed the lot to where the TRA men were standing shoulder to shoulder in a circle, facing outward, with the women in the center.

"What's going on?" Molly asked.

"They can't very well walk into the temple in their gear," Trina said matter-of-factly. "So they change in the parking lot."

The humor and ingenuity of the moment lifted some of the strain Molly had felt on the ride down the canyon. She alternated between grinning and giggling as the women doffed pants or chaps, shook out their shirts, and tucked in their tops. They spent a moment fluffing and preening before they traded places with the men, who transformed themselves into white-shirt-and-tie-wearing temple goers in the same way—except for the hair fluffing.

Watching Hank pack his gear away, Molly noticed that he also packed away the joviality he'd exhibited at The Hub. As he straightened his tie, brushed back his hair, and turned his face to the temple, the Hank that Molly knew best emerged—the responsible Hank, the reliable husband and father, the faithful priesthood holder.

The Hank who made her feel safe in the world.

Chapter 12

The next morning, Molly snuggled warmly against Hank, enjoying an early morning moment of cozy contentment while thinking about her first TRA adventure. She was grateful for the peace and serenity that had come to her in the temple. That, along with Ada and Trina's encouragement, had made the trip home on I-15 bearable.

Thank heavens I could keep Hank in sight, she thought, putting her arm around his middle.

He clasped her hand and pulled her arm more closely around him. "It was a good day yesterday, wasn't it, Miss Molly?" he murmured. "I don't remember the last time I attended a temple session where I was so focused on the work."

"Why do you suppose that was?"

"The whole experience, I think. Riding in the fresh air, enjoying the scenery, being part of the single purpose of the group."

"Pulling off your riding pants in the parking lot?"

She could feel his silent chuckle. "That was definitely part of what made it extraordinary. I hope you enjoyed yourself too."

"I did," she said soberly. "Except for when I was scared to death about you being on the road."

He rolled toward her and pulled her into a hug. "And here we are, both safe and together." He kissed her and then got out of bed, whistling as he went into the bathroom.

You didn't even hear me. You have no idea how I felt.

She padded into the kitchen, wondering if it would be worth it to ruin his pleasure in the day by telling him. She was pouring herself some orange juice when the phone rang.

"Hey, Mom," Wade said cheerfully. "How did it go yesterday?"

"Your dad had a great time."

"And you? Didn't you enjoy yourself even a little bit?"

"Yes," she admitted. "I liked the women I rode with, and going through a temple session always lifts me up."

"Then it wasn't all bad. Are we still on for lunch today?"

"Of course."

"Great. We can't wait to hear about Dad's first road trip. Lisa and Hayden haven't talked about anything else all week. And . . ." Wade paused. "Mom, I'm bringing the kids' helmets with me today. Dad said he'd take them for a ride if I did."

In a flash Molly's unresolved anxiety and fear from the day before came roaring to the surface, and she exploded. "Wade! What are you thinking? It's irresponsible enough that you risk my sweet babies on that wretched four-wheeler, helmets or no helmets. But letting them on that thing in the garage is . . . is . . . *reckless endangerment*. I won't allow it."

In the silence following her outburst, she could hear Wade breathing on the other side of the line. "Wade?"

"This isn't up to you, Mom. Heather and I are their parents, and we've decided that if Dad feels all right about taking them on his motorcycle, they can ride with him."

Molly dropped into the nearest chair, stunned at how deftly Wade had put her in her place. "It may be your decision, but I absolutely do not agree with it."

"I know you love the kids, and you only want to protect them. But I don't want your fear to get in the way of their relationship with their grandpa."

That sounded too much like what Micheline had said to ignore. In her need to protect the ones she loved, she ran the danger of infecting them with her fear. That wasn't what she wanted.

"Is Laurel coming?" Wade asked, interrupting her thoughts. "We haven't seen her for weeks. The kids miss her, Katie especially."

"She said she'd try to be here, but she's involved in some big litigation that's got her working late hours."

"Maybe that's why she's been a stranger. Heather was afraid we'd done something to upset her."

"Why? Has Laurel said anything?"

"No, it's more of a feeling. Tell Dad we're all looking forward to hearing about his TRA adventure."

Molly was making the healthy version of Hank's Saturday breakfast with low-calorie waffles and turkey bacon when he joined her in the kitchen. "Who was on the phone?"

"Wade. He called to see if Laurel would be here today. Heather thinks she might be upset about something."

"She has been a little distant since the retirement party." He poured juice into some glasses and put them on the table. "That job of hers takes a lot out of her."

"I hope that's what it is," Molly said, but her mother's instinct knew there was more. Now she had Laurel to worry about on top of wondering how she would manage to keep her mouth shut when Hank took Lisa and Hayden for a ride on the motorcycle.

Can I do that? Should I do that? she wondered. Even if Wade and Heather thought it was okay, was it right for her to stand by and let the kids do something so dangerous?

Driven by her concerns, Molly went through her morning chores like a dynamo.

"What's lit your fire?" Hank asked.

"The kids are coming," she said with false cheer. "I have frosty dogs to make."

He grinned. "Got to have frosty dogs if the kids are coming. Do you need my help?"

"I've got it, thanks."

"Then I'll take care of some things in the garage."

More like bond with The Beast.

Molly grabbed a handful of random CDs and put them in the changer to keep herself entertained while she concocted her grandchildren's favorite treat, hot dogs frosted with cheesy mashed potatoes. To a background of Josh Groban she assembled all the ingredients and started peeling potatoes. Working automatically, she let her mind wander to the time she'd first heard the songs of another famous crooner, Barry Manilow, back when Wade and Laurel were toddlers. How much simpler things had been then, busier but simpler.

Before she knew it, Molly had peeled, boiled, mashed, seasoned, and cheesed enough potatoes to frost dozens of hot dogs. Looking at the mound in front of her, she shook her head. *What was I thinking to make so much? No matter. Wade and Heather will take the leftovers.*

As she slit hot dogs and laid them out on cookie sheets, a disc from a conversational German class she'd taken the year before clicked on. *"Nach mir bitte. Die Sonne scheint,"* the deep voice said. "Repeat after me. The sun shines."

"Dee sohn-ah sheint," Molly repeated as she piped the last of the cheesy potato mix into the slit in the mustard-slathered hot dogs.

"Das mädchen ist schön. The girl is pretty."

Molly mimicked the words as she topped the dogs with an extra scattering of grated cheese and a sprinkle of paprika. Then she slid the cookie sheet into the oven.

"Der Junge ist kräftig. The boy is strong."

"Are you talking about me, Grandma?" Hayden came running into the kitchen from the garage. He skittered to a stop, pushed back the sleeves of his shirt, and pumped the muscle on his right arm.

"The boy is strong," he repeated in his deepest voice and struck a weightlifter's pose. "Something smells good. Are we having frosty dogs for lunch?"

He stopped talking only long enough to give her a quick hug. "Jan's here with Bozo. Can I save a hot dog for him? We brought our helmets. Did you know we get to ride on that killer bike?"

He couldn't have used a worse adjective. "That's Sister Peterson to you, young man," she corrected. "Yes, the frosty dogs are for lunch, and you may save one for Bozo if Sister Peterson says it's okay for him."

His surprised look told her that her tone was sharper than usual. She softened it to ask, "Who said Grandpa's motorcycle was a killer?"

"Cal." Heather came into the kitchen, Katie in front of her and Junie in her arms. A diaper bag was slung over Heather's shoulder. "He's out there with Dad and half of the neighborhood."

Molly picked up Katie, who was small for five. "What exactly did Cal say?"

"That Dad's bought himself one killer of a cycle. Wade said it was a heck of a ride. Jan's husband expressed the same opinion, but in a four-letter word. Then Cal said Dad should have flames detailed on the Gold Wing in honor of that very fact."

"Men!" Molly muttered. "What? You want to get down all ready?" she asked a wriggling Katie.

"I want Aunt Laurel. Is she coming?"

"I hope so, honey lamb."

She put Katie down, and then went to see what was going on in her garage. Cal, Micheline, the whole troop of Petersons, and Alex Alvarez were standing around The Beast. *Who's sending smoke signals?* she wondered.

Micheline waved when she saw Molly. "I wanted to show Cal the Gold Wing. We didn't know you had a houseful."

"It's The Beast," Molly said. "It's a giant magnet."

"What smells so good?" Jan asked.

"Frosty dogs. *The frosty dogs!*" Molly shrieked in dismay. She ran to the oven and flung open the door in time to rescue the dogs just as the cheesy topping began to turn from golden to brown.

"Boy, those look good." Jan was watching her from the doorway. "My girls had them when they ate over here with your grandkids awhile back. They haven't stopped talking about them since."

Molly wouldn't turn someone away from frosty dogs any more than her mother would deny a visitor bean soup. "Would you and your family like to have lunch with us?"

"Love to," Jan said happily.

Molly was surprised by her reaction to the invitation. It was only frosty dogs, after all. She motioned to Micheline. "You and Cal, too."

"Sounds good," Micheline said. "Do you need something for dessert? I made snickerdoodles last night."

"I've got rainbow sherbet in the freezer," Jan said.

While those two went for their dessert contributions, Heather put Junie down in the portable crib and helped Molly make a green salad.

Lisa, Katie, and the Peterson girls set the extended dining room table and card table with plates for everyone, including Laurel. She hadn't arrived yet, but Molly was hopeful.

The tray full of frosty dogs and the bowls of garden salad emptied fast as guests filled their plates at the center island before finding their seats. But Molly couldn't eat. Hearing Lisa and Hayden go on and on about the coming ride had robbed her of her appetite. She busied herself keeping glasses full of lemonade or milk, filling a plate for Laurel, and chopping up a plain hot dog for Bozo, who waited patiently at the garage door.

When she came back after putting Bozo's hot dog in front of him, she caught Wade looking at her. His expression said he understood how she was feeling, but he didn't call off the ride.

After the dessert of snickerdoodles and sherbet, Hank stood up from the table. "That was a great lunch. Thank you, Molly. Thank you, Micheline and Jan." He clapped his hands. "Okay, kids. How about that ride?"

No. Not yet.

Molly caught everyone's attention using her "mother" voice. "Wait a minute. Bean Night rules apply." When the grandkids groaned, she explained to the visitors, "Cleanup comes first."

"Let's get at it," Hank said. He and Micheline directed the kids, who jumped to their tasks.

Now they work double-time, Molly thought grumpily.

Hayden was busy sweeping the floor and the others were bussing dishes when Katie cried, "Look! Aunt Laurel's here!"

Laurel put down her computer case and swung Katie up into her arms. "Hi, everyone. Looks like I missed lunch. I hope there are some frosty dogs left for me."

"I have a plate for you right here," Molly kissed Laurel's cheek. "I'm so glad you came."

"Did you think I wouldn't?" Laurel lowered her chin and her voice. "*I'm* not the one who's gone missing. You and Dad are never here when I stop by or call. Seems like you're always off on one of your *adventures*."

"When did you . . ."

But Laurel had moved on. "Micheline, Jan, this is a nice surprise." She talked to the two women while she ate, Katie sitting on her lap.

To Molly's eye there were still things that needed to be done when Hank officially declared the kitchen clean. He held out straws for Lisa and Hayden to draw for the first ride. Hayden whooped when he drew the short straw and headed for the garage.

Molly watched him with a sinking feeling. She'd hoped that something would rescue her from this moment. Aliens knocking at the front door would have sufficed, but they hadn't obliged, and now she had to either let Hank take her beloved grandchildren for a ride on The Beast or fling herself as an offering in front of it.

"We'll be fine, Moll," Hank said as he passed her. "I'll stay in the neighborhood and follow all the rules for riding with passengers."

Filled with foreboding, Molly followed the group out to the driveway. She bit her lip as Hank backed the Gold Wing out of the garage and turned it to face the street.

"What do you call a helmet without a face shield?" he asked Hayden as he checked to make sure the boy's helmet strap was securely tightened.

"I don't know, Grandpa. What?"

"A bug collector."

Hayden giggled with a nine-year-old's appreciation of bug stories. Hank hoisted the boy onto the passenger seat, slid his leg over the saddle, and started the engine.

Molly had been praying that either something would forestall the ride or she would experience a peaceful feeling of rightness. Neither had happened. It was up to her. Arms in the air, she started forward. "Stop, Hank! You can't—"

Wade caught her by the arm. "Don't do it, Mom. You might not trust Dad to take care of Hayden, but Hayden does. So do I. Don't ruin it for them."

"But—"

At the steely look he gave her, she clamped her mouth shut.

Hank revved the engine and they were off. Wade and the rest

of the onlookers drifted toward the sidewalk to watch them turn the corner and wait for their return.

Molly couldn't bear to see her grandson on the Gold Wing, so she sat down on the steps to the kitchen, head in her hands. Jan and Micheline hung back with her.

"That's got to smart," Jan said.

"What?" Molly asked, not looking up.

"Hearing Wade say you don't trust Hank to take care of Hayden."

The audacity of Jan commenting on her family business snapped Molly's head up. "My not wanting Hayden on the motorcycle doesn't have anything to do with me not trusting Hank," she said sharply. "Motorcycles are dangerous. People get killed on them. No amount of trust can change that. No amount of fun justifies it. Anyone with a brain can see that."

Micheline's jaw dropped. "Molly!"

"I . . ." Jan's face was paper white. She leaned down as if to adjust Bozo's collar. "I think it's time for us to go. Right, Bozo?" She hurried from the garage, pausing only to say something to her husband.

Micheline shook her head, disappointment in her eyes. "Molly, Molly, Molly. That was not your best moment." She joined the others on the sidewalk, leaving Molly alone with her regrets.

What have I done? she asked herself. *Why did I say that?* Then she prayed: *Please help me get a grip on my emotions. Help me see what's important and what's not. Help me make it through this day.*

After Hank had given rides to everyone who wanted them—Alex excluded, since he didn't have his father's permission—the party slowly broke up. Jan's husband herded his children toward home. Micheline followed Cal after giving Molly a quick hug and some advice. "Relax. Take a deep breath. Don't say anything you'll be sorry for in the morning."

"Too late for that."

When only family was left in the driveway, Hank turned to Laurel. "There's my girl. How about it? Would you like a ride? Wade brought Heather's helmet for you to wear."

"Clever ploy, Wade," Laurel said. "But I'm not interested."

"Then I'm up." Wade started getting his gear on. "What was that T-CLOCK thing you were telling me about, Dad?"

As Hank explained the safety protocol they had learned at the TRA meeting, Molly reluctantly acknowledged how seriously he took safety issues. If his safety had depended solely on that, she would have felt better. But it didn't. The world was full of drunks, kids texting, and drivers blinded with road rage.

"How long are you going to be gone?" she asked Hank.

He and Wade exchanged a conspiratorial glance. "It might be a while."

"If you're going to be gone longer than an hour, call us."

"We're going to be gone longer than an hour," Wade said.

The hands on the clock moved with excruciating slowness as Laurel played games with the children and Molly talked to Heather. When an hour passed with no sign of the men, Heather put Junie and Katie down for a nap and sent Lisa and Hayden to the family room for quiet time.

Molly hoped to have a conversation with Laurel once the kids were taken care of, but Laurel picked up her laptop. "I'm expecting an important document, so I need to check my e-mail," she said. "Is it all right if I use Dad's office?"

"Of course." Molly smiled to hide her disappointment. It seemed to her that Laurel had been using Wade's children as a buffer between the two of them all afternoon. Now she was using work. Whatever had been stuck in her craw since the retirement party wasn't something she was ready to spit out yet.

With Laurel in Hank's office and Heather dozing on the couch, Molly watched the clock while she re-swept the floor that Hayden had given a quick once-over after lunch. Then she watched the clock while she mopped it. When the hands showed that almost two hours had passed, she started pacing. Where were her men? Were they safe? Were they whole?

She almost collapsed with relief when she heard the motorcycle pull into the driveway. Leaning against the center island, she took a deep breath and promised herself she would give Hank and Wade the chance to offer their excuses and apologize for making her worry before lighting into them.

They clomped into the kitchen talking and laughing. "Hey, everyone. We're home," Hank called, waking Junie and bringing Laurel from his office.

Wade gave his wife a big kiss and started taking off his gloves. "That was wicked. You've got to try it, honey. You too, Laurel."

Heedless of the tension in the room, the men described their trip up one of the canyons. Then they went down the hall toward Hank's office, talking animatedly about the difference between street motorcycles, sport motorcycles, and touring bikes. There was a camaraderie between them Molly had never seen before. A camaraderie that excluded her and Laurel.

She hoped Laurel hadn't seen it, but her daughter's eyes had the look of someone suddenly cut loose from her moorings. Her whole life, Laurel had been the one Hank invited into his office, the one with whom he'd shared confidences and had long conversations. Now he'd invited Wade into the place she'd considered her special province.

I know what she's feeling, Molly thought. That morning Wade had spoken to her in a way he never had before. And now, instead of sitting down to give her the details of his ride, he'd gone to the office with Hank. The balance of relationships in the family was shifting.

Where does that leave Laurel? Where does it leave me?

Chapter 13

Ghnaah, pfwooooo.

Ghnaah, pfwooooo.

Ghnaah, pfwooooo.

Molly had been lying awake for hours, listening to Hank's snoring while scenes from their Saturday went round and round in her head. The fact that he could sleep so soundly when he and his toy had been the cause of such tension made her mad enough to spit nails.

Ghnaah, pfwooooo.

She clapped her hands over her ears and scrunched her eyes shut in frustration. *If I have to hear that one more time, I'll stick a pillow over his head!*

Gnaah, ngh, ngh, pfwoooo-ooo-oo.

Homicide not being a legitimate option, she flung her covers back and bounded out of bed, not caring if she woke him.

The sound of his snores followed her down the hall to the kitchen. She stomped around the island and the table trying to work off her frustration, briefly considering going into the backyard and howling at the moon. She decided against that, too. Hank would probably sleep through it, but the neighbors might call animal control.

She fixed a cup of Sleepytime herbal tea and sipped it while sitting at the kitchen table. Twenty minutes later her eyes were still wide open, and her feet needed to be moving. Cup in hand she wandered through the upstairs and then padded down the steps to the basement. She didn't realize the Stay Out Room had been calling to her until she was at the door.

She stood with her hand on the doorknob for a moment, wondering if she truly wanted to see how badly Hank had mucked up what she called "visual organization" and he called a mess. Then she opened the door and stepped inside.

The room didn't feel like it was hers anymore.

Her sewing machine, which had been ministered to by the Sewing Machine Doctor, was shrouded in its plastic cover. Boxes of art supplies were corralled on one side of her large worktable. Hank's Play-Doh dog sculpture was sitting on the other, leaving a large, empty expanse before the task chair. The narrow path she'd created months ago to get to the wrapping paper had expanded to two-thirds of the floor space.

Nothing's where I left it. How am I ever going to find the things he moved?

Shuffling through the remaining piles, she came across a container of Silly Putty. She opened it, dumped the pink mass into her hand, and began massaging it. Then, on an impulse, she threw some of it at one wall, where it stuck in a blob. Giggling, she massaged and threw several other balls.

She studied the pattern of pink blobs as if it were a photograph or a work of art. Deciding it needed more color, she searched out egg-shaped containers of neon yellow, blue, and green Silly Putty, and for the next half hour threw glops against the once-cream wall, laughing all the while.

She ran out of Silly Putty and laughter at the same time, but her venture into performance art had cleared her head. She sat down on the floor, her back against the wall and knees drawn up to her chest, and thought about the day before. *What a kafuffle. We're doing and saying things that are totally out of character, and it's all The Beast's fault.*

But Molly knew that blaming The Beast was too easy. She picked some stray pieces of Silly Putty from the rug and molded them into a muddy ball, thinking that the coming of the motorcycle had brought out parts of each of them they didn't know they had.

A few hours of sleep early Sunday morning didn't alter her assessment, but she decided to act as if there hadn't been a change in the Mancuso household. Hank seemed to have made the same decision, because they carefully tiptoed around each other, especially when it came to talking about what had happened the day before.

"Everyone sure liked your frosty dogs yesterday," Hank said.

"Thanks, but you and the motorcycle were the hit of the day."

He started to say something else but then changed his mind.

Just as well, Molly thought. She put the ingredients for apple pork chops and sauerkraut in her Crock-Pot so dinner would be ready when they got home from services. Shortly before they left home, she went over the Easter songs she would be teaching the Primary children during singing time.

Sharon and Ronald Bixby were the first people to greet Molly and Hank when they walked into the foyer. They chatted about Friday's Provo trip as they followed Hank and Molly into the chapel. Not only that, but Ron followed Hank into "their" pew. Sharon motioned Molly to sit next to Ron and took the aisle spot Micheline usually occupied.

Having Sharon sit where Micheline usually did put Molly in a fix. She was wondering what to do when Cal rushed by and Micheline appeared at the end of the pew. She stopped, momentarily perplexed. When Molly caught her eye and apologized with a subtle shrug, Micheline sat down next to Jan on the other side of the aisle.

After sacrament meeting Molly had to hustle to get to the Primary room, so there wasn't time to explain to Micheline until after Primary was over. "Sorry about not saving a place for you," Molly said when she found her friend at the door of the Relief Society room. "It would have been rude to tell Ronald and Sharon to find other seats."

Micheline's reply was matter-of-fact, even a little cool. "Sacrament meeting isn't about where you sit. But if you do feel the need to apologize to someone, Jan is still upset by what happened yesterday."

"I did make a mess of that, didn't I? Hank taking the kids for rides pushed my buttons big time, and I didn't even think before I lit into her. How bad was I?"

"You want to know the truth? That was as nasty as I've ever seen you. First you invited Jan for lunch, and then you decimated her. If you'd been as mean to me, I wouldn't be talking to you right now."

Molly had spent a good deal of her sleepless night trying to convince herself that she hadn't been so awful, but she couldn't escape the truthfulness of Micheline's words. "I'll apologize; I promise."

"Put your money where your mouth is, friend." Micheline pointed down the hall. "Here comes Jan now."

Molly had had little experience apologizing for bad behavior. She took a deep breath and started toward Jan, thinking, *What should I say? How can I make up for being so thoughtless?*

She intercepted Jan partway down the hall. "I'm sorry for what I said yesterday, Jan. It was rude and uncalled for. Will you accept my apology?"

Jan refused to look at her, but she nodded, a gesture that was almost imperceptible.

Molly touched her shoulder. "I mean it. Please believe me. I hope we can still be friends."

"Friends" seemed to be the magic word. Jan looked up with a tentative smile and accepted Molly's invitation to sit next to her in Relief Society. Micheline sat on Jan's other side, and Sharon bookended Molly.

Curiouser and curiouser, Molly thought. *I wonder what's going to happen next.*

What happened next was lunch with Nails.

Molly was sitting at her desk the next morning sorting through piles of family photos when the phone rang. Hank answered it, so she kept on working.

That summer her parents would be celebrating their sixty-fifth wedding anniversary, and she and her sisters had decided to make a scrapbook for them. As a first step they were each going through their copies of family photographs looking for ones they liked.

In the 1943 wedding photo Molly held in her hand, Roy Finley stood ramrod straight in his uniform. He looked impossibly young, and Bess, who was so much shorter than he, might have been a child playing dress-up. On the back of the photo was written, "July 7th. Roy left for Europe the next day."

She put the photo in the to-use pile.

"Molly," Hank hollered down the hall. "Nails wants to talk to you."

Hoping his voice hadn't carried across the line, Molly picked up her handset. "Hi, Dorothy."

"Hi to you. Am I imagining things, or did I hear Hank refer to me as Nails?"

"Oh, dear." Molly flushed with embarrassment. "It's the name we gave you when we first saw you up at Silver Fork Lodge. It's because of your long, red fingernails."

Nails chuckled. "I like it. It brings up associations like 'tough as nails,' which of course I am."

Molly hoped she meant it. She would never be able to think of the woman as Dorothy.

"Ada's spending a few hours at the Family History Library," Nails went on. "How about joining me downtown for lunch?"

"I'd love to."

"Great. I'm craving Evil Jungle Princess Shrimp at Thaifoon in the Gateway Center."

When Molly told Hank their plans, he reminded her of all the ridiculous careers they'd imagined for Dorothy that day at Silver Fork Lodge. "Find out what kind of work she did. We can see if either one of us came close."

Lunch at Thaifoon was a treat. They ordered lettuce wraps for an appetizer and shared an order of Evil Jungle Princess Shrimp. While they ate, they told stories from their pasts. They'd barely started on the entrée when Molly decided that Nails was one of the most interesting people she'd ever met.

Married and widowed twice, she'd had three children with her first husband. She now had ten grandchildren and a great-grandchild recently born to a mother barely nineteen.

"I'm getting a Harley bumper sticker for my Jeep," Nails said. "It says 'Great-Grandmas Ride Too.' What do you think?"

"That you'll get a lot of attention." Molly took another mouthful of the shrimp dish. "You must have had your kids pretty young."

Nails nodded. "After my first love—he was a James Dean wanna-be—left town, I married a cowboy from down the road. We made babies and rode the rodeo circuit. Eldon was a bull rider and I was a barrel racer."

"Ada said you were a rodeo queen."

"Miss Rodeo 1963. That was the last year I competed."

"How come?"

"Babies. I got pregnant with our first on our honeymoon, and they just kept on a-coming. My gynecologist didn't want me riding in that condition—the kind of training I was doing was too rigorous—so that was that.

"Eldon kept on bull riding though. The last trip we took together was to a rodeo in Grand Forks. We left our three kids with my mom so we could have some time alone. We'd been there two days when he fell over dead in the shower. Brain aneurism."

Molly was taken aback. "I'm so sorry. I can't imagine what it must have been like to be a young widow with three little children."

"I managed. I moved in with my folks and took any job I could find. Riding instructor, dispatcher for a cement company, reporter for the Third District Court. I worked there twenty years and only left because Charles asked me to marry him."

"That's quite a list of occupations. When Hank and I saw you at the lodge last fall, we tried to guess what sort of work you did. Neither of us was close." Molly looked at her with frank admiration. "You're amazing. All I've done is play the violin and raise my kids."

"Raising a family is a big job. And I've heard of the Fiddling Finleys. I'd like to see you perform sometime."

"Come on the Fourth of July. That's the next time I'll be on stage."

When their server brought the bill, Nails said it was her treat and put a credit card in the folder for the server to pick up. "Molly, do you mind if I ask you a question?"

"Not at all. I've asked you plenty."

"I noticed you didn't ride behind Hank on the Provo temple trip. Do you mind me asking why?"

Molly jabbed her straw at the ice in her drink. "I've seen firsthand what happens when a motorcycle and a car collide. It's a bloody mess, and I'll never get that picture out of my head. If it were up to me, Hank would never ride that Gold Wing again."

"Now I'm surprised you came on that trip at all. I know women in your situation who would have stayed home and made their men miserable over it."

"I came close to doing that. There were moments when I wished I had." She paused. "Did Ada tell you I almost flipped out when we were going down Provo Canyon? I was so embarrassed."

"Why? What you feel is what you feel. After Charles died, I started working with people who wanted to overcome their fear of horses. Sometimes a specific event in the past causes the fear. Sometimes there doesn't seem to be a reason for it. It doesn't matter. Fear is fear."

Molly bit her lip. "Thanks for saying that. You don't know how much it means to be understood."

"Hank doesn't understand?"

"He tries to, but for him, reason trumps feelings every time. It's been thirty-five years since the accident in front of our Murray house. He thinks I should be over it by now."

"Feelings have a way of ambushing us when buttons get pushed."

"You can say that again. So I guess you were pretty successful in getting people to work through their fear?"

"Yes. One of the great pleasures of my life has been to see people previously paralyzed by it get into the saddle and ride around the ring. And have fun doing it."

"Nai . . . Dorothy?" Molly spoke slowly, thinking aloud.

"It's okay to call me Nails."

"Nails, do you think you could help me? Not so I can ride with Hank, but so my fear won't get in the way of him doing what he wants to do."

"I think so, yes. But anything we do won't work unless you absolutely want to make that change."

"Isn't *wanting* to want to enough?"

"Only as a place to start. If you're serious, we could begin right now. I moved in with Ada after my second husband died. Her house is in the Avenues, only fifteen minutes from here, even with all the stoplights. If you have time to follow me there, I can give you a copy of the desensiti-zation tape I used with my riding clients. And if you want, I'll introduce you to my motorcycles."

Molly's hands were sweaty as she followed Nails's car to a butter-yellow Victorian house with white trim. Crocus and early tulips were blooming in front of the south-facing house, and wicker furniture had already been put out on the pillared porch.

Molly parked on the street and then joined Nails in the driveway. "Will Ada be home by now?"

"I'm not expecting her until later." She led Molly through the de-tached garage and into a large extension where two motorcycles were parked. Next to the flame-red Harley Molly had seen Nails riding in the canyon sat a smaller, blue motorcycle with a sidecar.

With a grand gesture, Nails presented them as if they were royalty. "This is Springsteen, the Heritage Softail Classic I rode on the temple trip. The Honda with the sidecar is Sister Martha."

Molly squinted. "You name your motorcycles?"

"No. They name themselves."

"That's a bit . . ."

"Weird?" Nails finished for her. "It started with the barrel horse my folks gave me for my ninth birthday. The first time I rode her, she told me her name was Firefly. Since then, I've taken every new horse, car, and motorcycle I've ever had on a naming ride."

For the next quarter hour, Nails told Molly stories about how she found the Harley and some of her favorite rides. "One fall I came home from a tour up one of the canyons bursting with things to tell Ada about what I'd seen. She said she wished she could go on a motorcycle ride with me, and I thought, 'I can make that happen.' I took some money Charles had left me and bought Martha and the sidecar the next day."

Even after all Nails had said, Molly still didn't understand the *why* behind having a motorcycle in the first place. "What is it about riding that makes you want to take the risk?"

Nails pondered that for a moment. "The feeling of being alive, I think. Being part of the landscape I'm riding through. Smelling what's coming before I see it, like a field of mown hay. I love taking back roads and talking with people I meet along the way. I love being bone-tired when I get home, but still taking the time to clean up my bike, the way I used to groom my horses after riding."

"I bet you talk to it and pet it, like you did your horses," Molly said.

"Guilty as charged."

"Have you ever had an accident?"

"Are you asking about barrel racing or motorcycling?"

"Both, I guess."

"I've had some near-misses on my motorcycle, but the only serious accident I've ever had was when I got pitched off a horse and broke my arm."

Nails pulled a chair from her workbench. "Here, have a seat." She opened a folding lawn chair for herself.

Molly sat down, thought creasing her forehead. "And you got back on. Weren't you even a little bit scared?"

"I was always more worried about Eldon than myself, especially if he drew a mean bull. Those eight seconds were like eternity. I imagine that's how it felt watching Hank ride down Provo Canyon. But rodeo was in Eldon's blood. It was his passion."

"So you let him do what he wanted to do, even though you were afraid?"

"Yes. I'm glad I did."

"Would you say that if he'd been killed by a bull?"

"But he wasn't. I don't spend too much time thinking and worrying about life, Molly. I'd rather live it."

Nails rummaged in some storage boxes until she came up with a cassette tape. "Here's the visualization tape I told you about. To get the most out of it, listen to it twice a day—with the expectation that it will help. You'll have to think 'motorcycle' every time the word 'horse' comes up, but after the first couple of times, you'll do that automatically."

"Thanks. I'll give it a try." Molly took the tape.

"If you like it, I'll make a CD for you."

"Nails, please don't mention this to Hank. I don't want to tell him about it until I'm sure it's working."

On her drive home Molly relived the conversations she'd had with Nails that afternoon and decided they'd all been about courage. Not only had Nails lived through some tough situations, she'd handled whatever life handed her with grit and determination. Molly was so inspired that for a second she felt as if she could get behind Hank and ride without fear.

When she got home, he was in the family room reading an issue of *Wing World,* the magazine put out by the Gold Wing Road Riders Association. "How was your afternoon with Nails?" he asked when she came into the room.

"It was great fun. You wouldn't believe what she told me about her life. She is some woman."

"Tell me."

For the next half hour, Molly entertained him with the details she'd learned. He was especially eager to hear about the various jobs Nails had had over the years.

"Court reporter?" he said. "I never would have guessed, with those fingernails of hers."

"They're fake," Molly said, laughing. "And get this—she takes her motorcycles on naming rides. It's something she started doing with her horses when she was barrel racing. She'd take each new one out on a long ride and ask it what its name was."

Hank's eyebrows showed what he thought about that. "I suppose you'll tell me the horses answered?"

"They did."

"And she did the same thing with her Harley?"

"She did."

"And it answered?"

"It did."

"Okay, I'll bite. What did it say its name was?"

"Springsteen."

"As in The Boss." Hank smiled broadly. "I can see it."

"I think you should take the Gold Wing out on a naming ride."

His smile faded. "What would be the point, when you've already named it? Everyone knows it's The Beast."

Chapter 14

When Molly came back from running errands a few days later, she parked her SUV on the far side of the garage, as Hank had recently requested. That meant his sedan would now occupy the slot between her vehicle and the Gold Wing.

Uh-oh, Molly had thought when he made the request. *He's heard me wondering how long The Beast would last if I sideswiped it on a regular basis!*

There was no doubt now that the motorcycle was a permanent part of her life. She definitely needed to give Nails's tape a try. There was no time like the present—Hank was gone, so she had the house to herself. She took the phone off the hook and put the tape into her old cassette player. Then she kicked her shoes off, settled down on the family room couch, and pushed Play.

She was immediately drawn into the invitation to relax. After she'd reached the limp-noodle stage, the soothing female voice instructed her to create a mental picture of a place where she felt safe. She conjured up her favorite apple tree on the family property—one she'd leaned against as a teenager, daydreaming about her future.

Then the voice instructed her to imagine a horse (motorcycle, Molly amended), but far enough away that it didn't cause any unease. Slowly, step by step, she was instructed to bring it closer.

Every part of her resisted that, so she visualized the Gold Wing on the other side of the field from the apple tree and left it there.

Over the next few days Molly slowly inched it closer; she reverted to the relaxation and breathing techniques when her skin started to crawl. She did much better when she stopped trying to hurry the process and took Nails's advice to play with it. How could she take the Gold Wing seriously when she was sliding it sideways, dancing it on its rear wheel, and standing it on its handlebars?

As she brought Hank's cycle a little nearer each day, Molly learned she had far more control over her feelings than she'd realized. She eagerly reported her progress to Nails a few days later.

"Do you feel less tense when you see the Gold Wing in your garage?"

"I think so."

"That's a good indication that what you're doing is working. Have you told Hank about it?"

"Not yet. He'd either think it was a bunch of mumbo jumbo, or he'd want me to go faster than I can."

"Give him a chance. He might surprise you."

"I'd rather keep it to myself for now."

Molly listened to the tape every day until a burst of balmy April weather hit. She and Hank spent a sunny week working shoulder to shoulder on spring yard chores. The Beast remained in the garage. Even the word "motorcycle" was absent from their conversation. She felt closer to Hank than she had since his birthday, and the feeling of connectedness continued into the weekend. They watched the Sunday sessions of April conference sitting together on the family room couch, sharing insights and jotting down periodic notes.

Life like it used to be, like it ought to be, Molly thought before dropping into sleep that night.

The bubble she'd been living in continued on Monday when Hope and June came to work on the anniversary scrapbook, boxes of photos in hand. Hope asked to see The Beast when they first arrived, but Hank had ridden it to the bowling alley, so it wasn't available for show-and-tell. After that the topic never came up. They were too busy poring over the photos they'd each sorted out, as well as the ones their parents had said were important to them.

They found a photo of Bess standing over a campfire, waving at the unknown photographer. The girls were clustered around her in wrinkled, mismatched outfits. "We were probably on the way to some gig,"

Molly said. "You were the serious one even then, Hope. See how intense your expression was."

"And those clothes! We look like migrant farm workers." Hope ran her fingers lovingly over the image. "Mom and Dad worked hard to get from where they were to where they are now."

By noon, they'd finished a preliminary sorting and decided on the format and narrative. Molly was feeling warm and happy when she hugged her sisters and waved them on their way. It lasted until she heard Hank returning home on the motorcycle. Life as It Was reasserted itself, bursting the bubble of Life as It Ought to Be.

It was time for her to face reality and get back on track with Nails's tape. But reestablishing her routine of listening was harder than establishing it in the first place, she found. For several more days she kept finding excuses for not doing the work. Finally she kicked herself into gear and went outside to listen to it on the comfortable front porch bench.

Well, here I am, back at square one. But I'm going to stick with it this time.

She put in the earplugs and turned on the player. To her surprise, the minute she heard the familiar voice she dropped into a relaxed state. She had no sense of how much time had passed when she heard a voice coming as if from a distant point in the universe and felt a warm hand on her shoulder.

"Hey, Molly! Are you in there?"

It took effort for Molly to climb out of the deep place she'd been in. "Sorry," she said when she opened her eyes and saw Micheline sitting beside her. She took her earplugs out and turned off the tape. "I was in my happy place, imagining Hank's motorcycle as a noninvasive neutral element in my environment."

"Huh? What are you talking about?"

"I was listening to a tape Nails said might help me get over being so paranoid about The Beast. It's one she used back when she was working with people who had a fear of horses. Whenever I hear the word 'horse' on the tape I replace it with 'motorcycle'. . . ."

She trailed off at the bemused look on Micheline's face.

"Nails is the weird one from Bixby's motorcycle group, isn't she?" Micheline asked.

"Not weird. Unconventional."

"Is the tape helping?"

"I think it would, if I listened to it as often as I'm supposed to. What brought you my way?"

"It's been a while since we've walked. I was hoping to catch you when you were free to go with me."

Molly looked from the tape to Micheline and chose Micheline.

The next day was the first session of Molly's Street and People Photography class. Listening to the tape was the last thing on her mind as she searched through her photographs. The instructor, a young woman named Chris, had requested all students bring examples of their work that caught the moment. Molly chose the action photos of the motorcycles she'd taken on the way to Silver Fork Lodge.

She was nervous when she spread her choices out for the class to look at.

"Now, this is what I was hoping to see," Chris said, looking at them one by one. "You didn't think about these, you took them automatically. Shooting should become a reflex, straight from the heart. That's what we'll focus on this quarter."

She picked up a photo of Nails and held it at arm's length, scrutinizing it. It was Molly's favorite of the Silver Fork shots; it showed Nails angling her bike inward as she rode around the base of a huge sunlit cliff, her braid flying.

"Try enlarging this and printing it in black and white. There's enough contrast to make it quite dramatic."

Molly looked at the photo with new appreciation. *I'll try that. Maybe even give a framed print of it to Nails as a thank-you gift when I see her next.*

Nails was thrilled when she saw the print. "You took others that day, didn't you? Bring them all to the next TRA meeting. Trina's creating a photo history of our chapter, and I know she'd love to have copies of them." She paused. "If you're coming."

"We are. Hank and I talked it over, and we've decided to join. He's already marked every meeting and event on the calendar up through June. Going to the meeting is a given for him, like going to Bean Night is for me."

"Balances out nicely, doesn't it?" Nails said.

On the calendar, at least, Molly thought.

The Silver Fork photos were a hit at the April TRA meeting. Riders who were in the photos requested copies, and others in the chapter asked if she would take action shots of them.

Molly smiled with pleasure at the compliments. Knowing how much the group appreciated her work changed her mind about going on the May ride to Vernal. "I'll bring my camera and take as many pictures as I can," she told those surrounding her. "Or you can call me and we'll set something up."

Hank was delighted at the response her photos got and her decision to take the Vernal temple trip. "I always knew you were a talented woman," he said as they waited for the almond-crusted tilapia they'd ordered. "Better watch out or you'll get tapped to be the chapter's official photographer."

"I will not accept if nominated, and I will not serve if elected."

Hank smiled. "Who's that you're quoting?"

"General William Sherman, I think. It fits the situation."

"You're going to be one busy lady taking all those pictures you promised. Are you going to have time to hunt down that missing $57.50 in the checkbook, or do you want me to do it for you?"

"Checking up on me, huh?" Molly wasn't surprised. Despite her growing skill, Hank had kept a finger on the pulse of their finances.

"Just a bit."

"How about we do it together?" she suggested.

The highlight of the April meeting was the announcement Ronald made after other chapter business was complete. "Sharon and I are sponsoring a ride starting the Wednesday after Memorial Day. We are calling it the West Coast Loop Trip."

Together he and Sharon held up an oversized map of the Northwest with a route highlighted in lime green.

"The first leg of the trip is from Salt Lake to Boise, where we'll take in a temple session." Ronald traced the route with the end of a dinner knife. "Then it's up through Oregon to The Dalles and the Columbia River Gorge—"

"Seeing that will be worth the trip," Sharon interjected.

"We'll attend the temple here in Portland, take the Coast Road down to San Francisco, and visit the temples in Oakland and Reno before hitting the home stretch. We want to take our time, so it'll be a long trip, probably a week and a half or so."

At the mention of the Coast Road, Molly saw Hank's eyes light up. "That's something I'd like to do."

She hadn't forgotten what he'd said he wanted to do the evening of the bucket list game—buy a motorcycle and ride the Coast Road. He had the motorcycle. Now Ronald's trip offered the opportunity to realize the other part of his dream.

"But isn't it a long trip to make on a motorcycle?" she asked.

"Not really," Ronald answered. "The length of the route isn't as big an issue as the number of miles you ride in a day."

Molly remembered the statistic from the TRA Web site—250 to 300 miles a day. Counting rest and lunch stops, that could easily add up to six hours a day. *That's nuts*, she thought.

Ronald called everyone to attention. "Raise your hands if you think you'd be interested in it."

Across the table Molly saw Gabe raise his hand, to Trina's immediate objection. "Not a chance, big boy," she said. "I'm not spending my anniversary weekend following you cross-country!"

When Gabe grinned sheepishly and put his hand down, Molly was disappointed. If Hank went on this trip, she wouldn't be able to ride along with Trina. She could drive her own vehicle, but it wouldn't be any fun without company.

The tally of interested parties grew. It included some people Molly had been wanting to get better acquainted with—the Hesses, Doyle and Jeri Connelly, and Barney and RaNae Forrest. RaNae held up both hands to be counted. "Fricka's going too."

"How about it?" Hank asked Molly.

She hesitated, and then nodded, and they both raised their hands.

Nails gave her a thumbs-up from a nearby table and called, "If you're going, I'm going."

Howard, who was sitting beside Nails, put one arm proprietarily along the back of her chair. "Then I'm going too." He caught Ronald's attention and two more names were added to the list.

"That's a man with a plan," Molly whispered to Hank.

"Think so?"

"No doubt about it."

The meeting ended with Barney and RaNae Forrest taking center stage. Barney reminded Molly of a heftier, bearded, and long-haired version of her dad. RaNae was almost as tall as he. Flyaway red hair, a turned-up nose, and a flowing outfit gave her a campy look. But what caught Molly's interest most was the sleek little animal RaNae was wearing around her neck like a boa.

Fricka.

For the next five minutes the ferret, now in fine health, had everyone in stitches demonstrating her version of the cha-cha-cha and standing and sitting to Barney's rhythmic command.

"Between Fricka's dancing and Ronald's magic tricks we'll have a regular sideshow for anyone who's interested," Sharon said.

When Molly asked to meet Fricka, RaNae put the curious critter on her outstretched arm. Molly was enchanted as it crawled up to her shoulder and sniffed her hair. "What do you do with her while you're in the temple?" she asked.

"We've made lots of friends in the Gold Wing Road Riders Association and the TRA," RaNae said, "and we've picked up a few through our travel blog, too. There's hardly a place where we can't find someone interested in watching Fricka. When the Hesses aren't along, that is."

"How do you keep up a blog on the road?" Hank asked. "Do you take a laptop along?"

Barney puffed up in mock affront. "Do I look like the kind of guy who would lug electronics on a ride?"

"There's usually Internet available where we stay," RaNae explained.

Doyle had been looking over Molly's pictures on the display table. "If you come on the Loop ride, you could be our official photographer and post a picture history of our adventures on a blog."

"Slow down," Molly said. "Let's see how the photo shoot on the Vernal trip turns out."

Before leaving that night, Nails took Molly aside and gave her a CD of a new visualization she'd made. "This takes everything a step further."

Molly hadn't been listening to the tape as regularly as Nails had suggested. She wasn't sure she was ready for something else. "What's different?"

"Now you'll be imagining the Gold Wing with Hank on it. When you can deal with that, you'll start visualizing Hank with one of your grandchildren."

"Whoa." Molly raised her hands up in a warding-off gesture. "I can't do that. It would be like me putting one of them on it myself. "

"I know it's your worst nightmare, but there's a reason for it. It's not the motorcycle itself that upsets you. It's the possibility that someone you love might get hurt while on it. What you've been doing is preliminary. This is the real work."

Molly hesitated before taking the CD. "I'll listen to it at least once. After I transfer it to my iPod."

⌒

Wary, but willing to give it a try, Molly sat down the next morning with her iPod and selected the session. She enjoyed the first part of it, which was the same progressive relaxation routine as on the tape. But when she got to the part where she was to visualize someone she loved on the motorcycle, she had to push the stop button. When she tried again later in the day, she allowed herself to see Hank on it, but only for a few seconds.

She kept at it over the next week, assessing her fear level each time as Nails had taught her to do. Gradually, she was able to see Hank ride off on the Gold Wing without too much anxiety. She was even able to visualize him putting one of the grandkids on the passenger seat, as long as the motorcycle stayed in the driveway.

But Nails was a hard taskmaster. Every time Molly reached one goal, Nails was ready with another challenge. Like getting acquainted with Springsteen. "The more you know about how motorcycles work, the more comfortable you'll feel around them."

Or not, Molly thought the day she stood with Nails in the motor-cycle bay of her garage, holding the parts diagram from the Softail owner's manual. She stayed three steps back from Springsteen as Nails pointed out each part of the motorcycle and explained what it did.

"Battery, gas tank, front suspension, shock absorber." Nails touched each part as she named it. "Now you do the same. It will help you re-member the parts and how they work."

Ada had come into the bay during this recital, pushing her wheel-chair in front of her. "Come on," she encouraged Molly. "Put your hands on that bad boy. Springsteen won't mind."

"I wouldn't want to be fresh," Molly joked, trailing a finger along the gas tank in front of the seat.

Nails moved on, pointing to elements from the left handlebar to the right. "Turn signal, starter switch, kill switch, throttle."

"Kill switch? Nice name."

"It's only a 'stop' or 'off' switch. Very handy if your bike is going down and you need to shut off the engine."

"Great image."

When Nails had covered all the parts and purposes, she started over at the beginning. But Molly had reached saturation point. "That's enough. No more!"

"I was waiting for you to tell me so. Taking charge is an important part of getting over your fear."

Molly was going for her purse when Ada said, "Since you're doing so well, how about throwing a leg over before you leave?"

"You mean sit on it?"

"Right now there isn't a safer motorcycle on the planet."

"She's right," Nails said.

Molly stared at the Softail, which was leaning on its kickstand. "I'm afraid it will fall over."

"This machine?" Nails laughed. "I could stand on the high-side floorboard and it wouldn't move."

Molly took hold of the handlebars and slid her right leg over the saddle. Standing astride the parked motorcycle, she let out a slow breath.

"Bravo!" Ada cried, clapping her hands.

"Shall we stand it upright?" Nails straddled the front wheel, and together she and Molly righted the bike. "Now sit on it," Nails commanded.

Gripping the handlebars, Molly lowered herself onto the saddle. Keeping her left foot on the floor for security, she put her right foot on the floorboard.

Nails, who was keeping the bike steady, nodded encouragement. "You're doing good."

Gathering her courage, Molly did the same with her left foot. The motorcycle beneath her felt powerful and potentially dangerous, and it occurred to Molly that that might be exactly what Hank liked about his machine.

Molly came home from her hands-on meeting with Springsteen determined to get acquainted with the Gold Wing. In order to do that, she needed to find a time when Hank was gone but The Beast was in the garage. That wouldn't be easy. He seemed to be making up for lost time by taking out the Gold Wing as often as he could, sometimes alone, sometimes with TRA members who'd discovered that he would stop everything to go for a ride.

One day when he came back smelling of fresh air and brimming with enthusiasm, Molly realized she was jealous of what he was experiencing. *I wish I could figure out how to get some of that without the blasted Beast being part of it.*

She finally got her chance to get acquainted with the Gold Wing when Cal picked up Hank one evening for bowling practice. She waited a few minutes in case they came back for some reason. Then she went into the garage and sidled up to the Gold Wing, giggling nervously at the ridiculousness of the situation. There was no one to see her and nothing to fear, but she still felt as though she were spying on an alien life-form. All she needed to complete the picture was a stick to poke it with.

When the motorcycle didn't object to her presence, Molly observed it for a moment. It felt different from the Softail, perhaps because not as much engine was exposed and it didn't have as much chrome. It sat more upright on its kickstand, and the instrument panel was more complicated. It had hard cases on each side rather than the stud-decorated leather saddlebags that were part of the Softail's attitude.

Molly knew Hank kept the owner's manual in the Gold Wing's trunk. She got it out and opened it to the page with the diagram of the Gold Wing. Then she started at the front and went through the routine Nails had done with Springsteen. "Front wheel, fender, headlight, handlebar. Check. Windshield. Check." She stopped. "Fairing?"

Molly looked at the smooth silver covering that extended from the front of the motorcycle back over the engine. "Oh. That's what makes you look dressed up." She had the odd feeling the motorcycle was pleased by the compliment.

She walked around it several times, glancing periodically at the diagram. She talked as she walked, to herself or to the motorcycle, she wasn't sure which. When she felt she'd gotten to know it from front wheel to rear light, she stepped back and observed it for a moment.

"You're not so scary," she finally said. "I guess I'd better stop calling you The Beast."

Chapter 15

"Dealing with fear is all about balance," Nails said shortly before the Vernal ride. "Know what you can do, what you want to do, and what you absolutely will not do. And do frequent status checks to see which is which."

Molly was doing one of those checks when she realized something. *I want to take that trip to Vernal and see the dinosaurs and go to the temple. I want to take the photographs.*

Wanting to do those things made all the difference. When she drove with Trina to Vernal, instead of using up all her energy trying to stay calm, she used it to get the perfect portrait shots of riders who had requested them. Each time she caught a body in motion or a face in close-up, Molly became more aware of how much she liked these people and how their shared experiences were creating a subtle shift in her perspective.

Between taking TRA photos and working with Nails, Molly's time was increasingly being taken up with motorcycles. She didn't realize the extent to which that was affecting her other activities until she called Micheline to put off plans for a walk and talk for a third time in one week.

"What's bumped me off the schedule this time?" Micheline asked.

"I'm going for a ride in a sidecar. Nails says it's the next logical step."

"For the record, I don't much care for being second choice. Don't suggest another walk until you're as committed to it as you are to this motorcycle stuff."

"Have I stood you up that many times?" Molly asked. "I can cancel the ride—"

"You've already broken one commitment. Don't break another."

Thoroughly chastised, Molly left for her ride. *This balancing act isn't so easy*, she thought. But when she arrived at Ada's and saw Nails in the driveway checking over Sister Martha, the ride pushed everything else out of her mind.

Sister Martha. The name had struck Molly as way too odd until she made the connection with Martha from the New Testament, the woman who took care of the people, anticipating and providing for their needs. The machine took care of Ada, allowing her to do something she otherwise couldn't do.

She darn well better take care of me, Molly thought.

As she walked up the driveway she waved at Ada, who was watching from the porch in her wheelchair.

"Here I am," she said to Nails, shifting nervously from one foot to the other.

"I see you remembered to wear boots that cover your ankles. Do you need a minute before we try this?"

"Let's get it over with."

Nails handed her a pair of black leather britches. "Ada said you could use her gear. It'll be a little big for you, but nobody rides with me unless they are dressed for it."

Molly put on the pants, windbreaker, and armored jacket Nails held out for her. Last came gloves and a helmet. "It's heavy," Molly said, "and tight."

"It's supposed to be." Nails pulled the helmet strap snugly under Molly's chin and positioned the microphone so she could speak into it. "There. You're ready to ride."

Molly took a couple of steps. "I feel like the Pillsbury Doughboy in this garb."

"You'll get used to it." Nails fastened her own jacket, put on her helmet, and secured her gloves. "Ready?"

Molly shivered—from fear or excitement, she couldn't tell which. "It's now or never." She was glad she was getting in the sidecar, not on the back of the cycle.

When she was buckled in, Nails mounted Sister Martha, pushed a couple of buttons, and said, "Can you hear me?"

"Loud and clear. Where are you going to take us?"

"Up and down some neighborhood streets. There's not a lot of traffic, and we can take the turns nice and easy."

Molly gripped the rim of the sidecar as Nails revved the engine and started slowly down the driveway. Molly's vocabulary didn't include many swear words, but she did have one favorite one, and in the first few seconds she muttered it more than she'd said it in the last five years. Being so low was frightening. The road whizzed by right underneath her, and every little bump made her grip tighter.

She jumped when she heard Nails's voice over the intercom. "Breathe or you'll pass out."

Molly's body took a gulp of air without instructions from her. Only then did she realize that between her mutterings she'd been holding her breath. She started using her relaxation technique, breathing deeply and slowly.

Five disaster-free minutes into the ride, Molly realized that a bump or two wasn't going to send them careening into a parked car or across someone's lawn and into their house. Her shoulders, which had been hunched nearly up to her ears, dropped almost to their normal position, but her fingers still kept a death grip on the sides of the car.

She was relieved when Nails headed back down her street and into her driveway where Ada waited. She got out of the sidecar and held onto it a moment to steady herself.

"Congratulations," Ada said. "You survived."

Molly took off the helmet. "I did. And there was even a second or two when I enjoyed myself."

"I call that progress," Nails said. "A couple more times in the sidecar and you'll be ready to take a ride with me on Springsteen."

"When pigs fly."

⌒

As the month drew to a close, Molly had to wedge her sessions with Nails and follow-up sidecar rides between her photography class and the planning meetings for the Fourth of July performance. Wade and Heather usually put together the new shows, but because this one had special family significance, he'd asked Molly and her sisters to give their input too.

They met in Wade's office, which had been a workshop in the original barn. When they'd put together a program they could all agree upon, Wade studied the lineup, his eyebrows pulled together over his nose. "It's a bit *Prairie Home Companion*-ish."

"That's why Pops will love it," June said. "Especially the finale."

After a lineup of patriotic songs and skits, the finale would include the tribute to Bess and Roy. Three generations of family would join them on stage to play the fiddling tune, "Cattle in the Cane," and accompany the corny love song Roy had written for Bess during their courting days, "I Love It When You Fiddle, But Don't Fiddle with My Heart."

"How's the scrapbook coming?" Wade asked as they finished up. "Will it be ready?"

June nodded. "The three of us will divide up the last of the pages on Monday after Bean Night."

"What?" Molly's mouth was an O of surprise. "Monday can't be Bean Night."

"It was the last time I looked at the calendar."

"Where has the month of April gone?"

⁓

Molly missed that Bean Night. The phone rang as she and Hank were walking out the door. The caller was Marlys Kay, one of the sisters in Molly's visiting teaching district. She and her husband cared for her elderly parents, a mother with mild Alzheimer's and a father with several chronic health problems.

"Oh, I'm glad I caught you," Marlys said. "I need to ask a favor."

Molly could hear the plea in her voice. "What can I do for you?"

"Wally and I had plans to go out for dinner and a concert, but the person who was going to sit with my parents called a moment ago to cancel. I know it's last minute, and I know it's Monday night, but is it possible . . ."

"I'll be right there."

Hank, who was leaning against the doorjamb, said, "Sounds like I'm off the hook tonight."

"Pretend all you want. I know you love Bean Night."

Molly called her parents to explain the situation and then hurried over to the Kays' house. Marlys was waiting at the door when she arrived, a page of care notes in her hand. "Thanks so much for doing this. I owe you big time."

Molly's tasks that evening were simple, yet she realized how wearing it would be to do them day after day after day. She was grateful that her parents still enjoyed relatively good health. And that Wade and Heather lived close enough to go over to the cabin if they needed help.

But how about Hank's sister? I wonder if Helena and Russ ever get a break in caring for Joseph and Ruth? That train of thought was interrupted by a call from the bedroom, which she hurried to answer.

Ed and Marlys returned home shortly after ten. They'd looked harried and tired when they left; they now had a relaxed glow about them. That was all the thanks Molly needed. She started for home buoyed by the good feeling that comes with service rendered.

The minute she walked into the kitchen, Hank said, "Hope wants you to call her tonight."

"Is anything wrong?"

"I don't think so. She says she has news you won't want to miss."

Curious, Molly punched in Hope's number on her office phone.

"You picked one doozy of a night not to show up, Sis," Hope said. "We had a special guest. Bet you can't guess who it was."

"But you want me to try." Molly was too tired for the guessing game. She dropped onto the overstuffed chair that filled one corner of her office. "It's late, Hope of my heart. Just tell me."

"Oh, all right. It seems a certain single art teacher was on his way home to Ogden this afternoon after judging a middle school art contest in Provo. He took the Lehi exit on a whim to see if the Finleys still ran the theater."

Molly knew who it was immediately. "Garrett Stapely, Laurel's old boyfriend."

"Correcto mundo."

Garrett Stapely and Laurel had been an item when she was in law school at BYU and he was working on his masters in art there. When she brought him to Bean Night, he fit into the family as though they'd been waiting for him. But just when everyone was expecting an announcement, they quit seeing each other. Laurel had refused to share details of the breakup, and Molly, who'd liked Garrett and his laid-back brand of humor, had always wondered what had happened.

"Tell me everything."

"Wade was in the yard when Garrett drove up, and they got to talking, so naturally Wade invited him to stay for Bean Night. He seemed glad to see all of us. Especially Laurel."

"How did she react?"

"Stunned. Floored. Flabbergasted. She kept her distance at first, but by the end of the evening, the two of them were talking like they always did. They even walked out to their cars together."

"Oh, blast and darn. I should have been there." Molly ached to call Laurel and ask her about the evening, but she knew better. If her daughter told anyone what she was feeling about seeing Garrett, it would be Hank. But given the recent distance in their relationship, that wasn't likely.

When Molly told Hank what had happened, he pursed his lips thoughtfully. "Hmm. I always liked that young man. Do you suppose anything will come of it?"

"I guess that depends on why they ended it in the first place."

The next morning, Molly answered calls from Heather, Bess, and several of Laurel's cousins, all eager to share their own take on the evening.

Everyone has something to say about Bean Night except the person most involved, Molly thought. She wished she'd put more effort into creating a closer relationship with Laurel rather than assuming that Hank's relationship with her would be enough. Girls needed their mothers.

Hoping it wasn't too late to change that, Molly did something she'd never done before. She called Laurel at her office.

"I'm going to be in town this morning, and I thought you might like to meet me at the Garden Room for lunch."

"Thanks for the invitation," Laurel said, "but I have a business lunch today. And just as an FYI, if this has anything to do with last night, I'm not talking about it."

Chapter 16

The Saturday after Molly's conversation with Laurel, Molly had a ringside seat to another unexpected reunion. It occurred on an impromptu ride Nails set up, and it helped her understand how it must have been for Laurel to see Garrett for the first time in years with a mob of Finleys avidly taking in every reaction.

She was starting her morning chores when Nails called. "Ada woke up this morning feeling great. She says she's up for a ride in the sidecar. I know it's short notice, but we'd love it if you two would come with us."

"Where are you going?"

"Emigration Canyon. I thought we'd meet at the zoo at ten so we can start up the canyon while it's still cool. We'll drive until Ada says to stop. On the way down, we'll have an early lunch at Ruth's Diner."

In anticipation of the West Coast Loop trip, Molly was glad to have a chance to practice driving the follow car. She'd learned from observing how Trina drove that it took both skill and art. The driver had to pay exquisite attention, not only to road and traffic conditions, but also to the lane and speed changes of the line of motorcycles ahead.

"I'm sure Hank will want to go," Molly said. "And I can use the practice driving, although I'm not crazy about doing it alone."

"You won't have to. Sharon and Ronald are coming, and she said she'd be glad to ride with you."

Molly found Hank in the backyard working on the wood fence that had heaved and buckled in the spring thaw. When she told him about the invitation, he grinned like a kid who'd been handed a reprieve. "Tell Nails we're on," he said. He started pulling off his gloves. "I'll go fill your SUV with gas and get some cash out of the ATM."

That's so Hank, Molly thought. *He does take good care of me.*

Later, when she saw him in the garage polishing the chrome on the Gold Wing, she added, *and his motorcycle.*

Ronald and Hank arrived at the meeting point first, followed by Sharon and Molly in the SUV. Molly was ready with her camera when Nails pulled into the zoo parking lot on Martha. Ada was in the sidecar, which sported two small flags stiffened to be at perpetual attention, one with the TRA symbol and one with her name in fuchsia letters on a lavender background. Laughing, Molly took several photos framing Ada with the flags flying behind her, then one of Ada giving everyone two victory signs.

"Those are great flags," Molly said. Since she hadn't yet told Hank what she and Nails were doing, she lowered her voice before asking, "How come they weren't on the sidecar when I went for those training rides?"

Nails smiled at her sister. "Because they say, 'Look out, world. Ada on board!'"

It was the first time Molly had seen Ada in the sidecar, and it pleased her to see her friend looking bright and enthusiastic.

Nails reviewed the route they'd be taking. Then she clapped her hands. "Okay, people. Let's get this show on the road."

Driving up Emigration Canyon was nothing like driving up Parley's Canyon, but Molly found it challenging in its own way. Instead of multiple lanes of fast traffic whizzing by and 18-wheelers boxing her in, she had to deal with the twists and turns of Emigration's two-lane road, which had blind access roads and driveways feeding into it, as well as markers for deer crossings and children at play.

Molly was hugging the outside of her lane in order to better see what was around a blind curve when she almost barreled into a single line of bicyclists on the road ahead. With a squawk, she swerved toward the inside of the lane. She was immensely relieved when she passed the leader and a glance in the rearview mirror told her they were all upright and pedaling onward.

"What are those crazies doing out here?" she said.

"Training." Sharon slowly released the grip she'd had on the overhead handle. "Emigration Canyon is a favorite ride for competitive cyclists. But that was too close for comfort. You'd never get me riding a bicycle on this road."

A moment passed before the absurdity of that statement hit Molly. "Oh, yeah?" she said, laughing. "If you weren't with me, you'd be riding behind Ronald, thinking nothing of it."

"Too true. What can I say?"

Partway up the canyon, Nails signaled and pulled off the road onto a wide shoulder commonly used as a viewpoint so Ada could stretch her legs. They hadn't been on the road very long, but Molly could see how stiffly Ada walked and how shaky her balance was, even with Nails holding her arm.

The sweet intimacy between the sisters made Molly reach for her camera again. *I hope I can capture that,* she thought as she snapped away. Printed in black and white, the photos would be a striking study of love and compassion.

"I never cease to be touched by how tender Dorothy is with Ada," Sharon said when they were back on the road. "I wish she had someone who loved and cared for her as much as she does Ada. Even if she insists she doesn't need taking care of."

"Do you think Howard's a candidate?"

"Who knows? It's what Dorothy thinks that counts."

The road took them all the way up to Little Mountain Pass, where they spent a quarter of an hour enjoying the view of surrounding peaks and the Upper Mountain Dell Reservoir below. It was especially beautiful when the sun broke through the clouds, turning the water in the reservoir blue and sparkly.

"Time to start down," Nails said a few minutes later.

"Sorry to be a party pooper, but sun and heat . . ." Ada gave an apologetic shrug.

"This is your trip, Ada." Molly said. "You call the shots."

On the way back down, they stopped at the diner, parking near a row of four motorcycles. Ruth's was a popular destination, well-known for its building (a converted trolley car), quirky atmosphere, and good food. Luckily, they'd beat the lunch crowd, so they were seated immediately. Nails requested an inside table for Ada's sake, but one near the back windows where they could see the terraced patios and flower-boxes loaded with spring color.

"Bet those guys out there belong to the bikes in the lot," Ronald said, pointing to a group of men on the patio. After their orders had been taken he shoved his chair back. "I'm going to go trade stories with them. Call me when the food gets here."

Hank said, "I'm coming too."

Molly and Ada were sitting on the side of the table facing the windows, so Molly could see Hank and Ronald introduce themselves and sit down on the chairs that were pulled up for them. Nails glanced briefly over her shoulder at the group outside and then continued a conversation she was having with Sharon. Molly turned to Ada.

"How was your ride up, Ada?" Molly asked.

"Fantastic. I've missed going out with Dorothy. I—"

When Ada didn't finish her sentence, Molly glanced at her. She was staring out the window through squinted eyes. "It can't be," she said to herself.

"Ada?"

Ada rubbed her eyes. "Sorry. I thought I saw someone I knew from long ago. You were asking?"

Sharon called to Hank and Ronald when their orders arrived. They came inside full of stories to tell about their new acquaintances, their motorcycles, and the trips they'd been on.

"Any possible recruits into the TRA?" Sharon asked Ronald.

"Maybe. A couple of them are Latter-day Saints. They got a big kick out of hearing about Temple Riders. I got their numbers, and I'm going to invite them to the next meeting. We'll see."

All through the meal, Ada kept squinting out the window, a furrow between her eyebrows. Even after the group paid their waiter and left, she seemed to be puzzling over something.

I bet she does know one of those men, Molly thought.

Nails also noticed Ada's expression. "Do you need something, Sis? Should we start back down?"

"I'm okay." Ada smiled reassuringly. "Just a little tired."

"You can ride the rest of the way to the zoo with me if you need to," Molly said to Ada. "It's probably more comfortable."

"I think that might be a good idea."

"I'll ride with Ronald," Sharon said, "if I can use your helmet and squeeze into your jacket."

When they left the diner's parking lot, Sharon was behind her husband, and Ada was riding with Molly. They'd not gone far down the road when Molly noticed red taillights flashing on the motorcycles ahead of her.

She slowed down, doing her best to ignore the prickle of apprehension on the back of her neck. "Can you see what's happening?" she asked Ada.

Ada strained against her seat belt to get a better look. "It's the other group. I think there's a motorcycle down. Better pull over."

Molly did so, grateful that they were in the lower part of the canyon where the shoulder was wider. Feeling little shivers of anxiety, she opened her door and stood on the runner to get a better view. They were well back from the action, but she could see Sharon kneeling beside a figure lying partway off the shoulder.

It was her worst nightmare come true. "Is he hurt bad?" she called to Nails, who was hurrying her way.

"I don't think so. He's conscious and isn't bleeding anywhere that I could see."

Molly dropped back into her seat and tapped the wheel nervously. Nails put a calming hand on her shoulder. "Sharon's giving first aid, and an ambulance is on its way."

"This is not what I needed."

"I bet the guy on the ground feels the same way," Ada murmured. "Do you know what happened, Sis?"

"An idiot in a jacked-up pickup tried to pass all of the motorcycles at once. There's hardly any straightaway here. He had to cut back into the right lane too soon to avoid going around the next curve on the wrong side of the road. The rider tried to get out of his way and spun out when he hit the shoulder. Ronald and Hank are trying to get his bike back up the embankment."

"That's terrible. And the driver didn't stop?"

"What do you think?"

The anger in Nails's voice intensified Molly's anxiety. Her fingers tapped at a furious pace. "See? This is what I've been trying to tell you and Hank. It doesn't matter how careful a motorcycle rider is if the other driver is stupid or half-asleep. Or texting."

Ada put her hand over Molly's, stilling her fingers. "Don't go there, Molly. You're feeding your anxiety by jumping ahead to a worst-case scenario."

"She's right," Nails said in a calmer voice. "We both need to turn the temperature down some."

Molly nodded. If she didn't get control of her emotions, they would spiral downward and destroy everything she'd accomplished. She closed her eyes while she sought and finally found the safe place she'd created.

She was in a much better state when the ambulance arrived a few minutes later. The EMTs headed toward Sharon and the rider where they were swallowed by the circle of bystanders. Molly was wishing the EMTs would shoo everyone away so she could see what they were doing when she noticed a tall, gray-haired man from the other group looking their way. He started walking toward them. Then he broke into a run.

"Dot!" he called, waving his hand. "Dot, is that you?"

Nails stared and put a hand over her heart as if she couldn't breathe.

"Oh, my heavens, it *is* Walker Beck." Ada's eyes were huge. "I thought I recognized him at the diner, but I wasn't sure."

Walker covered the distance in long strides and pulled Nails into a kiss that reminded Molly of the famous World War II photo of a sailor kissing a nurse in Times Square. At first it looked like Nails was kissing him back, but then she broke the embrace.

"Walker!" she exclaimed.

"Dot."

He tried to kiss her again, but she bristled and pushed him away. "Back off, bud. You gave up your kissing rights fifty years ago when you left town without telling me."

"Aw, Dot," he said with a lopsided grin. "I was a dumb kid back then, and I made a lot of bad choices. We never would have made a go of it. Be glad I got out of your life."

"I am," she said evenly.

Molly's gaze ping-ponged between the two. *Who is this Walker Beck? What happened between him and Nails?*

He wasn't handsome in the refined way Howard was. His face was long and thin, with deep lines that looked like years of being in the sun or of hard living. But he wore his leathers with a rakish charm, and Molly could feel the power of his blue gaze and puckish smile.

Ada leaned across Molly and waved. "Hey, Walker."

"Ada." Walker looked through the window of Molly's SUV. "I've been wondering about both of you lovely ladies, and here you are. It must be fate."

"It's good to see you. I've thought about you a lot, wondering whatever happened to you."

"Long story. Who's this?" he asked, smiling at Molly.

"My friend, Molly Mancuso."

"Hello, Molly." The hand Walker offered for her to shake was large, his grip firm.

"Are you living here in Utah again?" Ada asked.

"Temporarily. I'm here on business." He looked at Nails. "But that could change."

A flurry of activity shifted their attention back to the side of the road. The EMTs loaded the injured man into the back of the ambulance. Molly was relieved that there were no sirens blaring or lights flashing as it drove away. Next, the tow truck arrived. With the help of several of the men, the disabled cycle was secured on the flatbed. The driver went up the canyon to a turnout where he made a U-turn and headed back toward the valley. Hank, Ronald, and Sharon shook hands with the other riders, who were getting ready to take off.

"Guess I'd better get going." Walker turned to Nails with a full-watt smile. "I'll probably see you at one of those Temple Bikers meetings. If not before."

"Temple Riders," Nails said dryly.

"Nice to meet you, Molly. Good to see you, Ada."

When he'd left, Ada rested her head in her hand. "Uh-oh. We're in trouble now."

"No, we're not," Nails said. "I'm not seventeen, and I haven't forgotten who left whom."

"Maybe so, but he can still make you blush."

When they got going again, Molly was glad she was driving the vehicle that was right behind Hank and the other riders. They wouldn't have to worry about *her* tailgating or making moves that would put any of them at risk.

"I can't believe we ran into Walker Beck," Ada said with a sigh.

"Ada, is he the guy your sister was in love with when she was in high school?"

"The very one." Ada rested her head against the back of the seat and closed her eyes. Molly noticed that the color that had made her look healthy that morning had drained away, leaving her looking exhausted and wan.

"Are you okay? Do you need something?"

"Upsets tire me out," Ada said, her eyes still closed. "Excitement, too. Walker always trailed equal parts of both."

There was something in her tone that made Molly think, *Poor Howard.*

Chapter 17

Hank had barely taken off his helmet after arriving home from the Emigration ride when he started asking Molly questions about Walker. "What's the deal with Nails and that guy? I didn't see it myself, but Ronald said he kissed her."

"Boy, do I have a story to tell you."

Molly was in the middle of dishing every detail when she recognized something in her own voice that reminded her of the eagerness that had been in Jan's voice as she told about Lori and Bruce Aldridge's split-up. She stopped midsentence.

"You know, this is exactly what made Laurel so upset when Wade surprised her with Garrett at Bean Night. She knew everybody who was there would be talking about the two of them, hashing over the details and maybe even inventing a few, speculating on what was going to happen next."

"Does this mean I don't get to hear the good stuff?"

"Sorry, but I don't want to be guilty of spreading gossip. Nails wouldn't like it any more than Laurel does."

"I'll bet everyone in the TRA knows about it by our next meeting."

"Well, it won't be because I blabbered."

"Speaking of Nails, she said you two were going to get together on Monday. You've been spending a lot of time with her and Ada. What do you women do when you're together?"

"Hang out. Talk. Whatever rings our bell."

It's only a little white lie, Molly thought, justifying her omissions. *No bigger than others I've told over the years.*

The actual plan for Monday was for Molly to go for a ride with Nails on Springsteen. Or at least it had been before the trip up Emigration Canyon.

In recent weeks, the focus of their work together had slowly shifted from Molly getting over her fear of motorcycles to maybe some day being able to ride on the Gold Wing with Hank.

The change had sneaked up on her as her desire to share riding with Hank grew and her friendships with the Bixbys, Nails, and the Temple Riders as a group became more important to her. Both times she'd gone to their monthly dinner meeting, she'd found herself enjoying the company of interesting, smart, and thoughtful people who loved and lived the gospel—and also loved riding their motorcycles. She'd had to acknowledge that reasonable people could have another perspective on the issue of motorcycles, despite the risks.

The biggest measure of the change and what it meant was her decision to give Springsteen a try.

In preparation for her ride, she'd been listening to the CD several times a day, and her confidence had been growing. Being at the scene of the motorcycle accident in the canyon had dealt her a significant setback. Nails's reminder to use what she knew had helped her regain some lost ground, but she was not at all sure that she would be able to go through with the plan.

She called Nails with her concerns the night before the ride. "What if I can't get on Springsteen?"

"Then we'll do something else. This isn't a test, Molly. You aren't getting graded on it."

"What if I do get on but freak out?"

"I'll stop and let you get off. Listen, you'll either get on Springsteen or you won't. We'll either go around the block or we won't. It's not the end of the world either way."

Once she knew that Nails wouldn't push her into doing something she wasn't ready to do, Molly said, "Okay. I'll come, and we'll see what happens."

When she arrived at Ada's Monday afternoon, Ada was sitting on the steps to the porch, holding the gear Molly had worn when riding in the sidecar. Nails was standing beside Springsteen in the driveway.

Molly had the strange thought that Springsteen looked a little evil, with his abundant chrome and candy red paint glinting in the afternoon sun. But she didn't have time to dwell on that whimsy or to bring up all the questions she had about Walker, because Nails and Ada hustled her into the leathers and helmet.

When Molly was dressed, Nails got on the Softail and said, "Your move."

Molly stood to the side, looking long and hard at the sleek machine. The passenger seat was higher than the scooped driver seat. There was nothing between the two for Molly to hold onto, and the passenger backrest was no more than a padded rectangle attached to the motorcycle with chrome bars.

"How am I supposed to get on behind?"

"Like you did before. Swing your leg over."

Molly eyed the backrest. *I have to get it over that,* she thought. She took a deep breath and heaved her leg into the air with such force it knocked her off balance, and she fell on her tush with a grunt.

Nails slid off Springsteen. "Are you okay?"

Molly looked up at her. "Besides being embarrassed, I'm short, I'm stiff, I feel stupid, and I have concrete boots on."

"You haven't lost your sense of humor." Nails helped her to her feet, got back on the motorcycle, and steadied it. "Hold onto my shoulder and use the passenger peg as a step this time."

Once astride, Molly put her feet on the footrests and shifted a little to get more comfortable.

"Hold onto my waist," Nails said. "Keep your knees and elbows tucked in. Don't panic when I lean into a curve. And never try to counter it by shifting the other direction."

Molly had to slide forward to put her hands on Nails's waist. The unaccustomed position made her feel unstable and vulnerable, but she gave Nails an okay when Nails asked if she was ready. With a rumble of the engine and a little jerk, the motorcycle started forward. Molly grabbed fistfuls of Nails's jacket in a panic. The first time they hit a bump, she squawked and nearly buried herself in Nails's back. She felt every crack and buckle in the road as if it were an assault. When several cars passed them in rapid succession, her heart tripped and her breath came in short gasps.

"It sounds like you're hyperventilating," Nails said through the headset. "Take some deep breaths. We're on our way back."

Molly got off as quickly as she could after Nails brought Springsteen to a stop. Seeing how upset she was, Nails led her through a reliable defusing technique right there in the driveway.

"Okay, I'm feeling better," Molly finally said.

"Good. Now you can get back on Springsteen for at least a few seconds before you call it quits."

"Get back on the horse that bucked you?" Molly looked at the motorcycle parked in the driveway. *Maybe I can. It's not going anywhere.* She threw her arms up in surrender. "Why not?"

She got off as soon as she got on. Ada called them to the porch, offering sympathy and lemonade, and they sat on the steps to talk over what had happened.

"I think this is my first and last time riding on a motorcycle," Molly said. "It's too scary."

"But you did give it a try," Ada said. "Kudos for that."

"Hang on a minute," Nails said. "This isn't the end, it's a bump in the road. And it's my fault. I shouldn't have put you on the Softail for your first ride, Molly. A bike like Hank's Gold Wing would have been much better. You'd have felt more protected with a driver's backrest in front of you, armrests on each side, and a more substantial passenger backrest."

"Kind of like a highchair with the tray down in front?" Molly said, grinning.

"Pretty close," Nails said with a chuckle.

Ada refilled the glasses. "Cookies, anyone? I think I have a bib somewhere in the house, if needed."

Ada and Molly traded jokes about bibs and highchairs, but Nails seemed preoccupied.

"How would you feel about riding behind Ronald on his Gold Wing?" she asked when their laughter died down.

Molly was taken aback by Nails's suggestion. She'd been thinking—

with relief—that her motorcycle adventures were at an end. "I don't know about that."

"While you consider it, I think I'll see what Ronald has to say." She left the room.

Molly nibbled nervously at her cookie. "That Nails. She never lets anyone off the hook, does she?"

"Not even after fifty years."

Molly's ears perked up. "Has something new happened with Walker?"

"He looked up my name in the phone book and came over Sunday afternoon without calling first. You should have heard the conversation that went on in my living room. He explained. He apologized. He asked for forgiveness."

"What did Nails say?"

"Something like, 'I forgave you a long time ago, but it doesn't mean I want you on my doorstep.'" Humor twinkled in Ada's eyes. "I had to remind her that it was actually *my* doorstep."

"Why, Ada. I think you're on Walker's side."

"I like the idea of true love, even true love delayed."

"He's unattached, then?"

"Long-time widower. Personally, I think he's settling in for the long haul. Sharon says he's already been on a short ride with Ronald and some of the guys. Things are getting interesting, and I've got a front-row seat."

Molly was finishing off her cookie when Nails returned. "I had a long talk with Ronald. He's more than happy to take over as your teacher. He says if he's any good, he'll have you riding behind Hank on the West Coast Loop."

"Yeah, right." Molly snickered. "That would take a miracle."

"They do happen," Nails said. "But if you end up driving, you'll want a traveling companion to keep you company. Who would you take with you?"

"My friend, Micheline, of course."

Molly had scheduled and shown up for several walks with Micheline after getting reprimanded. On one of them she'd told her friend about the latest steps she'd taken toward overcoming her fear. Micheline had been as proud of her progress as she was.

"You're a gutsy woman. But while you're doing that with Nails, don't forget the camp song," Micheline had said. "You know the one that says, 'Make new friends but keep the old. One is silver and the other, gold.' I'm the gold-standard friend, and don't you forget it."

Inviting her to go on the trip would be the perfect chance to show her that she'd not been forgotten.

The next day, Molly took Micheline to lunch at a Mexican restaurant they both enjoyed. She waited until the flan was served before she told Micheline about the West Coast Loop ride. "This is going to be a fantastic trip. It goes through some spectacular country that I've never seen before. But it looks like I'll be driving by myself." Molly paused. "Unless you'd like to come with me?"

Micheline had been about to take a mouthful of flan. She set the spoon back down. "Are you serious?"

"Absolutely. Think of the fun we would have. We could talk a blue streak while we listen to our favorite CDs and chomp on chips and chocolate."

"You're sure?"

"Sure I'm sure, unless by some miracle I'm suddenly transfused with the courage to ride behind Hank. How likely is that to happen?"

"Not very. Okay. I'm in."

They spent the rest of the afternoon talking about the trip, what music they would take, what snacks they would pack, and what board games they would stuff into Molly's SUV for evening entertainment. It was going to be grand.

Then Molly went for a ride with Ronald.

I'm getting to be a group project, Molly thought when she saw that Ada and Nails had also come to the Bixbys on the day of the ride. She parked and walked past Ronald's pearl brown Gold Wing to join them on the porch, where they were comfortably chatting. She expected them to hurry her into Sharon's gear, which she would be wearing for these training rides, and onto the motorcycle, but they continued to talk. Molly's nerves were about to get the best of her when Ronald slapped his knees and rose. "Shall we, Molly? Gracie's waiting for us."

"How did she get that name?" Molly asked.

"The first night we had her home, Sharon couldn't get me out of the garage. Finally she grabbed me by the arm and said in her best Burns and Allen imitation, 'Say goodnight, Gracie.' The cycle's been Gracie ever since."

Molly knew the moment she was situated in the passenger seat that riding Gracie was going to be totally different from riding Springsteen. *Nails was right,* she thought as Ronald took her for a spin around the neighborhood. *I feel as safe as a baby in a highchair. No bib necessary.* That was a complete surprise. But the greater surprise was that she enjoyed herself so much she thought the ride was too short.

Considering where she'd started, it was a miracle. Not enough of one to make her change her plans with Micheline, but enough to make her wonder where the road she had started down was leading.

It was enough to make Ronald wonder too. After they'd scheduled another ride, he said, "I think you should tell Hank what you're doing, Molly. If I were in his place, I'd have a hard time understanding why my wife hadn't included me in something so important to both of us. Unless this is all part of some greater plan, like springing it on him during a temple ride."

Molly knew he was right. Hank needed to hear about it from her, not from someone who'd seen her on the back of Ronald's motorcycle. Even so, something in her still resisted. "I'm not ready yet."

When Ronald started to argue his point, Sharon stopped him with a wifely hand on his shoulder. "It's up to you, Molly. We'll do whatever you want."

Molly scheduled several training rides with Ronald when she knew Hank would be busy or gone. She listened to the relaxation routine on her iPod before each trip, but as time went on she felt more comfortable and rarely needed Nails's coaching. Now whenever Nails showed up for one of her rides, it was to join Sharon as a cheering section.

At first, Ronald kept to neighborhood roads, with short forays onto the major streets running east to west. Then, with Nails's approval, he proposed a ride up to and along a portion of Wasatch Boulevard, a much busier, faster thoroughfare.

Molly sucked in a breath. That was definitely out of her comfort zone. "Okay. If you both think I'm ready for it."

The day of that ride, Molly made her own version of the yellow emergency-information card Hank had filled out before the Provo ride and laminated it. She took it with her to the Bixbys.

"You have got to get your own gear one of these days," Sharon said when she handed Molly her helmet. "The better the fit, the more comfortable you'll be."

"This stuff is expensive. I don't want to shell out the shekels until I'm sure I'll use it."

"You've done great so far," Nails said.

"On city streets and not exceeding forty-five miles an hour. Today will be the litmus test." Molly was about to get on the motorcycle when she remembered the information card. She pulled it out of her purse and showed it to Nails and Sharon.

"Why, Molly Mancuso, you're beginning to think like a real motorcycle rider." Nails returned the card. "Keep it zipped in your inside pocket."

Ronald started out on the streets he'd taken her on before. Though traffic was heavier than she'd expected when they turned onto 7200 South, Molly felt comfortable as they traveled east toward the mountains. Remembering Ronald telling her Sharon was his second pair of eyes, she tried to be the same, looking out for cars getting ready to enter their lane, being aware of the conditions they were driving through.

At the intersection with Wasatch Boulevard Ronald caught a red light. While they waited for it to turn green, he asked, "Are we a go for taking Wasatch?"

She gave him a thumbs-up.

When the light changed, Ronald waited three counts and then accelerated through the intersection. Molly wasn't prepared for the sudden burst of speed. She gripped the armrests, telling herself, *I'm all right. It's all good.* But being in heavy traffic going at higher speeds was disconcerting. Especially when she'd heard riders say more than once,

"Drivers don't see motorcycles." That wasn't a happy thought when there was a car in front of them, a car to the left of them, and, worst of all, a car behind them.

Twenty minutes later they neared Parley's Canyon. "Decision time," Ronald said over the intercom. "Do we go west on I-80 to State Street or stay on surface roads?"

"Can we bail out after a few miles if I need to?" she asked Ronald.

"Sure 'nuff."

Flush with her success so far on the ride, Molly gave him a go.

She knew she'd made a mistake within seconds. She'd panicked on the trip to Provo when she'd seen big trucks in the lane next to the group of riders Hank was with. Now she was the one on a motorcycle with cars and 18-wheelers speeding past immediately to her left.

They hit a rough patch, and Ronald pulled closer to the inside lane where a rattling construction truck whooshed along next to them. Diesel exhaust made it hard to breathe. Molly bit down on an involuntary sound of distress, trying to remember everything she'd learned about managing fear. But when she heard the air brakes of a big truck right behind her, it was too much.

"Get me out of here!" she cried into the microphone.

Ronald took the 1300 East exit and turned into a nearby gas station and convenience store. Molly got off the motorcycle as fast as she could and leaned against it, her knees quaking.

Ronald put a steadying hand on her back. "Breathe."

"Why does everyone keep telling me that?" Molly snapped. But she straightened and took several deep breaths.

"I'm so sorry, Molly," Ronald said. "Dorothy is going to skin me alive for messing up all our good work."

They stood by the motorcycle for a quarter of an hour drinking the water he bought in the store and talking while Molly decompressed. Finally her heartbeat went back to normal and the shaking stopped.

"What do you think?" Ronald asked. "Do I need to call Sharon to come get you?"

Molly's first instinct was to have Sharon come. Then she remembered how much she'd enjoyed some of the shorter rides. "If we can go back on residential roads, I'll be fine. I think. I hope."

"If it helps any, most motorcycle owners find freeway travel a challenge, especially when they're just starting out."

The ride home was uneventful, but it took some sessions with Nails and several additional short rides before Molly was ready to brave Wasatch Boulevard again. She refused to consider another freeway ride, but she did sign up for the passenger safety course Nails suggested. That coaching increased her awareness of being a partner in her own safety while on the back of a motorcycle.

All this time, what Ronald had said about telling Hank hovered in the back of her mind. It was time to tell him, but she'd kept it from him so long, she didn't know how to go about it.

She could say, "Uh, Hank. I knew how much you wished I could get over my fear and ride with you on your motorcycle. So I've been getting help with that behind your back. The Bixbys know. Cal and Micheline know. Ada and Nails know. I bet even Howard Norton knows. In fact, you're the very last person to find out."

That would go over big.

Maybe she could try the straight-up approach. "Hey, big boy. How about a ride on your wheels?" That might work, but after scraping him up off the floor an explanation would still be required.

She remembered how insignificant she'd felt when Laurel had refused to share what was happening with her and Garrett. Now she'd done the same to Hank. He'd asked how she was spending her time, and she hadn't told him the truth.

Chapter 18

The day Molly triumphed over her fear by riding behind Ronald up Little Cottonwood Canyon, Sharon said, "Do you know what this means? It's time to seriously consider riding behind Hank on the West Coast Loop trip."

"You're forgetting the freeway factor," Molly said, folding Sharon's outerwear. "That counts me out."

"Not necessarily," Ronald said. "Our route avoids freeways whenever possible, and the ones we will take typically don't have the kind of traffic we experienced in Parley's Canyon that day. The only stretch that might be a problem is I-80 from San Francisco to Reno, but you'll have had enough time in the saddle by then to handle it."

"I'm not so sure."

Nails had been listening to their exchange. "I agree with Ronald. But just because you could doesn't mean you *should*. It has to be something you really want to do and feel good about."

"Then I think I'll pass."

Molly was not as certain in her decision as she sounded. Thinking that she might go riding with Hank *sometime* was a lot different from having people she trusted say she was ready to ride with him on the West Coast Loop trip. And the idea that she might be able to give Hank the surprise of his life wouldn't leave her alone. Nor would the questions it brought up.

What if there were a way to get her past the worst of the freeway congestion between Sandy and Ogden? What if she pushed past the line in the sand her fear had drawn and took that leap of faith? She could imagine how surprised and delighted Hank would be to have her behind him on his Gold Wing.

She could also imagine how disappointed Micheline would be if they didn't take the trip together.

She was still mulling over the Loop ride as she approached Hank's motorcycle in the garage the next day. She had gotten so comfortable on Gracie that she'd decided it was time to make friends with Hank's set of wheels. Since Hank had gone with Ronald to scope out the big Harley-Davidson facility in Lindon, she had the garage and the Gold Wing to herself.

She sat on the steps for a while looking at it. "I wish I knew what your name was. I'm okay with The Boss, Sister Martha, and Gracie because I know who they are."

The motorcycle didn't move, blink, or speak.

She approached it slowly, running her hand over the custom driver and passenger seats, admiring the supple, luxurious feel of the leather. She pulled the armrests back so she could get into the seat easily. Then she put her left foot on the footrest.

The motorcycle waited.

She grabbed hold of the driver backrest with both hands and swung her right leg over the cycle. When she was in the seat, she pulled the armrests into position.

"You feel as nice as Gracie. Maybe even nicer." Molly leaned into the backrest that supported her in the perfect place. "I think I could get used to this." She shifted in the seat again and then used her foot to nudge the outer bar of the footrest into a higher position.

"Can we talk?" While Molly practiced shifting the footrests from one position to the other she told the Gold Wing what she thought about Hank buying it the way he had, the conflict it had caused, and all the ways she had tried to resolve it.

When her ramblings progressed to her worry about Laurel, Molly began to feel silly. "I can't believe I'm sharing my most intimate thoughts with two wheels, a seat, and a pair of handlebars. The least you could do is tell me your name." She nudged the bars back down to where they lined up with the lower footrests, shoved the armrests back, and got off the cycle.

She gave it a pat and was on her way into the kitchen when a single word popped into her head. *Zelda.* She turned and stared at the motorcycle. "Zelda?" she said aloud.

Zelda the Magnificent.

"Oh, good. There's a megalomaniac motorcycle in my garage."

I rule.

"I must be going crazy."

Later that morning she opened the door to the garage and looked out again. The motorcycle seemed to take up most of the space, even though Hank's sedan and her SUV were parked there as well.

"All right. You rule."

Laughing at herself for talking to a motorcycle, Molly called Nails. "I think I know the Gold Wing's name. Zelda the Magnificent. I might be able to get away with calling her Zelda, but I wouldn't dare call her Zell."

"Sounds like you have a real character on your hands," Nails said with a chuckle. "One you might enjoy getting to know better."

Molly had come to the same conclusion. "Nails . . . I think . . . I'm considering . . ." She was scared to say it out loud. Once she had, there would be no going back. "I want to ride behind Hank on the trip."

Nails whooped. "What made you change your mind?"

"It's strange. All of a sudden I could feel what it would be like, and I knew I wanted to do it. But don't say anything to Hank. I want it to be a surprise."

"That should take care of trying to figure out how to tell him about your training."

Molly danced around the room after she'd hung up the phone, chanting rhythmically, "I'm going to ride! I'm going to ride." She opened the garage door. "Did you hear that, Zelda? I'm going to ride!"

Then the import of her decision hit her, and she sat down. After chasing her thoughts for several minutes, she decided to pray. She expressed everything: her hopes, her doubts, her fears, her longings.

Am I doing the right thing? Will riding with Hank bring blessings to both of us? Will we be kept safe from harm?

She knew as she asked that there were no guarantees, but she was filled with the assurance that no matter what choice she made and what the consequences might be, she and Hank would be fine.

She was less sanguine about the situation with Laurel, who wasn't talking to either her or Hank these days. When she did return one of Molly's numerous calls, it was at a time when she knew no one would be home so she could leave a voice mail message: "It's Laurel. I'm fine, just busy." It was a far from satisfactory communication.

Maybe she's talked to Heather, Molly thought, punching in that number.

Wade answered. "Hey, Mom. What's up?"

"Have you heard from your sister? I'm worried about her."

She must have sounded apprehensive, because Wade said, "Take it easy, Mom. She's fine. She's started seeing Garrett Stapely again."

"Did she tell you that?"

"He did. He says she's not too happy with any of us right now. I think we teased her too much on Bean Night about having a second chance at love."

That would do it, Molly thought. But she knew Laurel's distance from the family was more than that. It had started when Hank had retired and had doubled the day he brought home the motorcycle.

When another day went by with no direct communication with Laurel, Molly's concern demanded she take action. She called Laurel's secretary and asked if her daughter had some time free around noon. When the answer was yes, Molly said, "Write me in; I'm bringing her lunch."

She spent the morning fixing the layered sandwiches Laurel had loved as a child. She added other favorites to the cooler, including a salad of baby greens with Stilton cheese and pears, and lemon bars. That done, she put on a shirtdress in a fresh floral print she thought Laurel would approve of. Looking in the mirror, she applied clear red lip gloss and pulled strands of her newly frosted hair in place.

When Molly arrived at the office, the secretary told her to go on in.

Laurel was working at her desk when Molly knocked on the door frame. "I came to share lunch with you. There's a sunny spot and some open tables on the pavilion next to the Joseph Smith Memorial Building. I thought we could eat there."

Laurel stood with a grudging smile. "You are one determined woman, Mom. I don't have the time to go somewhere for lunch, but we have a nice cafeteria up one floor."

"That sounds fine."

They found a free table in a quiet corner, and Molly started unpacking the cooler.

Laurel immediately noticed the sandwiches. "I haven't had one of those in years. I always loved it when you made them." She watched with interest as Molly brought out the other offerings. "All my favorites. I think you're trying to ply me with good things to make me talk."

Molly patted Laurel's arm. "You're right."

Laurel did talk, but not about Garrett. She directed the conversation to Wade's children, the herb garden she'd started on her balcony, the plans for her grandparents' anniversary tribute, and, finally, the motorcycle.

"You two are getting to be thick as thieves with that Temple Riders group, aren't you?"

"I guess we are doing a lot with them." Molly started to tell Laurel about the work she'd been doing with Nails and the rides she'd had with Ronald.

Laurel almost jumped out of her chair. "Let me get this straight. You're getting on a motorcycle? After everything you've said about them being instruments of death?"

"Hard to believe, isn't it? But I'm getting more comfortable all the time. In fact, I'm going to surprise your dad by riding behind him on the Loop trip."

"What are you going to do? Show up the morning of the ride and say Ta-da?"

The tone of Laurel's voice deflated her enthusiasm over what had previously been a delightful thought. "Something like that."

"I'm not in favor of surprises. Neither is Dad."

"It was quite a surprise when he brought the Gold Wing home."

"He thought you knew what he was up to."

"I didn't. But this is completely different. I'm surprising him with something that I know will please him to no end."

"Maybe so, but not all surprises turn out to be welcome." Laurel set aside her unfinished salad.

"Are you talking about Garrett and Bean Night? Surely seeing him wasn't unwelcome."

"Seeing him for the first time in years with the whole family gawking at us was."

"Wade said you weren't happy with the clan."

"The Finleys aren't very subtle. Wade kept teasing us like we were teenagers on a first date."

"He told me he was afraid he'd overdone it." Molly paused. "He also said that Garrett told him you two have been on a few dates."

Seeing Laurel's expression harden, she immediately wished she could retract that comment.

"I thought I'd made it clear that whatever's going on between Garrett and me is our business."

"You did, but I was hoping you would change your mind and share that part of your life with me." Slowly Molly began packing the dishes away, wondering why she had thought this lunch was a good idea.

Laurel handed her the container the salad had been in. "Have you told Micheline about your change in plans?"

"Not yet."

"You'd better, and soon. I ran into Micheline's daughter yesterday. She says Micheline's been telling everybody about it. She's even bought some new clothes."

"Oh, boy."

Laurel gave Molly a lawyerly look. "You know, Mom, you can't keep throwing monkey wrenches into your relationships and not expect there to be consequences."

There will be consequences, all right, Molly thought on the way home. *That's why I haven't told Micheline about the change in plans yet. I don't want to deal with them.*

Micheline had asked her repeatedly as the trip neared, "Are you sure about us doing this together?" And Molly had repeatedly replied, "Absolutely." Now she was going back on her word. It had been easy to make up for missing a few walks, but she didn't know how she could possibly make up for choosing to ride with Hank.

"I'll tell her when we go for our walk tomorrow," Molly promised herself, but she went to bed wishing there was a way to get out of it.

They'd gone once around the large loop at the park before she had the courage to begin. She slid into it sideways, saying, "You know how upset I was after I freaked out on I-80?"

"Uh-huh. You'd pretty much resigned yourself to riding only on short day trips. On back roads."

"You won't believe this, but I worked back up to giving Wasatch Boulevard another try. Then a few days ago, Ronald took me for a ride up Little Cottonwood Canyon on Gracie. There were some tough moments, but I kept breathing, and you know what? I had fun."

"I suppose next you'll be telling me you've decided to ride behind Hank on the trip."

"Actually . . ." Molly began.

Micheline stopped in the middle of the path, her eyes blazing. "I knew this would happen. I made all my plans and I even got a few things, but all along I had this feeling you'd ditch me. So much for gold-standard friendships."

"I feel awful about it. I know how much you were looking forward to us going together—"

"I thought we were *both* looking forward to it." Micheline took off in a jog, and Molly had to run to catch up with her.

"Please, Micheline. It's important that I do this. It would mean so much to Hank."

Micheline stopped, arms akimbo. "Playing the Hank card, are you?"

"Yes, I won't apologize for it," Molly said. "Remember when Hank brought the Gold Wing home? You said if Cal had a motorcycle and invited you to ride, you'd do it in a nanosecond."

Micheline jabbed at the blacktop with the toe of her shoe. "I did, didn't I?"

"I have a chance to ride behind Hank, and I'm going to take it. But I promise to go someplace with you after he and I are back. Then you can wear all those travel clothes you bought."

"Don't promise, Molly."

Micheline's tone was distant. Molly knew something had been lost, and she didn't know what to do about it.

They walked several minutes without speaking. Then Micheline said, "Are you really going to ride all those miles on the back of the Gold Wing? It's a lot different from a few rides with Ronald. Frankly, I can't see it."

"Hank would say the same thing—if he knew."

"You mean you haven't told him either?"

"Nope. I've kept it a secret, and I can't wait to spring it on him."

Micheline stared at her. "Do you have any idea how he's going to react? Secrets and husbands don't mix well."

"Call it a surprise, then."

Micheline shook her head. "Whatever you call it, it's not a risk I'd take. How are you going to pull it off?"

"That's the tricky part. If I surprise him before we leave, I'll have to ride through the wretched I-15 traffic past Ogden, and I don't want to start out having to deal with that. I need to figure out how to get myself and my gear up to the first rest stop north of Brigham City and surprise him there."

Molly was halfway hoping that Micheline would offer to help, but all she said was, "That shouldn't be too hard."

"The thing is, Hank will be expecting you and me to be driving my SUV. If someone else takes me there, he'll know something's up."

Micheline pulled a face. "I see where this is going."

"It's the only way to make it work," Molly pleaded. "You and I would start out in the SUV the way we planned. At the first stop, I'll have someone distract Hank while I put on my gear."

"You've bought some of your own?"

"Not yet, but it's on my to-do list. When Hank's ready to go, I'll pop out in front of him, helmet in hand."

Micheline grinned. "Has he had his heart checked lately?"

"As far as I know, it's ticking along quite fine."

"Then you and Hank ride off into the sunset, and I drive your SUV back home."

"That's the idea. I know it's asking a lot after ruining your plans."

"They were *our* plans, Molly, and it is asking a lot."

Molly made a helpless gesture. "I don't know what else to say."

"What is there to say? You're going to do it."

Micheline let those words hang a few moments before allowing the corners of her mouth to turn up ever so slightly. "And I'm going to help you. I wouldn't miss seeing Hank's face for the world."

Chapter 19

After telling Laurel and Micheline her plans, Molly decided she'd might as well call the rest of her family and get it over with.

Her father boomed across the line, "Bess knew it yesterday. She had that feeling she gets, and she was right." He told Molly to say her prayers and to remind Hank to look both ways before driving through an intersection. It made her feel like she and Hank were kids leaving home for the first time. She found it sweet.

Wade said, "You wild woman. How did that happen? You were close to losing it the day the kids rode with Dad."

She told him the short version, with the promise to go into detail when they got back. In return, he promised he wouldn't do or say anything that might tip off Hank.

As the trip neared, Molly kept checking with Micheline to make sure she had all the particulars straight.

"What's with this?" Micheline finally asked. "Are you nervous, or are you afraid I'll pull a Molly? Don't worry, I'll be there."

Marking off the days on the calendar, Molly had a hard time keeping both her excitement and her nerves in check. She was sure Hank would realize she was up to something, but luckily he attributed her pumped-up state to pretrip jitters.

"Relax," he said, when he saw her fussing over her trip lists. He took them out of her hand and made her sit beside him on the family room couch. "If we forget something, we can pick it up along the way. Remember, I've made an appointment to have your SUV washed and serviced tomorrow. Can't have you behind the wheel of a vehicle I don't know is roadworthy."

"That's so nice of you."

"I've also checked the emergency box to make sure nothing's missing."

"You're taking care of me. Are you doing the same for yourself? I can't have you riding a motorcycle I don't know is roadworthy."

"Been there, done that. And I've added some things to the emergency kit that came with the bike. Extra tools, tire repair kit, spare headlight. Duct tape."

"Duct tape?"

"Don't you know?" He looked at her with mock astonishment. "You can fix a thousand things with duct tape."

"Guess I forgot to take that class."

"By the way, I'm not going to put a suitcase in your SUV. I want to pack all my things on my bike. I want the whole experience of being on the road."

"Even your Sunday clothes?"

"The others are doing it."

"It's fine by me." Inside she was jumping with joy. One more logistical issue cleared up. With Hank's things already packed in the hard cases, all she had to do was figure out how to pack her luggage so that it could be tied down on Zelda's trunk.

The next morning Molly drove the SUV to the car shop, Hank following. When he took her home before leaving to run errands, he said, "I'll be gone most of the day. Are you sure you'll be okay without a car?"

"Nails is picking me up. We're going shopping together," Molly said. She didn't mention she would be buying riding clothes.

Nails first took her to Cycle Gear, a motorcycle parts and accessory shop in Draper. "Be prepared; this is going to cost big time," she said as she parked her Jeep. "But it's worth every penny."

When Molly walked into the shop, she entered a world she'd never imagined. Near the door was a stack of helmets nearly reaching the ceiling. On the other side of the store was an equally high stack of tires. Motorcycle-related items from exhausts to clothing to toys filled every inch of space.

"Oh, boy," she said. "How am I going to find what I'm looking for in this place?"

"See that woman over there?" Nails pointed to a tattooed saleslady straightening a display of helmets. "She knows everything there is to know about riding gear. I'll get her to help us."

After listening to the woman explain the relative merits of various types of protective outerwear, Molly chose a black and pink cordura jacket and black pants, two pairs of gloves in different weights, and a full rain suit. Cold-weather clothing was next, lightweight items worn under protective gear that could be plugged into each other and then into the motorcycle for blessed warmth.

"If you're on a road trip, you always pack rain gear and heated clothes, no matter what time of year," Nails said.

Last, Molly added a quality helmet to the pile. "How am I going to pack all of this on the cycle?"

"You'll be wearing most of it. A couple of duffel bags will hold the rest, plus everything else you're going to take. A bungee net will hold them on the trunk."

The final total, including two duffels and a bungee net, made Molly gasp. "I hope Hank doesn't check the credit card statement online before we leave. I'd have to tell him what this was for, and it would ruin my surprise."

"I thought you were doing the finances."

"I am, mostly. But no matter how good a job I do, he's always double-checking. It's like he's waiting on the sidelines for me to drop the ball."

"That would drive me crazy," Nails said as she loaded the packages into the rear of her Jeep.

"It does." Molly leaned against the vehicle, running her finger down her shopping list. "Why didn't we get my boots here?"

"Because there's only one place to go for boots."

Nails's grin made Molly suspicious. "You don't mean—"

"The Harley-Davidson place. But don't worry. Lots of ordinary people get their gear there. Not all of them ride Harleys, and some don't even ride motorcycles."

"Hank and Ronald went down a while back, did I tell you that? They thought it was massively cool. Hank bought a biker wallet with a chain he can hook to a belt loop. Very practical."

The large Harley-Davidson building in Utah Valley was designed to look old, as if it had been part of the defunct Geneva Steel Company. The harsh industrial-looking interior was softened by dozens of tropical plants growing out of oil cans. It was filled nook and cranny with all kinds of interesting items with the Harley logo.

Molly had thought the array of goods at the other store was amazing, but this was more so by far. She tried to keep her focus on what she'd come for, but she walked out with a sack in each hand. In addition to a pair of black leather boots sporting an embroidered Harley-Davidson logo on the front and ringed ankle straps, she'd purchased an orange and white long-sleeved Harley T-shirt with a V-neck and rhinestone trim, plus a black-and-white do-rag with the half-skull logo printed across one corner.

It was past noon by then, so Nails led Molly to the restaurant connected to the Harley building, where they ordered the house specialty, little sandwiches with gourmet fixings called sliders. "Hank's going to think I corrupted you," Nails said as they waited for their food.

"You didn't. I picked out the T-shirt and do-rag all on my own."

Molly dug through her purse for the packing list she'd put together and laid it on the table. "I wouldn't have any problem packing a suitcase for this trip, but I don't know how much I can take on Zelda. Any suggestions?"

Nails pushed the list back toward Molly. "I don't have to read it; I can tell already it's too long. Added weight affects how a motorcycle handles, so you don't want to take any more than is absolutely necessary."

"But I'm already down to the basics."

"Oh, honey." Nails laughed. "You're a long way from the basics."

Molly had been too distracted to notice it before, but now she saw that Nails was wearing a touch of blush on her cheeks and color on her lips. Her ponytail was caught in a ribbon instead of a scrunchie and her nails had been given a coat of light pink polish. *I wonder who she's dressing for? Walker or Howard? Or herself?*

"What are you taking on the trip?" Molly asked her.

Instead of a direct answer, Nails told a story. "I took a long road trip on my own once. It was five months after Charles passed away, and I needed to prove to myself that I could take on life without him. I decided to ship my bike to Nauvoo, and then ride it back following the Mormon Trail. I read a lot about the trail before I went."

"That sounds like me," Molly said. "I've been looking up the places we're going on this trip and printing out information. Sorry I interrupted. Go on."

"When I was reading about the handcart companies, I found out that each person could take only seventeen pounds of personal items with them. I decided to limit myself to that amount, not counting my gear, as an exercise to see what I could live with. And live without."

"That's not much. Are you doing the same this time?"

"Yes, but I won't weigh it. I don't have to. Since then I've learned to travel very light. It simplifies things."

"Simple is good, but what if there isn't room for my camera equipment or extra socks or things I might buy on the road?"

"No problem. Ronald and Sharon always have a spot in their Tag-a-long for that sort of thing. I think they bought it as much for the rest of us as for themselves."

Their sliders arrived then, so Molly put her list away.

"Bon appétit," Nails said.

Once more, Molly noticed how alive and bright she looked. "Have you seen Walker lately?"

"He comes over every few days. Visiting Ada, he says."

"And?"

"He can hang around if he wants to."

Molly thought she could see the barest hint of a smile, and she could almost hear the words, *I don't object.*

Later, as she crossed unnecessary items off her list, Molly thought about the handcart pioneers and what they'd gone through. She was surprised to feel a deep connection to them. She and Hank wouldn't be going into the unknown like the pioneers had, but they would be going west in the company of other Latter-day Saints and doing the Lord's work in the temples they visited.

But we are going into the unknown, in a way, Molly thought. *Hank and I are going to be spending two weeks in close proximity for the first time in years. Who knows what will come out of that?*

⌒

Three days later, Molly met with her sisters to practice the fiddling tune they'd decided to play for the Fourth of July program. Her head was so full of motorcycles and the trip, it was hard for her to switch gears, but once they started practicing, she was totally absorbed in it.

When they took a break, Hope said, "Rehearsals will be well underway when you get back, Molly. There'll be less than a month before the big event."

Molly nodded. "And then it will be over. Funny how we spend so much time anticipating and preparing for something, and before we know it, it's come and gone."

"And ends up a short comment in a scrapbook," June said, "if that. Sometimes I wonder what moments God would put in a scrapbook of our lives. Probably ones we thought were insignificant or don't even remember."

"If you spend too much time dwelling on that, you could drive yourself crazy," Hope said. "Is this one of those moments? Maybe this is one?"

June's laugh was clear and happy. "Don't worry, I'm not doing that. But I am trying to pay attention to life as it happens."

"I have some scrapbook moments coming up myself," Molly said.

"No kidding," June said. "You make me feel quite unadventurous. While you and Hank are on your road trip—on a motorcycle, no less— I'll be doing the same-old, same-old."

"But paying attention while you're at it," Molly kidded.

On the way home, Molly wondered what moments of her life God might put in her scrapbook. *Is this one of them?* she thought as she turned into the driveway in Sandy. The garage door was up, and she could see Hank standing by Zelda, a satisfied look on his face.

"What are you up to?" she asked, getting out of the SUV.

"Packing. I wanted to see if there was room in the cases for the things I want to take."

There was nothing on the floor beside Zelda and nothing piled on the hood of his car. "What exactly? I don't see anything."

"That's because it all fit." He opened one of the cases and pulled out the soft inner bag he'd packed his items in. It was full but not bulging. "See, I even have some room left over for things I might buy on the trip."

"That's the engineer in you," Molly said, glad she didn't have to worry about where to put her purse and camera.

He put the bag back into the case and then picked up a chamois and began polishing the cycle's gas tank in a circular motion.

Noticing how enthusiastically he was going at it, she said, "If you don't watch out you'll rub Zelda's paint off."

He stopped in midcircle. "Zelda? You called my bike *Zelda*?"

"That's her name."

"How do you know? I'm sure you haven't taken it out for one of Nails's naming rides."

"I know it sounds strange, but she told me."

"Please tell me you're not carrying on conversations with a machine."

I have, but I'll never tell. "Don't worry. I'm not going bonkers."

"I'm glad to hear that," he said with an amused glance. "But if small appliances start talking to you, promise you'll make an appointment with a shrink."

"The minute it happens."

He started polishing again. "I asked Laurel to come for supper the night before we go."

"Any special reason?"

"Aside from the fact I'd like to see her? I want to show her the file case I put all of our important papers in. It's been awhile since we went over that."

Molly leaned against his sedan. "I'm not sure that's a good idea. She doesn't approve of what we're doing. Hand her those, and she'll think it's a bad omen."

"Not Laurel. She's trained to think like a lawyer."

Training goes out the window when it comes to family, Molly thought.

Tuesday, the day before they were to leave, Molly got an attack of the heebie-jeebies. She called Micheline yet again to make sure everything was still a go. She called Nails for reassurance that she really was ready to make the trip. Then she called Ronald to go over the logistics of the surprise.

For the surprise to work, it had to look as if she were making normal trip preparations. She packed the things she wanted on the trip in one of the new duffels and hid it behind the driver's seat. Then she put a decoy suitcase and the smaller cases holding their temple clothes in the back. Sharon had promised to put those in Molly's second duffle when they pulled off the switch.

While Molly was doing those things, Hank was busy mowing the lawn and stopping newspaper and mail deliveries, checking off his own list as he went. He was overflowing with cheerful excitement when he joined her in the kitchen to get ready for Laurel's visit. "What can I do to help?"

With him assisting, it didn't take long for Molly to assemble the corn chip and chili casserole she'd decided to make. Once it was in the oven, they started on a salad.

"I've been thinking about something," he said as he sliced green onions.

A preface like that could only mean trouble. "Yes?"

"As long as we're so close to Mom and Joseph, I'd like to peel off from the group in San Francisco and visit them. If Micheline doesn't mind the change in plans."

"How far is it from there to Cucamonga?"

"About four hundred miles. We'd need to take I-5, but if we start out early in the morning, we can put some miles behind us when the traffic is relatively light. By California standards."

Molly's heart plummeted. He had no idea what he was asking—he still thought she would be driving with Micheline. She felt confident about riding the planned route on Zelda, but to go an extra four hundred miles on the freeway from hell?

"Molly?"

"Sorry, my mind was somewhere else." She tried to look enthusiastic. "I think visiting your folks is a great idea. Although I imagine showing off Zelda to Chester and Lennie is part of the reason you want to go."

"You got me there. Lennie's been giving me a hard time for getting 'the retired man's motorcycle,' but he's happy that I'm back on two wheels."

"Lennie does like his Harley, doesn't he?"

"Oh yeah. The chrome he's put on that baby . . ."

"You add chrome to a cycle after you buy it?"

"Fender trim, frame covers, footrests . . . that's what makes every cycle individual." He reached for the plates and began setting the table. "I hope you don't mind us missing out on the second day of the San Francisco tour."

She returned her attention to the lettuce. "Not if you take me another time."

"I'm for that."

Laurel arrived just as Molly was putting the casserole on the table. She asked Hank to bring the salad over and Laurel to pour some milk for her dad. She sneaked glances as Laurel filled Hank's glass, trying to figure out what was different about her daughter. *It's the blouse,* she thought. Laurel usually wore clothing in shades of blue, black, and gray, but this blouse was a mauve that softened and warmed her face. She also wore uncharacteristically high heels with fashionable pointy toes.

"Your shoes are very stylish. Are they new?"

"I bought them a while ago."

After Bean Night, I bet.

Dinner conversation was mostly between Laurel and Hank, who was always interested in the cases she was working on, the ins and outs of office politics, and her views on local happenings. The subject of the trip didn't come up until Molly brought a dessert of fresh fruit to the table.

"I can't stay long," Laurel said. "What was it you wanted to tell me?"

Hank cleared a space in the center of the table and spread a map in front of her. "I bought this for you and marked the route so you can follow our progress when you read our blog."

"*Hank and Molly on the Road*," Molly said. "Wade came up with that name when he set the blog up. He also gave us a short course on how to post text and photos."

Hank began telling Laurel about the points of interest they would be visiting along the route, but Laurel didn't look very interested. Molly tried to catch her attention with tidbits of information, with no success.

Hank finally gave up. "You don't want to hear this, do you?"

"I can see you're excited about this trip, but I wish you weren't going on it."

"We've made all the right preparations," he said. "We'll take every precaution."

"Which means exactly nothing. All it takes is one driver not paying attention and you're toast. All my life I've looked to you as the example of doing what was right and best for the family. Now this."

Say the right thing, Hank, Molly thought, although she had no idea what that might be.

As the silence lengthened, she realized he didn't either. All the time she'd been worrying about Laurel, he'd been confident in his relationship with his daughter. Now Molly knew he was being forced to look at the gap opening between them.

"I was going to show you something," he finally said, "but this is clearly the wrong time."

"I'm here, so whatever it is . . ."

He hesitated and then got the file container from his office. "I've been reorganizing things. All our important papers are now in this case. Power of attorney, health-care directives, and things like that. Just in case."

"The just-in-case case? Very funny."

When she didn't take it from him, Hank said, "I'll leave it on top of my desk where it'll be easy to find."

"That's fine." Laurel rose from the table and picked up her purse. She seemed eager to leave but also reluctant. "Do you need me to do anything while you're gone?"

"Not unless you want to pull the weeds before they take over," Hank said.

Laurel shook her head. "I don't think so."

"There is one thing. If I could remember what it was." Molly frowned, and then snapped her fingers. "The African violet!"

She fetched the plant from its place in the living room. "Remember this? Lori Aldridge gave it to your father at his retirement party. She thought it might be the start of a new hobby for him."

"What a strange idea." Laurel smiled slightly.

"The poor thing. I've neglected it, and I don't think Hank even sees it. I'm amazed it's not dead." Molly handed her the plant.

"What am I supposed to do with it?"

"Keep it alive. Make it bloom if you can. I haven't been able to."

Laurel studied the care tag attached to the tiny dowel Molly had never removed from the pot. "Have you been following the watering instructions?"

"Basically I water it when it droops."

"Do you fertilize it?"

"Uh . . ."

"Plants may survive on water only, Mom, but they won't bloom without food."

"I'll do better when we get back. I promise."

Chapter 20

That night, Molly dreamed she and Hank were huddled together in a sandstorm that raged around them and a broken-down Zelda. Then the image shifted. She was standing alone on the side of a bleak road in the middle of nowhere, watching the TRA members disappear over the horizon without her.

She awoke in the early morning with a start and the horrible feeling that she'd been left behind as real as it had been in the dream. She jumped out of bed and dashed into the garage, flopping down on the steps in relief when she saw Hank rearranging items in one of the fabric bags.

"Good morning." He smiled broadly. "Today's the day."

"Yes, it is. How much time do we have?"

Hank checked his watch. "It's six thirty. We need to be at the meeting point at eight, so we should be leaving here in an hour. Go get dressed, and I'll fix us some breakfast."

"I don't think I can eat."

"How about I fix us a banana smoothie? That ought to hold us until our first stop."

If I don't throw it up, she thought. Excitement made her hands tremble, and her stomach did flip-flips as she showered and dressed.

Micheline arrived right on time. Molly met her in the garage and opened up the rear of the SUV so Hank could see them put Micheline's pretend luggage in the back.

He did a final walk-through of the house and led them in a short prayer. Then he rubbed his hands together. "This is it. I'll head out. You two follow." He got on his motorcycle and gave the *Star Trek* "Engage!" gesture.

Molly followed him north on State Street to Little Dave's Deli on West 33rd near an entrance to I-15. There were already five motorcycles parked on one side of the building. A cluster of people dressed in protective apparel stood in a circle nearby. She could tell by their gestures and focused attention they were examining something.

Hank parked Zelda in the line of cycles. Molly pulled into a parking space by the exit. "Come on, Micheline." She climbed out of the vehicle. "Let's go see what's up."

As they approached, the crowd parted to reveal Merrill Carter sitting on a big, electric blue motorcycle—with three wheels. Enid stood beside him, her apricot hair glistening in the sun.

"What in the world?" Molly said.

"It's a tricycle," Micheline said.

"A Spyder Fastback." Merrill's pride was obvious. "We were tired of missing the longer trips because we didn't think we could handle them. Now we're back in business."

"Take a good look at it," Ronald told Sharon. "We'll be in the market for one of these ourselves in a few years."

"Fine by me, if it'll keep us riding. When did you get it, Enid?"

"We picked it up yesterday afternoon. We thought we'd show it off and send you off at the same time." Enid reached into a bag and started handing out sugar cookies cut in the shape of the Honda trike and frosted in the same bright blue with silver sprinkles.

While Molly and Micheline were enjoying their cookies, Nails joined them. "Introduce me to your friend."

"Micheline, this is Dorothy," Molly said. "You've heard me talk about her."

Micheline reached out to shake the offered hand. When she saw the flame-tipped fingers, she cried, "You're Nails!"

The attention of others in the group swung toward them. "Oh, dear," Molly said. "I didn't mean for that nickname to get around."

Nails laughed. "Too late now, but I don't mind."

The rest of the group introduced themselves in turn: Sam and Rose

Hess, the Connellys, and the Forrests and their ferret. An astonished Micheline had to see the cage securely affixed to the right side of the Forrests' Gold Wing before she would believe they were really taking the animal on the trip.

Then Ronald called everyone to order and reviewed safety protocol and the formation they would be riding in. "I'll be lead rider and Doyle will be the gunner," he said. He briefly outlined the first leg of the day's trip—north on I-15 to I-84, which would take them northwest into Idaho. "We'll spend a couple of hours in Twin Falls to see the temple and Shoshone Falls. Then we'll eat lunch at the home of Barney's sister, Janet."

"I sure wish the Fastback had come in earlier," Merrill said. "Enid and I would have packed our bags and gone on this trip with you."

Then it was time for the travel prayer. The group made a tight circle and Merrill asked for a blessing on the riders. Then he and Enid said their farewells, the motorcyclists mounted up, and Molly and Micheline got into the SUV.

"Here we go," Molly said to Micheline as she followed the motorcycles into the flow of traffic on I-15— after the requisite thirty-second count. She was glad her friend had so many questions about the people she'd met. She needed something to keep her nerves in check.

It worked for a while. But as the signs for Hill Air Force Base and then Odgen flashed by and she saw the exit for Brigham City by the side of the road, every worry Molly had ever had resurfaced with a vengeance. By the time the motorcycles took the prearranged exit ramp, Molly was ready to let go of the steering wheel, fling her arms into the air, and yell, "What was I thinking?"

"Do you know what excuse Ronald's going to use for stopping?" Micheline asked.

"He doesn't need one." Molly followed the motorcycles to the first convenience store on the road. "Groups take a short break and gas up every hour or so. We've been on the road for an hour and a half." She found a parking spot and turned off the engine. "Now we wait until someone gets Hank out of the way."

Howard did the honors. He said something to Hank and led him artfully into the store. Then Nails, Ronald, and Sharon hurried over to Molly.

"Showtime," Nails said.

Working quickly, Sharon put the temple cases in the second duffel. Then Ronald took both duffels and the bungee net and started toward Zelda.

"Wait," Molly said, holding out her purse and camera. "These should fit in one of the saddlebags."

"Consider it done," Ronald said. "Now get your gear on before Hank realizes something's up."

Luckily the ladies' room wasn't occupied. Once inside, Nails handed Molly her armored pants. Molly pulled them on over her jeans, and then put on her boots, the armored jacket, and her gloves. She moved her arms up and down, and then leaned from one leg onto the other, testing for comfort. "I'm glad I took the time to wear the newness off these a little."

Nails gave her the once-over before handing her the helmet. "Looking good. Do you have a scarf to go around your neck if it gets windy?"

Molly patted her pocket. "I've got that Harley-Davidson do-rag, balm for my lips, and my emergency card. Rose said she'd fill the water container that fits in my cup holder."

"You're all set. I'll find a place to put your tennies."

Molly headed toward the parked motorcycles feeling like the reveal portion of an extreme makeover show. The TRA members surrounding Barney Forrest, who was showing off Fricka, made an effective barricade between her and Hank. It was time to yell, "Move that bus!"

"Hey, Hank," Nails called. "You've got company."

He looked up as the crowd parted, at first puzzled, then astonished. "Molly? Molly! What in the world?"

Molly's laughter pealed across the parking area. "Why, Hank Mancuso. I do believe you're speechless."

The group hollered, "Surprise!" and started clapping.

Ronald put an arm over Hank's shoulders. "Your wife is riding with you on this trip, brother. She's been working with Dorothy and me to get over her fear of motorcycles. It took some time, but we got her so she's comfortable in most situations."

Molly stood proudly in front of Hank. "Busy freeways are still a bit of a problem. That's why I surprised you here instead of at home. But Ronald promised me that from here to Boise won't be too bad."

Hank grabbed her in an enthusiastic hug and then held her at arm's length to take in the sight of her decked out in riding clothes. "I can't believe this is for real."

"I even got everything I needed in two duffels, one for my things, one for our temple clothes," Molly bragged. "Ronald has tied them down on Zelda with a bungee net."

Hank looked at his cycle, shaking his head as he noticed the extra baggage. "Amazing!"

"Looks like we're ready to go," Ronald said.

"Well, whaddaya say, pilgrim?" Molly asked Hank with the Duke's inflection.

Hank picked her up, twirled her around, and kissed her soundly to the applause of all watching.

It was hard for Molly to say good-bye to Micheline. "Thanks for helping me with this. I couldn't have done it without you," she said as they walked to Molly's SUV.

"I wouldn't have missed it for anything."

"Be sure to read our blog."

"Every day."

Molly watched Micheline drive away, a buzz of excitement running up her spine. There was no turning back now.

Hank gestured grandly toward Zelda. "May I escort you to your chariot, madam?"

She caught her breath at the adoration in his eyes. She hadn't seen such a look for a long time. It made everything she'd gone through worth it.

Riding behind Hank was different from riding behind Ronald. Molly hadn't expected that their years of shared experiences and her confidence that he would take care of her would affect how she felt riding on the Gold Wing, but they did. As Zelda eased up the on-ramp and back onto I-15, she allowed herself to sit back and enjoy the moment.

Traffic was light, and the group made good time from stop to stop on their way to Twin Falls. At each break she was inundated by Hank's questions. "What made you decide to do this?" "When did you take your first ride?" "How did you feel?" "Do the kids know what you're doing?" She was so happy to finally be able to tell him that the story came out in a gush.

At one stop he said, "I see you're well outfitted. Where did you get your gear?"

"A shop in Draper Nails took me to. We got almost everything I needed there, including a rain suit and heated garb. But my boots are Harley-Davidson, from that place down in Lindon you and Ronald went to."

"That had to cost a pretty penny. You must have put it on a charge card, because I didn't see a check made out to that place."

"Yes, I did." She worried what his reaction would be. After she'd started handling the finances they'd agreed to discuss any large purchase with each other.

"Well, I hope you didn't skimp on what you got to try to save money."

Molly laughed. "Don't worry. I didn't skimp."

Despite periodic stops to get gas and work out the kinks, the two-and-a-half-hour stretch from Brigham City to Twin Falls was grueling. Even with the additional cushioning of an aftermarket seat Molly was uncomfortable. She waited as long as she could before alerting Hank that she was going to shift position or adjust her footrests. The relief she gained was disappointingly temporary, hardly worth the effort.

As fatigue set in, her conviction that everything would be all right weakened. Hank had to be getting tired too. Would he doze at the wheel? Veer into oncoming traffic? Hit the soft shoulder and careen off the road? None of those things happened, but her relief was profound when they turned south toward Twin Falls and stopped at a viewpoint on the north side of the Perrine Bridge crossing the Snake River Canyon.

Barney uncaged Fricka, put her on her leash, and poured her a little bowl of water. "Remember when Evel Knievel tried to jump his cycle across the canyon?" He pointed to the southwest. "The actual site is farther west where the canyon is narrower. My sis, Janet, and I actually saw him crash."

He had more to tell, but Molly didn't catch much of it. She was busy taking photos of the dramatic cliffs and the green canyon floor with the river running through it.

When they mounted up again, Barney was lead man, taking them through town and over to the Twin Falls temple, an elegantly simple rectangular design with a single spire rising upward. They left their motorcycles in the parking lot and walked around it, talking quietly. A pair of gardeners working on the grounds eyed them curiously, but didn't question their presence.

"Too bad we didn't have the time to schedule a session here as well as in Boise," Barney said. "Counting our trip to Idaho Falls in August, we would have done sessions in all three Idaho temples this year."

"What trip is that?" Molly asked.

"Only the national rally. You and Hank won't want to miss it. It's going to be fantastic."

I guess I know where we'll be in August, Molly thought.

A quarter of an hour later, Barney led the group five miles east to Shoshone Falls, descending into the canyon on a narrow road that led to a riverside park.

"Five minutes, people," Ronald called as the group headed for viewing platforms at the upper and lower falls. "Janet's expecting us soon."

Molly joined those who took the stairs to the viewing platform above the lower falls. "See if you can get a picture of that," Jeri said, indicating the perpetual rainbow in the spray above the river at the bottom of the wide falls.

"Don't forget you're supposed to be taking pictures of us, too." RaNae struck a pose with Fricka on her shoulder.

Molly obliged, catching owner and pet nose to nose.

She took RaNae's reminder to heart and made sure everyone in the group would have at least one visual reminder of the stop. Her final shot was her favorite—Howard and Nails standing at the rail as they gazed at the sparkling refracted light arching over the water below.

Janet was thrilled to welcome them to her home, and they spent a delightful hour enjoying good food and conversation. But Molly's back and legs stiffened up during the lunch break as the many hours of riding in one day took its toll. She groaned when Ronald said it was time to saddle up, and she needed a boost from Hank to get back on Zelda.

"Hang in there. We'll be in Boise in a couple of hours."

"Define couple."

"With stops, a little over two."

It sounded like forever.

"Take a nap, it'll go by faster." He patted the top of her helmet.

"That's what I'm going to do." Rose Hess said as she swung easily onto the back of their bike. "Sam says he always knows when I've crashed, because I fall forward and conk my helmet against his."

As much as she wanted to, Molly couldn't sleep. She kept herself occupied checking passing traffic and watching for "black alligators," as Hank called chunks of retread on the road. When she saw Mountain Home listed on a distance sign, she started singing "Our Mountain Home So Dear" from the Church hymnbook. That lifted her spirits for a while, but by the time she saw the City of Boise sign, all she was trying to do was make it from one minute to the next.

The Boise hotel Ronald had booked for them was perfect for a TRA stop. It was inexpensive but clean and comfortable, not too far from the Boise temple, and allowed small pets if they were kept in cages. The minute Molly got into her and Hank's room, she took off her jacket and flopped on the bed, exhausted.

"Don't get too relaxed," Hank said. "We have to leave for the restaurant soon."

Molly moaned dramatically. Members of the Boise area TRA had invited the group to have supper with them at a local restaurant that featured home-style cooking. The last thing she was interested in was food, but she didn't want to miss out on anything. She forced herself to get up, wash her face, and apply moisturizer and lip balm. *I suppose I ought to do something with my hair,* she thought, but it didn't seem worth it when she was going to have to put her helmet back on. She settled for a single comb-through before she and Hank left the room.

Four couples from the Boise chapter were waiting for them at a long table near the back of the restaurant when they arrived. There was a flurry of greetings followed by order taking. Then conversation flowed as the two groups got acquainted and exchanged stories.

Ronald got everyone's attention. "Wanna hear a joke? What's the difference between a man on a motorcycle and his wife?" Pause. "She needs a destination; all he needs is a direction!"

Encouraged by the laughter, Ronald came up with another joke. "How do you know if you're a biker?" Pause. "Your only three-piece suit is a leather jacket, leather vest, and chaps."

"How about this," a Boise man said. "You know you're a biker if taking your wife on a cruise means going down the interstate."

Barney put in his two cents' worth. "You know you're a biker if you can identify bugs by taste."

The guffaws were still echoing when Molly got up to visit the ladies' room. As she passed a table of twenty-somethings, a skinny man wearing an AC/DC T-shirt and a soul patch beneath his lower lip caught her attention with, "Hey, lady, how do you know you're a biker? When you think helmet head is a fashion statement."

The man's companions reacted as if he'd said something tremendously clever. *Do I look that bad?* Molly wondered as she went through the door to the ladies' room. She'd finger-combed her hair after arriving at the restaurant, but a check in the mirror showed that hadn't been enough.

Later that evening the men gathered in the Bixbys' room to look over maps of Idaho and Oregon. Molly, revived by a good dinner and interesting company, invited the ladies to grab a soda and come to her and Hank's room for a chat. When everyone had found a place to flop, Rose said, "Okay, Dorothy. Now that it's just us ladies, I want to hear about that kiss everybody's talking about."

"Don't make more out of it than it was," Nails said with an arch look. "It was just a greeting between old friends who haven't seen each other for years."

"It didn't look like that to me," Molly said, fanning her face.

"Who is this Walker Beck anyway?" RaNae asked.

"Dorothy's first love," Sharon said. "That's what Ada says."

"That Ada." Nails's voice was exasperated, but she wore the smile reserved for her sister. "Wait until I get my hands on her."

"What does Howard have to say about Mr. First Love showing up?" Rose asked.

"That's something you'll have to ask Howard."

The tone in Nails's voice put an end to that topic. After a few moments of limbo, RaNae said, "So, Molly, what did that rowdy say to you in the restaurant?"

"He made a snide remark about my hair. And here I thought I'd fluffed it adequately after I took my helmet off."

"The perennial problem for ladies who ride," Rose said. "That and dry skin."

"What's your secret?" Molly asked, admiring the freshness of Rose's complexion.

"Are you ready? I use mayonnaise on my hair and mashed avocado on my face."

"Darn. I didn't think to pack those."

It was late and they were all tired. RaNae, who was on one of the beds, stretched and yawned. "I suppose we ought to pack it in, but I don't want to move."

"Me either," Rose said. She dug a package of honey-roasted peanuts out of her pocket and poured a few into the hands held out for them. "How are you doing, Molly? A full day on the back of a motorcycle on your first trip must have been rough."

"Other than every joint in my body aching, I'm fine."

"I know how that feels," RaNae said. "That's why I always bring some analgesic hot patches on these trips. I'll share, if you want."

"And I've got some liniment," Nails said. "It stinks like the dickens, but it does the trick."

Molly scrunched up her nose. "Thanks anyway, but a hot shower, some ibuprofen, and a good night's sleep should do the trick."

"Good," Rose said. "Hank was concerned, and he asked us all to keep an eye on you to make sure you're okay." She paused. "That husband of yours certainly does take good care of you."

Molly smiled in acknowledgment, but she wasn't sure how she felt about Hank discussing her status with others when they'd been on the road only one day. It seemed too much like the concern he had when he double-checked her work on the finances. *Is he already thinking that I can't go the distance?*

"What a day," Nails said. "I don't think I'll ever forget Hank's expression when he saw you in your gear, Molly. You took him completely by surprise."

"That was really something, wasn't it? It was almost as good as when he surprised me by bringing home the Gold Wing on his birthday," Molly said.

"Hold it," Rose said. "You didn't know Hank was buying a cycle?"

"I would have if I'd been listening."

"Had he ever ridden before?" RaNae asked.

"Yes. He quit when I asked him to. I thought it was too dangerous, and it didn't fit with my idea of what a good Latter-day Saint man was like."

"Goes to show you never can tell," Sharon said.

Nails began buffing a chip out of one of her stick-on fingernails. "I like to read the motorcycle For Sale ads. The other day I read one for a cycle that had only eleven miles on it. It said, 'Wife not happy with this motorcycle.'" She made a noise of sympathy. "Poor bloke. The only time that he got to ride his bike was when he brought it home from the dealership."

Molly thought back to the way she'd reacted when Hank drove Zelda home. "It could have been Hank placing that ad."

"Could have been, but wasn't," Nails said. "You didn't push him to it."

But I came close, Molly thought. *So close.*

Chapter 21

The next morning, they dressed in their Sunday clothes to go to an early session at the Boise temple. Molly felt silly pulling on her riding pants under her skirt, but Nails looked funnier when she demonstrated her technique, pulling the front and back of her broomstick skirt up like a diaper and stuffing the rest down the legs of her chaps.

The whole stuffed and layered group met in front of the hotel. Ronald had put on a gray bow tie with small burgundy dots, Molly noticed.

"He always wears bow ties on temple days when we're on a TRA trip," Sharon told her. "But not his goofy ones."

Everyone waited while the Forrests exchanged cycles with the Hesses. Then Rose and Sam, now equipped with cage, treats, and ferret, headed off for a school visit that a member of the Boise chapter had arranged. The others started for the temple.

Once in the temple parking lot, Molly held back from joining the ladies in the dressing circle. "Everyone feels a little shy the first time they drop their drawers in a temple parking lot," Sharon teased. "You'll get used to it."

Turning away from the circle of men facing outward in the parking lot, Molly slipped off her outerwear. Then she put her hand on RaNae's shoulder for balance, took off her motorcycle boots, and replaced them with flats.

When Jeri gave the men the all-clear, they switched places with the women and doffed their riding pants. Molly could see why Hank had picked out a pair of motorcycle boots that didn't have straps and buckles announcing their purpose—he didn't have to change shoes to be appropriately dressed for the temple. As the men put on their ties, Molly observed that strange transformation she had seen before, from bikers to serious servants of the Lord.

As they headed for the entrance, Hank took Molly's hand. "I don't think we've ever gone to so many different temples as we have since joining this group. Provo, Vernal, and now Boise."

"It still seems strange to me," Molly said. "Motorcycle riding combined with temple attendance."

"It's the juxtaposition. A worldly passion combined with a holy purpose. These people love going to the temple."

I hope some of that rubs off on me. Molly always felt uplifted when she went to the temple, but she still wasn't sold on going the way the Temple Riders did.

Her testimony of the gospel was like the air she breathed, something that just *was*. She'd struggled with depression when she had three miscarriages after Wade's birth, but even then, she'd never doubted God's love for her or grappled with questions of faith and meaning. All the things she did—reading scriptures, saying her prayers, attending church, serving when and where she could, and going to the temple— flowed from her native faith. She experienced deep pleasure and satisfaction from them, but not the kind of exalted feelings some Church members described in testimony meeting.

"Maybe it's because I'm not a deep thinker," she'd once told her mother.

Bess had gently run the back of her hand over Molly's cheek. "But you do have a unique capacity to love and find joy in life. Those are spiritual gifts too."

After the Boise session was over, the group went back to the hotel to change into riding clothes, load their cycles, and check out. Then they went to a Denny's restaurant for a late breakfast, parking their machines in a row.

An elderly gentleman dressed in pressed khaki work clothes eyed their cycles with interest. "You picked a good day for a ride."

Doyle described the loop they were taking. The man nodded. "Are you a club? Do you have a name?"

"Temple Riders," Ronald said. "We combine the love of being on the road with serving the Lord through going to the temple."

"You're Mormons."

"Yes. Are you?" Doyle asked.

"No. I haven't gone to a church since I was . . . oh, about seventeen."

"Do you know about our Church?"

A mischievous look crossed the man's face. "Nope. I never asked and nobody ever told."

"We can change that." Sharon pulled a Book of Mormon from one of the motorcycle saddlebags.

When she, Ronald, and the Connellys clustered around the man, Barney said to the others, "Let's go on in. We don't want him to feel outnumbered."

They were giving their orders to their waitress when the Bixbys and Connellys joined them.

"One Book of Mormon handed out." Jeri's eyes gleamed with satisfaction. "Doyle's already asked one of the Boise TRA members who was with us in the temple this morning to follow up with Willard."

"What a great way to start the day," Ronald said. "A temple session and a missionary opportunity."

Doyle sat down beside Jeri. "That's what we're all about."

As they ate, they talked about the route they would take to their next overnight stop, a little town on the Columbia River named The Dalles. "We should be on the road by eleven. It'll take us a good five hours to get there," Ronald said.

"Five hours!" Molly cried. "How am I ever going to do that?"

Jeri patted her shoulder. "One hour at a time. You'll make it. And if you need to, you can go straight to bed after we eat dinner."

"The ride will be worth it," Sharon assured her. "The Dalles is where the really great scenery on the Columbia River Gorge starts. We'll have time for sightseeing in the morning, because we don't have to be at Bette's Place in Hood River until noon. We're meeting some TRA people from Portland there for lunch."

At the mention of sightseeing, Molly remembered the information she'd gleaned from the Internet about the town with the strange name. "There's a lot to see at The Dalles, did you know that? It's at the end of the Oregon Trail. Pioneers loaded their wagons on rafts there and floated down the river."

She pulled a printout from her shoulder bag. "In the downtown area, there's the Fort Dalles Museum, the oldest bookstore in Oregon, and some murals depicting historical events painted on store walls."

She was scanning the page for information about the dam above The Dalles when Hank touched her shoulder. "I think we'll need to save whatever else you have until later. The Hesses just pulled in, and it's time we were on the road."

"Oh." Looking up, she saw that the others were ready to go and were waiting on her. Embarrassed, she folded her paper. "Sorry. I get carried away sometimes."

Howard put a tip on the table. "Hey, we're not complaining. We like having our own tour guide."

I hope he's not saying that just to be nice, Molly thought.

When she went to stand, she felt like an old lady. Not only was she stiff, she was pooped. *Where did all that energy of yesterday morning go?* she wondered. She could imagine Micheline saying, "Adrenaline rushes don't last forever, Molly."

She devoutly wished for one when Ronald called them into a group in the parking lot and outlined their route. "We'll be on the interstate until after we cross the Oregon border and on 'red roads' after that."

Molly was using her fist to rub her hip as she listened. She made an involuntary sound when she hit the sore spot.

Hank was at her side in a flash. "What's wrong, Molly?"

Everyone turned to look at her. "Nothing," she said through gritted teeth. "Don't fuss over me, okay?"

But when she got on the motorcycle, her hip protested loudly. Every part of her protested, to one degree or another. She crossed her fingers, hoping that the big dose of ibuprofen she'd taken would get her body through the next five hours. Just as she hoped the serenity and peace she had experienced in the temple would sustain soul and spirit through the coming ride.

It was tough going. Before long, Molly's right leg ached and her sitz bones felt like they were pressing into solid rock. She tried not to shift without warning Hank first, but when her hip shrieked, she moved without thinking and got a sharp reprimand from him over the intercom. He barked at her again a few miles later when she panicked during a deep curve and leaned in the opposite direction.

"For heck's sake, Molly. Didn't Ronald teach you anything?"

From that point on, she sat as straight and still as she possibly could, no matter how she hurt. Every minute seemed like an hour. She could tell her riding companions realized how miserable she was by the way they encouraged her at every stop and periodically used the CB connection to draw her attention to something interesting they were passing by.

She was numb when they finally arrived at their historic hotel in the center of The Dalles. When Hank held out his hand to help her dismount she tried to move her knees but couldn't. Her hips were frozen too. Hank lifted her from the passenger seat and set her feet on the ground. When her legs buckled momentarily, he caught her with an arm around her waist.

"I was afraid something like this would happen," he muttered. "Let's get you to our room and out of that gear."

"Just get me to our room. I can do the rest myself."

"Don't be silly, Molly. At least let me help you get your boots off."

Once they got into the room, he not only pulled her boots off, but he also helped her get out of her riding pants and turned on the hot water for her shower. "I'll check up on you later," he said as he left.

She stood under the warm spray for a long time, but she didn't get into her pajamas and into bed as she longed to do. She and Hank were alternating posting on their blog, and today was her turn. She was determined to get that done, after which she might as well go to supper with the group.

She considered what she might write as she went to the hotel's computer alcove. Most of the miles they'd covered were blurred by pain except for a few vivid mental snapshots. An old shack standing in a field of grass. The road ahead winding through stands of tall pines. A huge truck with a load of logs passing them from the opposite direction. The first tantalizing views of snow-capped Mount Hood as they neared the Columbia River.

And the row of cups in the diner outside Prineville where they'd stopped midafternoon for lunch. That's what she wrote about, after deciding there was no place in *Hank and Molly on the Road* for her pain and Hank's disappointment.

> The people we're riding with have an interesting habit. They stop at a greasy-spoon café at least once on a long trip. It's a change from chain restaurant food, which begins to taste the same after awhile. They also have criteria for deciding whether to stop: are there any motorcycles parked in front?
>
> The café we stopped at had two Harleys, a Honda, and a Victory in its parking lot. Right inside the front door was a shelf holding coffee cups with names on them. The sign below them read, "If you're a regular, take your cup and take your seat." The names on the cups made me think of the Seven Dwarves: Duff, Wally, Ezra, Ron, Charles, Emory, and Will.
>
> It was a good stop. My hamburger was up there with the best I've ever had and the fries were hot and crispy. The only problem was that I had to get back on the motorcycle when we were done!

After publishing her post, she glanced at the clock in the hotel's computer alcove. She had time to check their e-mail before supper. Of all the messages in their in-box, the only one she opened was from Heather. It was full of chatty family news and a sentence at the end that popped out as if written in all caps.

"Garrett and Laurel came to dinner! I can't say any more. She'll kill me if I do."

Molly wrote back, "I'm dying of curiosity. Wouldn't it be wonderful if they fell in love again? And made it past whatever tripped them up before?"

She was logging off when Hank found her. "What are you doing here? I thought you would be in bed."

"It was my turn to blog," she said.

"I would have done it." He looked at her doubtfully. "We're about to leave. Do you want me to bring you something back?"

"I'm coming too. I don't want to miss out on all the fun. Besides, I have photos to take."

The group ate at a restaurant in the historic downtown, and then walked through the nearby streets to see the huge murals on store walls. Molly loved the visual images they added to the history she'd learned from her research and would have lingered longer before each if she'd been on her own. One showed Lewis and Clark looking out over the gorge, another Celilo Falls, the ancient fishing grounds that were flooded when the dam above The Dalles was built.

The walk did her good, too, helping her work out her stiffness.

The long summer twilight cast a golden glow on the streets as the group started back to their hotel. Nails and Howard were walking ahead with the Hesses, carrying on an easy four-way conversation. When they reached the crossroad leading to the hotel, Nails said, "There's a mural Howard and I want to see a few blocks over. You go on. We'll see you later."

As they walked away Molly noticed Howard move closer to Nails and rest his hand on the back of her waist.

"Does Howard know he's got competition?" Rose asked nobody in particular.

"You mean Walker?" Ronald said. "He isn't here. Howard is."

"He'd better take advantage of it," RaNae said.

"You women," Barney groused good-naturedly. "You're always thinking about romance."

That reminded Molly she hadn't told Hank what Heather had written about Laurel and Garrett in her e-mail. She tucked her arm through his and told him about it and what she suspected.

"Sounds to me like they're picking up where they left off," Hank said.

"Will you be glad if they get serious again?"

"I'll be glad if she's happy. Whatever it takes."

"Me too." But Molly realized that she had no idea what outcome would assure that.

Since Molly wasn't moving very fast, they lagged behind the others.

"It's good to see you're feeling better, Moll," Hank said. "You were looking pretty rough before dinner."

"I'm better now. But I do need to toughen up."

"You amaze me."

She glanced at him. "Why?"

"I never thought you would go through so much for me."

"I did it for myself, first," she said, choosing her words carefully. "To keep fear from ruling my life. Then I did it for you. For us."

"I don't care what got you going. The fact you did means a lot to me. More than you know."

Something in his tone caught her attention, and she stopped in the middle of the sidewalk. "What do you mean, 'More than you know'?"

"Nothing. It just came out that way." He gave her a lavish hug. "I'm so glad you're here. I'm a lucky man."

Despite the reassuring words, it didn't feel like nothing to Molly.

Chapter 22

"Molly?"

Molly groaned as Hank gently shook her shoulder.

"I'm going out early to do a nuts-and-bolts check on Zelda before people get moving."

She forced her eyes open. "I'm awake. Wait for me." Determined to prove she could be part of the whole motorcycle experience, she heaved herself out of bed and pulled her clothes on.

Even after a stop in the motel breakfast room for cereal and milk, they were a full hour earlier than the start time when they went out to the parking lot. And they found that someone else had gotten a jump on them. Howard was already at the line of motorcycles, polishing the mirrors on Nails's Harley.

"When you're done there, my windshield could use a cleaning," Hank kidded.

"Been there, done that. Did it yesterday morning too." Howard laughed at Hank's surprise. "You thought bugs magically avoided your windshield?"

"It did look way too clean, come to think of it. Thanks, Howard."

Howard grinned. "Don't expect this every morning. Dorothy is the only one who gets that special treatment."

Hank started his walk-around of Zelda, explaining to Molly what he was checking and why. Others of the group had begun to show up by the time Hank patted Zelda and pronounced her in fine shape. When everyone was present and loaded up, Ronald went over the plans for the day, which included lunch with TRA members from Portland. Then Doyle offered the travel prayer.

He'd just finished when a motorcycle entered the parking lot too fast and drove straight toward them. The rider stopped with a rev of his engine and took off his helmet with a dramatic gesture.

"Walker!" they all said at the same time.

Molly wished she'd had the nerve—and the reflexes—to take pictures of the group's reactions. Howard looked perturbed. Barney looked intrigued. Nails's face was a study in conflicting emotions.

Ronald shook Walker's hand in welcome. "What are you doing here, brother? I thought you were tied up with business."

"I got finished sooner than I expected. It's a good thing I've done some Iron Butt endurance rides. Except for a few z's at Prineville, I've been burning the road up to get here before you left."

He turned his persuasive grin on Nails. "I hope you don't mind me tagging along."

"It's a little late to ask, isn't it?" The words could have sounded angry, but they didn't. "You're here."

"Guess our formation will be different now," Hank said.

Everything will be different now, Molly thought.

An easy camaraderie had formed in the group during their two days on the road. Walker's arrival knocked it out of balance. Molly saw it when they parked their cycles at The Dalles Dam visitors' center at Seufert Park. Nobody left the lot—they were all waiting to see what Nails would do and with whom.

With an exasperated huff, Nails headed toward the visitors' center.

Walker looked at Howard and Howard looked at Walker. With a strangely similar grin, they both followed her. Molly caught Nails and the odd couple on her camera.

"This is better than a soap opera," Rose said as they looked at the image on the back of the camera. "What do you think she's going to do with those two?"

"Ignore both of them, I imagine," Molly said.

Rose grinned. "I can see her doing that. When we get to Portland, will Walker go to the temple session or hang out with Sam and me and Fricka?"

"Don't know. We'll find out when we get there."

After an hour looking at the educational displays at the visitors' center, the whole group slowly gathered at a viewpoint on the river's edge. It was the closest they could get, since dam tours had been cancelled after 9/11. While they were there, a bus from a day camp pulled to a stop and disgorged a swarm of children. They scattered the minute their feet hit the ground, shouting and shoving into each other and anyone else in their path. They were followed by a pair of harried teenagers doing their best to herd them back in line.

"Those are the counselors?" Nails asked. "They can't be more than fifteen."

Molly tsked. "They're definitely out of their league."

When the swarm headed their way, Ronald and Barney exchanged glances. They didn't say anything to the children, as Molly was tempted to do. Instead they created an irresistible attraction.

Ronald pulled a quarter out of the air and danced it back and forth across his knuckles where one of the ringleaders would be sure to notice. He had a captive audience when he made the coin disappear from that hand and reappear in the other. Barney pulled Fricka out of her favorite nesting spot inside his jacket. She scurried up his arm and perched on his shoulder, catching the attention of the children nearest him. "If you back up and stand quietly, she'll dance for you."

Molly caught images of the children's faces as Barney and Ronald entertained them for the next five minutes. *What amazing men they are,* she thought. She was chagrined to realize that before the advent of Zelda, she had never looked past Ronald's church image to discover the fine and funny man beneath. *I probably would have overlooked Barney and RaNae, too, if I had been introduced to them earlier.*

When it was time to go, Hank said, "Mount up, my little paparazzo."

"I guess I am a bit like one," Molly said. "The scenery is fantastic, but people are much more interesting."

The morning's ride, which followed the wide, curving Columbia River as it flowed through forested hills and red cliffs, was blessedly short. They arrived at Bette's Place in Hood River moments before the Portland TRA contingent.

The two groups got acquainted while talking motorcycles on the side street where they'd parked in a row of bright color and chrome. When everyone was seated inside and lunch had been ordered, Ronald made the formal introductions. Molly tried to fix them in her memory as he spoke. Tom and Mary Wentworth—older, owners of a vintage touring bike with fringed leather saddlebags. Anton and Linda Sanchez—younger like the Hesses. George and Kip Rabosky—a father and son duo who'd found riding a way of reinvigorating their relationship.

She listened to the various conversations going on around her as she ate her smoked salmon wrap. Her ears perked up when she heard Sam say, "If we want to know anything, we ask Molly. She's either looked it up on the Internet, or—"

The Utah bunch listening to him shouted in unison, "She took a class."

Linda, who was seated across from Molly, spoke over the laughter. "I think that's wonderful. The more you know about the world around you, the more you appreciate it."

"Linda's our encyclopedia," George said from the other end of the table. "She comes prepared when we go someplace new."

"Me, I'm an in-the-moment kind of guy," Walker said.

Molly was surprised that he'd entered the conversation, because he'd been keeping a low profile all day.

"What does that mean?" Linda asked.

"Sometimes I take off on a trip without knowing where I'm going to go or what I'm going to see. I like experiencing where I'm at without what I *think* I know getting in the way. "

Mary nodded. "You and Tom. He loves how our grandchildren react when they discover a bit of the world for the first time. He wanted to do the same, so he came up with this routine he does whenever we stop for a view. He closes his eyes for a few seconds, and then pops them open and tries to take in everything at once. As if it were all brand new."

Molly's attention was still back with what Walker had said. *Without what I think I know getting in the way?* That didn't make a lot of sense to her. She'd spent her whole adult life pursuing the education she'd felt the lack of as a young mother and wife. Wasn't it important to know where you were going and why?

By early afternoon the combined group of riders had turned onto the Historic Columbia River Highway. This was the most spectacular stretch along the gorge, and Molly had been looking forward to it. The names of their stops were well known to her from her reading: Multnomah Falls, the famous and much-photographed Vista House, and Crown Point.

The sight of Multnomah Falls from the parking lot made Molly forget Walker's curious lunchtime comments. The lot was a ways from the viewing area, and Molly was eager to get up close. She automatically grabbed her printouts and hurried up the broad walkway leading to the falls.

Multnomah Falls was a ribbon of white dropping in two tiers from a great height into a pool below. A bridge crossed over the lower cascade. Molly and several others gathered at the rail in front of the pool.

"It's so beautiful and so tall," Rose said, staring upward.

"It's the fourth largest falls in the U.S." Molly scanned the pertinent printout. "Six hundred and twenty feet from top to bottom." She was about to say more when she noticed Tom with his eyes shut. He popped them open, looked quickly from right to left, and smiled hugely.

Seeing the pleasure on his face, Molly wondered, *What would it be like to go for the impact without the preparation?*

"Anyone like to climb to the bridge?" Linda asked. "We've got time, and the view's worth the effort."

Everyone except the Connellys and the Wentworths decided to make the climb. Nails forged ahead; the odd twosome of Walker and Howard brought up the rear. The path led through tall trees and undergrowth of an intense green Molly had never seen before. Now and then the red, yellow, or white of wildflowers caught her eye. She could feel the moisture from the falls in the air.

As they climbed, Molly listened to George and Kip tell Hank how they came to be riding together.

"I have a son about your age, Kip," Hank said. "Seeing you two makes me think maybe Wade and I could do the same."

"Don't leave Molly out." George glanced at her with a smile. "My wife insists I have to give her equal time."

"Hear, hear," Molly said.

They'd reached the bridge by then. No one spoke for a moment after they walked out onto it. Then Sam said, "It's amazing. A true wonder."

"It starts at some underground springs on Larch Mountain," Molly began. She glanced at her sheet and was about to share more interesting facts when she noticed Walker looking at her with a thoughtful expression. "What?"

He made a gesture that took in the whole landscape. "Does this really need an explanation?"

Molly didn't know what to say. He'd spoken kindly, but his words felt like a rebuke. She'd been having fun sharing what she'd learned. It made her feel like she was contributing to her companions' enjoyment of the trip. Now she wondered if she was getting in the way of their experience.

"Hey," Walker said, "don't let me ruin your moment. It's only a thought."

She nodded acknowledgment that she'd heard him, thinking, *It's a little late for that.* She folded up her sheet and put it in her pocket.

On the way back to the parking lot, she told Hank what Walker had said. "Do you think I should stop sharing what I know?" she asked.

"You heard what Sam said at lunch. And Howard yesterday. They like hearing what you have to say."

"Then I don't ruin what they're seeing by telling them about it?"

"I don't think so."

She waited until they'd negotiated a steep section before asking, "How about you? Do I embarrass you when I share what I've learned?"

He put an arm around her. "No. I just think, that's my Molly."

⁓

It was a short gusty ride to Crown Point, a cliff high above the water topped by a structure called Vista House. They parked their cycles facing the buffeting winds and trudged out onto the bluff. Molly was about to tell her companions about the Kasota limestone construction of the comfort station, when the sudden impact of the dramatic vistas took the words right out of her mouth.

Hank looked at her questioningly. "Molly?"

Molly held up a finger. "Having a moment here. Catch me later."

"You sure?"

She nodded. As the group trailed away a few at a time, she walked toward the edge of the dramatic drop-off. She didn't need to check her printout to see how many feet above the river she was. She could *feel* it. Holding her breath, she gazed out over the wide gorge to the rows of blue hills that faded into the distance on the other side. Then she squeezed her eyes shut, and after a moment popped them open as Tom had done. For a second the colors were brighter and the edge of the horizon sharper. Molly laughed with pure delight. If she could have, she would have embraced the whole world, the love she felt for it was so great.

She was still smiling when Walker quietly joined her. "I see what you mean," she said.

"Then I'm not *persona non grata*?"

"No."

"I'm glad. It wouldn't help my plans to romance Dot if one of her friends didn't like me."

"That's the plan?"

Walker nodded. "There's something still between us; I knew it the minute I saw her again. Only she doesn't quite trust me yet. I need to show her who I am now, as opposed to who I was then. That's why I flew back to Austin to get my temple recommend renewed. I want to go to the temple sessions with you all. And Dot."

Molly was impressed. "Howard likes her, you know."

"Oh, I know." He grinned mischievously. "But I bet she hasn't kissed him the way she kissed me up Emigration Canyon."

In twos and threes the rest of the group joined them for a few minutes of quiet appreciation at the rim. Then they slowly started back to the parking lot. Molly was curious to see what Walker would do, now that he'd declared his intention. She was surprised to see that instead of singling out Nails, he joined the group and began talking pleasantly to those around him as if he'd always belonged.

Hank was rearranging the items in a saddlebag when Molly got back to Zelda. He looked up at her and smiled. "How was your moment, Moll?"

"Amazing. I tried Tom's pop-the-eyes-open technique. It works. I've never seen the world so bright and fresh before."

"Hmm. Maybe I should try it."

Molly stowed the camera case and was about to do the same with her printouts when that moment on the cliff came back to her. She moved the papers up and down as if weighing something. Then she fished all of the information sheets out of her duffel, not caring if they got wrinkled or torn in the process.

Hank stared at her. "What are you doing?"

"Getting rid of all this stuff. I'm going to try seeing things Tom and Walker's way for a change."

Chapter 23

"Freeway ahead," Hank said over the intercom. "We'll be on them from here all the way to our hotel."

Great, Molly thought. She'd been so carried away by the magnificent scenery that she'd forgotten they would be taking freeways through the Portland area to Lake Oswego, where the temple was located. Ronald had assured her that he'd planned their trip to avoid such roads whenever possible. What he hadn't said was that more often than not, it wasn't possible.

Resigned, she did what she knew to do. She plugged in her iPod and selected the relaxation routine.

The combined groups stayed together until they reached the metro area and the Portland TRA members dropped off one by one with a honk of their horns. Molly barely heard them because her body had responded automatically to her routine. That helped, but part of her mind was still aware of the fact that they were on major freeways, and it seemed to take forever to get to the motel.

Once Molly got to their room she didn't leave it. Three days of unaccustomed travel had caught up with her. After assuring Hank she didn't mind if he had dinner and spent the evening with the group, she took a shower, ordered room service, ate while watching a sitcom rerun, and went to bed early. When a sound nudged her from a deep sleep in the morning, she felt as if she had to swim up from a great depth before she was fully awake.

It was Hank setting a tray of juice and bagels on the desk.

"Good morning," he said, brushing the damp off his jacket. "There's a cloud sitting in front of our door. I had to walk through it to pick up breakfast. It's chilly, too."

Molly rolled into a sitting position and rubbed the sore spot on her hip. Then she flexed her ankles and knees several times. "Maybe that's why my bones ache so much. Do you think it'll rain?"

"Someone I talked to in the breakfast room said that here, mist counts as rain. Good thing we have ponchos." He smeared a bagel with strawberry cream cheese and handed it to her.

"Thanks for bringing me breakfast."

"If I hadn't, someone else would have. Everyone's worried about you."

"They don't need to. I'm fine." She took another bite of bagel.

"You weren't fine last night, and to tell the truth, you're not moving very fast this morning." He sat down on the chair opposite her. "We'd all understand if you stayed here and rested while we go to the temple."

"We? You talked about me to the others again?" She put the rest of her bagel on the plate. "I'm stiff and tired, but not so bad off that I can't go through a session."

"I'm sure that's true—only after that we'll be back on the road again. I think you'd be better off if you took a long, hot bath or used the motel pool to work the kinks out before you got back on the motorcycle. You don't have any idea how physically hard this kind of trip can be. It's a lot different from a couple of hours riding behind Ronald."

His tone made her bristle. "Why do you make it sound like the work I did with Ronald was trivial?"

"I didn't know I was."

"You've done it more than once. You're not mad that I didn't tell you what we were doing, are you?" She saw something flicker in his eyes. "You are, I can see it."

"Okay, I am. A little. I wanted to be the one to help you past your fear. I was hoping you'd ask me."

"Do you really think we could have worked together on something so sensitive? Our ability to communicate when it comes to motorcycles wasn't the best."

"Maybe not, but you left me out of something that was very important to you."

"Only so we could do something together that was important to *you*. If I hadn't, I wouldn't be here right now. You *are* glad I am, aren't you?"

He huffed in exasperation. "How did we get to that? All I wanted was to make sure you could handle the next leg of the trip."

"You're right. Forget what I said. I do appreciate you and the others caring about me. And bringing me breakfast."

When that didn't erase the lines between his brows, she perched on his knee and kissed his forehead. "Don't frown. And don't worry. I'll be fine."

Kiss and make up smoothed things over, but Molly knew there was much unsaid between them. It would come out sooner or later, and probably at the most inopportune time. But not now.

Now she wanted to focus on getting ready to go to the temple, and she had a lot to think about.

Before leaving The Dalles the previous morning, she'd checked her e-mail again, hoping for more news from Heather. What she'd found was a message from June reminding her not to miss the moments God would choose for her scrapbook. Then she'd had the moment on Crown Point, which inspired her decision to not muddy new experiences with what she thought she knew. Taken together, those things made her want to be present at today's temple session in a new way.

She considered what that meant in practical terms while she got dressed and put on her makeup. *Giving equal time for head, heart, and spirit,* she decided.

Her mood was pensive as they arrived at the temple and prepared for the session. *I know I haven't given my whole self to this experience in the past,* she prayed silently. *But, oh, help me be more open and aware this time.*

As she prayed, the words of the Lord to Moses came to mind: "Put off thy shoes from off thy feet, for the place whereon thou standest is holy ground." She felt her heart expand and the Spirit affirm as never before that this was the House of the Lord, and she was engaged in doing His will.

She moved carefully toward the chapel as if what she carried in her heart was a fragile ornament that could break at any moment. Nothing had changed, but everything felt different. As the session began, a new awareness seemed to illuminate what she heard and saw, making each moment a miracle. Even when it gradually faded, that sense of the miraculous remained, joined by overwhelming gratitude and love.

It must have shown in her face when she sat down next to Hank in the celestial room after the session was over. He seemed to recognize what she was feeling. He took her hand, and they sat quietly together until he whispered, "I think we need to go."

Outside the temple, various groupings of the two TRA chapters were chatting in the watery sunshine. Molly didn't feel like talking, so she and Hank walked hand in hand around the immaculate grounds. They stood for several quiet moments at the reflecting pool, the diamond shape of which accentuated the image of the eastern aspect of the temple shimmering on its surface. That's when Molly, overwhelmed by all she'd experienced that morning, started to cry.

Hank put his arms around her and drew her close. "I love you, Miss Molly," he whispered in her ear.

"I love you too, Hank."

⌒

There was no time for Molly to make a graceful transition from the peaceful atmosphere of the temple to the noise and bustle of the world. Back at the hotel, they changed, checked out, and were starting to load up when the Hesses returned, riding Barney's bike. They'd taken Fricka on a nursing-home visit arranged by Linda Sanchez's sister.

RaNae gave Fricka a snuggle and a once-over, and then offered her water and a treat while Ronald went over the day's route.

"This will be another long day," he said to Molly. "We'll have to use freeways from here until we get west of the metro area, but once we get on the Coast Road, you'll think it was worth it."

"Oh, joy," she responded.

"Think of it as practice for when we go to Cucamonga," Hank said. "*If you still want to make that leg of the trip with me when we get that far.*"

Molly frowned. "What else would I do?"

"Call it a day and fly home from Oakland." When he saw her expression, he added, "It's an option, that's all."

She wasn't looking forward to hours on the road, but the thought of giving up was the farthest thing from her mind. "Great. I love it that you've made a contingency plan in case I bail."

Ronald made a time-out sign. "Go to your corners, kids. Nothing has to be decided right now."

The weather cleared as they dropped down to the Coast Road near Lincoln City. The two-lane highway hugged the coastline, with steep green hills to the left and rugged drop-offs to smooth beaches on the right. Beyond the beaches, the silvery expanse of the Pacific stretched to the horizon. Here and there, huge, craggy rocks stood just off the shore, surf roiling at their bases. Some had strange conical shapes, others had flatter tops on which trees grew.

"I didn't think anything would rival the gorge for beauty," Molly said to Hank over the intercom. "But this is fantastic."

"It sure is. Better even than what I was imagining New Year's Eve."

Molly hoped that by focusing on the beauty she wouldn't be so aware of how her body was feeling. She was already uncomfortable when they stopped for lunch at a restaurant in Lincoln City, but she was determined to hide it from Hank. She was glad when his attention was captured by a friendly if heated discussion of the virtues of the touring bikes represented in their group—Harley, Gold Wing, and BMW. It gave her a chance to down a couple of painkillers when he wasn't looking her way.

When the discussion led to an impasse, Barney began peppering Walker with questions. Walker answered good-naturedly, addressing the group as a whole, but Molly had the feeling he was speaking directly to Nails.

He'd left Utah, he said, because both the rules and the mountains were closing in on him. Plus, he'd wanted to see what life was like outside of the valley.

"And how was it?" Howard asked, one eyebrow raised.

"Big. Exciting. Full of things and places I'd never imagined. Also hard, ugly, unforgiving."

"Why didn't you come back?" Rose asked.

Walker made a self-deprecating sound. "Stubbornness, at first. By the time I'd gotten some sense knocked into my head, my dad wasn't interested in having me back."

No one said anything as he crossed one booted leg over the other and sat in thought. Nor did anyone make a move to go. With a wry grin he continued.

"I eventually got a job with Joe Don Lovett, a fine Latter-day Saint man who owned a shipping company in Austin, Texas. Drove cross-country for him until I married his daughter, Crystal. Then I traded my cab for an office desk.

"Crystal and I had four children. We had seventeen grandchildren when she died eight years ago. They're my pride and joy. I've got photos of all of them in one of my saddlebags, if you're interested."

"That's sweet," Nails murmured.

"Where are your kids?" Rose asked.

"All over, from Texas to Philadelphia."

"So what brought you back to Utah now?" Howard asked.

"I'm helping start up a new branch of the Lovett shipping company. After that, I'm going to retire. I'll be able to go where I want for as long as I want. I can grow roots anywhere." His gaze shifted to Nails. "If I have a reason."

"Lucky man," Howard said under his breath.

The group was trailing out of the restaurant when Doyle exclaimed, "Hey, guys. Look over there. It's an Indian."

Molly was about to make a comment about political correctness when she realized Doyle was pointing toward a motorcycle on the far side of the lot.

Of course. How stupid can I get?

That movie, *The World's Fastest Indian*, wasn't about a track star. It was the story of an old duffer who broke the world land speed record on a motorcycle he'd modified, an Indian. There had been TV news segments on it when they filmed in Utah on the Bonneville Flats.

When she joined the others standing around the bike, Molly could see why it had drawn them. It had two-toned fenders—teal along the top half, aqua on the bottom—that swooped slightly upward in the back. On the front fender was a chrome ornament of a chief in a headdress. The brown leather saddle had a fringed skirt and was decorated with studs and conchos. Long brown leather fringe hung from the handlebars.

There was so much to look at she almost missed the miniflaps with short fringe at the backs of both fenders.

"That's money you're looking at, folks," Walker said admiringly. "I don't think this is a new version of the classic. I think it's the real deal—and in mint condition."

"It's got a Wyoming license," Barney said. "Whoever owns this beauty has put some miles behind them. And this is no touring bike."

"Speaking of miles," Ronald said, motioning toward their motorcycles with his thumb.

Back on the curvy two-lane road, they immediately got stuck behind an RV that was in no hurry. Molly didn't mind the slow going. The painkillers were working, and she had a lot on her mind. The thaw between Nails and Walker. Hank thinking she would give up and fly home from Oakland. But most of all, her extraordinary experience in the temple.

She ached to share it with Hank but didn't know how to put it into words. Looking over his shoulder at the line of cycles in front of them, she felt deeply grateful for the Temple Riders and all they'd done to make this trip possible for her. Without them, she wouldn't have been in the temple that morning. It meant a lot to know they'd been there with her.

The Heceta Head Lighthouse was their next stop. "We've got half an hour, people," Ronald said as people started in different directions. "Don't wander too far off."

"Yes, Dad," Rose said with a fond smile.

Everyone moved quickly, determined to see as much as they could in that short time. Hank spent his time inside the lighthouse. The Hesses and Forrests took Fricka down a path to the beach below. Molly started out taking photo after photo, but then she realized she was seeing what was before her through a lens. She spent the last minutes of the stop sitting on a rock, simply looking.

They'd rejoined the others in the parking lot when Howard said, "Well, I'll be. It's the Indian."

When the rider pulled up next to them, Ronald said, "We were admiring your machine in Lincoln City. She's a beaut."

"She's in better shape than I am," the rider said.

Molly silently agreed when he took off his helmet. His ears were long and hairy, deep grooves parenthesized his mouth, and his salt-and-pepper ponytail was thin.

"Did you rebuild her yourself?" Barney asked.

The old guy smiled, showing surprisingly good teeth. "She was a wreck when I bought her in back in '60. Ran her into the dirt more than once, rebuilt her every time."

These men, Molly thought. *They never meet a motorcycle they don't like.*

"Where are you headed?" Ronald asked.

"Marin County."

"We're bound for Oakland."

The man touched his hand to his forehead. "Gus Winthrop. Looks like I might see you on down the road."

It was late afternoon by the time they reached their hotel in Brookings, north of the California border. "Dinner first and then ice cream," Barney declared. "We haven't had any since before The Dalles."

They went to a seafood place where they were seated at a cluster of three tables. "Look," Molly told Hank as both Howard and Walker went to pull out Nails's chair.

Howard outmaneuvered Walker, throwing him a look of triumph as he motioned Nails to sit. Walker didn't miss a beat. He took her napkin up from the table, shook it out with a snap, and, in the best maître d' fashion, placed it across her lap.

"You have to hand it to Howard," Hank said. "He's not ready to give up yet."

After supper, the group rode their motorcycles in search of the ice cream parlor recommended as the best in town. When they'd all been served they walked out onto the deck overlooking the harbor and saw that Gus had beat them to it. The old man with long ears was sitting by himself at one of the outside tables enjoying a huge cone.

"You were behind us at Heceta Head," Nails said. "How did you get here first?"

"I reckon you went to a restaurant for supper." He held up the cone. "I ate a big lunch, so this here's my supper. One scoop each of praline, rocky road, and chocolate mint."

Sharon held up her own cone of chocolate mint. "There's a man after my own heart."

"I noticed your license plate is from Wyoming, Gus," Nails said. "How long have you been on the road?"

"Four days. I started out in Buffalo, on the east side of the Big Horns."

Doyle grimaced. "That's a lot of miles on a bike not built for touring."

"I'm a tough old bird."

"I believe it," Barney said. "But tomorrow's Sunday. Taking a day of rest, like we are, might not be a bad idea."

Ronald nodded. "After that we're headed for Orick. We'd be pleased to have you ride with us."

"Thank you kindly," Gus said, "but I've covered a lot of road on my own since I left Buffalo. I think I'll keep on that way." He paused, and then pointed at the logo on Doyle's vest. "What does TRA stand for?"

Terrific Riding Associates, Molly thought.

When Doyle and Ronald told Gus about the TRA and its connection to The Church of Jesus Christ of Latter-day Saints, he said, "Some of my people are Mormons."

"Really?" Now Molly was curious.

"My mother and sister joined while I was stationed in Germany in the late '50s. They had the missionaries talk to me when I came back, but they couldn't rope me in." He smiled as if apologizing for how his last words sounded. "I couldn't get past those prohibitions."

"Does your family live in California?" RaNae asked.

"My mother passed over a long time ago. My sister, Annabelle, has a general store in a small town called Sleepy Hollow. I haven't seen her for nigh onto thirty years. Never met her son, but when he was a youngster I sent him presents now and then."

"I bet they'll be thrilled to see you," Rose said.

"Remains to be seen." Gus's smile was wistful. "They don't know I'm coming."

Molly couldn't imagine what would keep someone away from family for so many years. The Finleys were all very close. Molly was always on the phone with her sisters, her parents, and Wade. None of them ever missed sending birthday cards and anniversary cards. Hank never paid attention to things like that.

The thought of birthdays was like a bucket of cold water waking her up. *Oh no. I bet Hank didn't send Helena a card for her birthday.* It was now Hank's job to keep in touch with his family, but Molly regretted not having reminded him that date was coming up.

Ronald got the whole group going shortly after that with a reminder that they needed to do Sunday shopping before they got settled for the night. He'd booked rooms that had refrigerators and microwaves and had arranged for their use of the motel's breakfast room for a Sunday potluck.

"What should I buy?" Molly asked RaNae as the group descended on a local grocery store.

"Whatever you like. We did this once before on a trip Ronald and Sharon sponsored. Everyone buys their favorite microwaveable foods and snacks. You wouldn't believe what we ended up with. Think of it as a junk food extravaganza."

It's certainly going to be that, Molly thought as she scanned the carts in the check-out lane. The choices ran in the direction of frozen pizza rolls and other cheesy treats, salty snacks, and gooey desserts. In defense of her waistline, she added fresh fruit and veggie trays to the mix. Hank dropped in a large bottle of pink stomach remedy.

Once back at their motel with the food items properly stowed, everyone stood in the lobby talking about the potluck and speculating on Gus's past and what he did in Wyoming. No one seemed ready to pack it in, so they eventually migrated to the chairs and tables in the breakfast area.

"I wish Gus would take Barney's suggestion and join us," Sharon said as she dropped into a chair.

"He won't," Ronald said. "He's definitely a Lone Ranger."

"I've never known anyone who kept a motorcycle that many years," Sam said. "I've had three, counting the Gold Wing."

"I've had, let's see . . ." Barney counted on his fingers. "Five."

That was enough to get the men trading stories about when they'd first started riding and what brands of cycles they'd owned.

When the attention of the group turned to Hank, Molly expected a factual response. Instead, he told the story of how he'd grown up working in the first Mancuso Auto Shop. He was in an unusually expansive mood that evening. Not only was he more talkative than usual, he was funny. Everyone loved hearing about his uncles Phil and Leo, especially when he started telling about how some of the Harleys they'd worked on in the early '60s had belonged to men who'd formed the original Hell's Angels club in his hometown of Fontana. "The old uncs said they never had any trouble with those boys. Probably because they did such good work on their cycles."

That's something I've never heard before, Molly thought.

"We all know how you surprised Molly when you brought home your Gold Wing, Hank," Doyle said. "What made you buy it when you did?"

"You mean besides retiring, reading an AARP article about not putting off doing what you really want to do, and having a birthday?"

Everyone looked at him expectantly, and Molly was suddenly nervous about what she was going to hear.

"My father's grandparents were from the old country," Hank began. "They passed their immigrant's drive to succeed on to their children and grandchildren. Dad grew up knowing it was his responsibility to work hard and contribute to the welfare of the whole family so the next generation could have a better future.

"I was thirteen when he died. The last thing he said to me was, 'Henry, you need to be a man now. A real man takes care of family first. That's his duty, no matter what. Work hard. Stay the course. Then you can think about yourself and what you want to do.'

"I never forgot that. When I married Molly and we had our family, I knew what my job was, and I did it. I stayed the course for almost forty years. Retiring was like getting a permission slip saying, Now you can do what you want."

Sam gave him a high five. "I'd say you did, in a big way." Other positive comments such as "Right on" and "Good for you" overlapped one another, but Molly wasn't part of that cheering squad.

Was that really what life with the kids and me was like? Drudgery and obligations, with Zelda as the payoff?

Hank looked at her and smiled, happily oblivious to how his words sounded. *Maybe he didn't mean it the way I heard it,* she told herself. *Maybe I'm making something out of nothing.*

Then again, maybe not.

She'd hoped this trip would serve up answers to the question of Hank, but instead it had presented her with yet more questions. She hoped he was as talkative when they were alone in their room. There were things she wanted to ask him about.

Only Hank didn't go upstairs with her. When Ronald suggested it was time to hit the sheets, Hank said cheerfully, "I'm wide awake, Molly. You go tuck yourself in, and I'll write something for the blog. It's my turn."

So much for conversation. Molly trudged up the stairs to their room alone. She tried to stay awake, but she fell asleep before he returned.

Chapter 24

When they gathered for breakfast in the motel dining room Sunday morning, Ronald had a surprise for them.

"I got an e-mail this morning from a TRA member who's been reading my official trip blog. His name is Dusty Gilbert and he lives in Novato. He saw we'd be going through there on our way to Oakland, and he wants to know if we'd be willing to talk to his ward's Young Men and Young Women groups Tuesday evening."

The group erupted with excitement and questions. They quieted down when Ronald knocked on the table. "If we accept the invitation, it will add another day to our schedule. That won't work for some of you."

"Us, for sure," Sam said. "We've got jobs to get home to."

"Unless we all agree to scrap our second day in San Francisco. What do you think?"

The group—minus Molly and Hank, who'd be splitting off anyway—quickly voted to cross off the sightseeing day in favor of the fireside and finishing the trip together.

"I wish we didn't have to leave the group." Molly felt peevish. She sounded that way too.

"We're only missing out on a couple of days," Hank said. "It's not like you'll never see them again."

"I know, but it's like leaving a movie right before the best part."

"We made these plans weeks ago. Mom and Joseph are expecting us. We can't disappoint them."

Molly sighed. "I know, I know."

As predicted, it was foggy and cool that morning. They drove though pockets of cloudlike moisture to one of the local LDS churches, where they attended sacrament meeting. Then they went back to the hotel for their potluck, which was every bit as entertaining as RaNae had promised. They spent the rest of the day quietly—reading, napping, and writing on the backs of postcards they'd purchased the day before.

The next day brought no improvement in the weather, but they set out anyway. It was eerie. Fog shrouded the landscape and dampened sounds. It condensed on windshields and face shields, and Molly kept having to wipe the moisture away so she could see. Ahead of her and Hank, the taillights of the cycles and other vehicles glowed a muffled red.

It wasn't until they'd crossed the Oregon–California border and turned inland that Molly noticed the fog lifting. The sun fought to break through as they skirted the first of the redwood forests, where the trees stood tall with mysterious scraps of clouds caught in their high branches. They stopped for lunch in Eureka and then forged on to the Redwood National Park near Orick.

There had been times in Molly's life when she'd felt small, even unimportant, but being among the redwoods was the first time she'd felt insignificant. She was grateful they were in no hurry. They were close to their destination for the day, so they drove slowly and stopped often.

As she had at Heceta Head, Molly put away her camera after trying but not succeeding in capturing the wonder of the beauty around her. She was content to walk through the trees with Hank, tipping her head upward to catch glimpses of blue sky and breathing in the smell of the damp, loamy soil underneath the trees. Her attention was diverted only once—when she saw Walker and Nails, fingers entwined and heads tipped toward each other, deep in conversation.

She nudged Hank. "See that?" she whispered, nodding in their direction.

"Uh-huh. That's why we're taking this other path."

Orick was a little burg in the big woods that catered to campers and hikers. When they reached their motel, a now-familiar sight greeted them—Gus's Indian. Gus himself was lounging in an Adirondack chair on the porch. "Howdy, folks," he said, coming down the steps to greet them.

"Fancy seeing you here," Ronald said.

Gus grinned. "I got socked in by the fog just over the border, so I had a day of rest after all. When I got on the road this morning, I decided your idea of stopping here was a good one."

"Have you told your sister that you're coming?" Rose asked.

"And lose my advantage? Some fortresses you have to take by surprise."

"You got that right," Walker said.

Nails kicked a playful puff of dirt in his direction.

"The prodigal son gets the attention," Howard murmured.

Whoa, this isn't so entertaining anymore, Molly thought. *Howard has seen which way the wind is blowing.*

While people were unloading, Molly caught Nails alone for a moment. "You need to talk to Howard."

"I know," Nails said. "I'll take care of it tonight."

After stashing their bags in their room, Molly and Hank explored the old lodge they were staying in. It was run-down—it had been built in the '50s—but clean and comfortable and full of charm. The large lounge had a fireplace, log furniture, a game corner, and a shelf of loaner novels. There was a laundromat as well, and an attached home-style restaurant. Next door was a classic garage that reminded Molly of the Mancusos' Fontana shop.

"Bet we can wash our motorcycles there," Hank said.

While Hank cleaned Zelda, Molly gathered their soiled clothing and carried it to the laundry room. She wasn't the first one there. Barney was sitting on a low stool, and RaNae was trimming his beard.

"I'm doing his hair next," RaNae said. "Can't have him scaring the youth of that ward we are going to visit."

"Are you open for business?" Molly asked.

"Sure. Send Hank in. Unless *you'd* like a trim."

"*I* would." Molly hadn't noticed Gus until he spoke. He stood with one hand on a pile of folded clothes, a shy and diffident air about him.

"A trim or a real cut?" RaNae asked.

"Just make me look good." Gus rubbed his stubbled cheek. "I can't have Annabelle see me looking like this."

When Gus joined the group that congregated in the game corner after dinner, Molly saw that his ponytail was a thing of the past. RaNae had cut his hair Sunday-School short. She had trimmed his ears and given him a shave as well. He looked years younger and quite spiffy in his new-looking jeans and western-style shirt with mother of pearl snaps on the pocket flaps.

He also looked quite uncomfortable.

It's like the closer he gets to his sister's, the more uncertain he becomes, Molly thought.

"Who's this handsome man?" Nails said with exaggerated astonishment. "I don't think I've seen him before."

Her teasing turned Gus's cheeks ruddy. "I'm not sure I have either. A man doesn't worry much about how he looks when he lives on a sheep ranch."

"Ah. Herder. That's what the HRDR on your license stands for," Sam said.

"Yup. Been herding sheep on the Big Horns since '65. During the winters I do whatever needs doing on my boss's ranch."

"That's a lot of years," Rose said. "Guess you thought it was finally time to quit."

"Nope." Gus shook his head. "I'd be up on the range right now if I hadn't let myself be talked into going up to the main house to see that *Bucket List* movie. You know it?"

"It's a great movie," Hank said.

"Remember the scene where the rich guy visits the daughter he hasn't seen in many years? It made me think of my sister and that nephew I've never met. The next day I told the boss man I was going on a trip come spring and he should get himself a new herder. He found a Basque fellow to do the job a few weeks later."

Bucket lists can be dangerous, Molly thought. *Especially if you're honest about what's most important to you.*

She'd never had a chance to say what would be first on her bucket list New Year's Eve, because they'd stopped playing after Hank said he wanted to ride the Coast Road. *What would I put first on my list if we were playing now?* she wondered.

Go to the temple for my daughter's marriage.

No. That doesn't count, because I can't make it happen.

Take a cruise with Hank.

Hah! He'd say, "What do you think we're doing now?"

Make this retirement thing work for both of us.

She sat a long time with her chin in her hand, wondering if that were possible.

⌒

When they pulled onto Highway 101 Tuesday morning, the configuration included Gus. The rhythm of a day on the road was now familiar to Molly, as was the ache—mostly dull, now and then sharp—that always showed up in her right hip after being on the road awhile. "Why don't you try putting your foot on my thigh," Hank said when she'd needed to shift positions several times in a row. "I've seen RaNae do that with Barney."

"You wouldn't mind?"

"Not at all."

Getting in that position was a bit tricky, because her legs weren't as long as RaNae's, but when she did, the pain immediately lessened. "Much better," she said. Then she chuckled, realizing that someone seeing her like that would think she was completely comfortable riding on a motorcycle. *You've come a long way, baby,* she congratulated herself.

Gus was still with them when, in late afternoon, they reached the Novato mall where Dusty Gilbert was going to meet them. A motorcycle man himself, Dusty wanted to be riding in the front of the group when they rumbled into the parking lot where the unsuspecting youth would be gathered.

Molly felt sorry for Gus. Novato was only a short distance from Sleepy Hollow, and the old guy was a morass of conflicting emotions—eagerness to see his sister and fear that she might reject him. Accompanying them to the church gave him an excuse to postpone the moment when she would open her door and see him standing there.

They'd parked their cycles in a row and had been waiting only a few minutes when Dusty arrived. "Would you look at that," Gus said.

Dusty's motorcycle had the same swoopy fenders and chrome ornament as Gus's machine. It was all black, even the exhaust pipes, which made Molly think of Darth Vader.

Dusty parked across from them. "Welcome to Novato. I'm Dusty Gilbert. Which one of you is Ronald?"

"The one wearing the American flag bow tie," Doyle said.

Dusty shook Ronald's hand. "It's so cool you guys were willing to come. Our young men and young women are in for a real treat."

Ronald introduced Dusty to everyone. When he came to Gus, Dusty grinned. "I see one of you knows what a good motorcycle is."

Gus saluted. "There aren't many of us. What made you buy yours?"

"When I was little, my uncle sent me a little toy cast-iron Indian. It was red and had rubber tires and spoke wheels. Even had a detachable rider, a policeman in a blue uniform. I loved that motorcycle."

"Sounds like you and your uncle were good pals," Gus said.

"We might have been. If I'd had a chance to know him."

"Why didn't you?" Nails asked Dusty.

"Long story." He took a step toward his bike, but then stopped. "I don't know why I'm telling you this, but the only time he ever visited, he was smashed out of his gourd and stunk to high heaven. My mom told him to leave and not come back. What she meant to say was, 'Don't come back until you're sober.' But we never saw him again. She's always felt it was her fault."

"That's sad," Sharon said.

"She had a private investigator look for him, but no luck. He's either out of the country or living completely off the grid."

"I'd say a sheep ranch in Wyoming is off the grid," Gus said dryly.

Everyone turned his direction, and Molly felt the hair on the back of her neck stand up.

"What's your name, son?"

Dusty looked bemused. "My given name? Norman."

"That's right. Norman. Your mother is Annabelle. Before she got married she was a Winthrop." Gus paused. "Like me."

Dusty's jaw dropped and his expression went from shock to wonder. "You don't mean . . . you can't be . . . Uncle Gus?"

A wide grin transformed Gus's face. "You're looking at him. I've been sober for a decade, Norman. Do you think that's long enough that your mother will allow me a visit?"

Sharon grabbed Molly's arm. "Oh, my goodness. Dusty is Gus's nephew!"

"Un-be-*liev*-able," Barney said as the two men embraced.

"Oh, give me a break." Howard's tone reflected the mood he'd been in since Nails had started spending her time with Walker. "Things like this don't happen in real life."

"They do so," Sharon said earnestly. "I read about them all the time. Like the childhood sweethearts separated by World War II who bumped into each other fifty years later in the elevator of an apartment building in Brooklyn."

"Right." Howard's voice dripped sarcasm.

Like Nails and Walker finding each other on a motorcycle ride up Emigration Canyon. Molly didn't say it aloud. It was the last thing Howard needed to hear.

"I saw something similar on a prime time news program," RaNae said. "People kept telling these two guys who worked at a Home Depot that they looked and acted enough alike to be related. And you know what? They actually were brothers who'd been separated at birth."

Molly put a hand over her heart and sighed. "There's a reason they say truth is stranger than fiction."

The rest of the evening was full of excitement and delight, but it was that initial moment of recognition that shone brightest in Molly's mind. And the impromptu talk that Dusty gave to the young men and young women while standing in the parking lot of the church building.

He stood with his arm around Gus, speaking of the mysterious ways the Lord works to bring about his purposes. "For years, my mother has been grieving over the hard words that drove her brother, my Uncle Gus, away. It's been especially hard on her this last year, because she's been ill. Her dearest wish and most heartfelt prayer was that she could see her brother again and tell him she loved him. I've been praying for that too.

"Who would have guessed that me joining the Temple Riders Association, Brother Bixby—he's the one with the bow tie—planning a trip, and Uncle Gus watching a movie would set in motion a series of events that would bring us to where we are tonight. You might call it a matter of chance that Uncle Gus met these fine folks on the road about the same time I asked them to come talk to you. I have no doubt it was the answer to prayer."

"I wish someone had filmed this," Molly whispered to Hank. "Mormons, motorcycles, and the mission of the Church couldn't come together in a more inspiring way."

The next morning was a Wednesday, eight days since Molly had surprised her husband in Brigham City. *It seems like two weeks*, Molly thought as she packed her duffel. *So much has happened.*

They drove on winding roads through the green hills of Marin County and then crossed the Golden Gate Bridge to San Francisco, where they met an area TRA member who'd offered to be their tour guide. He took them past Fisherman's Wharf, along a picture-postcard street of the Victorian homes called Painted Ladies, up to Coit Tower, and down the zigzag of Lombard Street. Then they crossed the bay to Oakland on a double-decker bridge and drove by the temple on the way to their nearby hotel.

Molly felt restless and sad during the ride, and her mood lifted only slightly during the ice cream social they had that night with Bay Area TRA members. She was concerned about Gus, who'd worked his way into her heart. He'd been beaming when he'd said good-bye and had gone home with Norman, but she feared the road ahead of him would be bumpy. The impending separation from the other TRA members was also weighing on her. Yet there was something more that eluded her until the middle of the night, when she awoke with the knowledge that, for her, the trip was complete.

All the promises it had held had been fulfilled. She'd taken on her fear and gained the upper hand, if not entirely vanquishing it. She and Hank had spent more time together than they had in years, and they'd survived it, despite the unanswered questions his recent comments had raised. She'd discovered a love for temple service after the profound experience in Portland. And she'd witnessed how following the promptings of the Spirit could work in wondrous ways to bring families together.

I want to go home, she thought. *No, I want to be home. Right now. Where there's time and space for me to think about all that's happened.*

But the next day, she and Hank would be starting out for Cucamonga. No matter how much she wished it, her journey was far from over.

~

The group gathered at six in the morning to give them a send-off.

"We're going to miss you," Molly said. "Without you all, me riding with Hank would never have happened. Thank you all."

"Give yourself some credit," Nails said. "For a novice, this trip was an endurance trial, and you've passed with flying colors." She held out a package. "Here's a little something to mark the occasion."

"You didn't," Molly squeaked when she saw what was in the package—a set of stick-on nails. Red with silver flames on the tips, they were as long and as outrageous as the ones Nails wore on the road.

Molly giggled delightedly as she applied one after another. Then she held her hands out for everyone to admire. "What do you think?" she asked Hank.

"They look . . . dangerous. Don't grab onto me with those things."

The men chuckled appreciatively.

"And don't get any ideas about me adding red flames to Zelda so she matches."

When it was time for prayer, Doyle put a hand on Sam Hesse's shoulder. "Would you favor us, please?"

Sam's face flushed with pleasure as he stepped forward. His prayer was couched in phrases and delivered in a cadence different from what Molly was used to hearing, but it was sweet and heartfelt.

Then it was time to leave. Molly didn't apologize for her tears during the last round of hugs. She'd come to love these people. More than that, she'd depended on them for their freely given acceptance and encouragement. She would miss Sharon's no-nonsense approach to whatever popped up, Ronald's humor and coin tricks, and Nails's wisdom and support. She would miss Walker, whose comments at the falls had precipitated a change she didn't have words for, though she kept trying to find them. She would even miss Fricka's bright eyes and curious nature.

"Here we go," Hank said over the intercom, revving Zelda's engine. "It's just you and me, babe."

Chapter 25

Three hundred sixty-three miles of crowded California freeway lay between them and Cucamonga, and Molly was not a happy camper. When traveling freeways with the group, Ronald had always assigned her and Hank the outer lane, putting other motorcycles around them as a buffer between them and traffic. The sense of safety that had given her was now gone.

This is insane, she thought as they sped down the road with vehicles on all sides of them, in gear that offered pitifully inadequate protection against steel and tarmac. Before they'd started out, Nails had said, "Keep your iPod handy and use your relaxation routine *before* you really need it." She needed it now, and they hadn't even turned south on I-5.

The trip was torture, plain and simple. The routine helped Molly at first, but the sheer length of time spent in the nerve-wracking traffic wore her down. It wore Hank down too. She could see from the set of his shoulders the intense concentration it took to mind the road, other motorists, and Zelda. And she could see it in his irritation at her needing to shift so often to alleviate the pain in her hip or make yet another rest stop.

Molly called Helena on her cell phone when they were almost there, so the family was waiting in the front yard when Molly and Hank finally reached the end of their long day's journey. Helena was immediately concerned when Hank had to lift Molly off the motorcycle and steady her for a moment.

Molly made herself smile. "I'm okay; I just need to move." She took off her helmet and ran her fingers through her hair.

"You've got fancy nails!" Helena exclaimed. She grabbed one of

Molly's hands and exclaimed again. "Well, aren't you full of surprises! Not only do you arrive on a motorcycle, you're decorated to the hilt."

She pulled Molly toward Ruth, who stood near the front of the house leaning against her walker.

"Look here, Mom."

"Oh my," Ruth said, inspecting Molly's press-on nails as if they were treasure.

"It's good to see you back riding, Hank," Joseph said. "I remember how you and Lennie and Chester used to take off on your bikes whenever you could. The Mancuso Boys."

"Those were the days," Hank said.

"The boys worked as hard as you can imagine to get permission," Ruth said to Molly. "I think that's what kept them out of trouble."

"I would have thought having motorcycles would get them into trouble."

"It did a few times, but not the kind you're thinking of." Joseph turned to Hank. "Remember when Lennie ran out of gas on one of your long rides?"

Hank guffawed. "How could I forget? After that, he started carrying extra gas in the trunk of his bike."

"Still does," Russell said.

When they all went into the house, Helena shooed Hank and Molly toward the guest room. "There's time for you to freshen up and take a nap before Lennie and Chester and their wives come for dinner. They couldn't wait until tomorrow to check out your machine. Molly, don't even think of taking those nails off. I want everybody to see them."

A nap is a wonderful thing, Molly thought when she woke up after a short, deep sleep. She showered and dressed in her sparkly Harley-Davidson T-shirt because she knew Hank's cousins would get a kick out of it.

Hank had already shown off Zelda to the Mancuso boys and their wives when Molly joined them in the family room.

"There she is, the woman of the hour." Chester picked her up and gave her a whirl-around. "I would have bet my own wife and children that you would never get on a motorcycle. Shows how much I know. And you stuck it out on that long trip. You're one gutsy woman." He gave her an admiring glance. "And a hot mama to boot."

"Love the shirt," Lennie said. "I'd like to get my wife one like it. By the way, I lost money because of you. After Hank called Helena from Portland, we laid bets on whether you could make it or not. I lost."

Molly turned to her husband. "Hank?"

He had the grace to look embarrassed. "When you crashed in Portland, I told Helena I was afraid the trip was going to be too hard for you."

"Guess you don't know your own wife," Chester said.

Molly was glad that the attention went back to motorcycles when they sat down at the dinner table. She didn't want any more admiration and congratulations unless it came from the man who meant the most to her. Still a little ticked at Hank, she got some satisfaction out of listening to his cousins rag him for buying a Gold Wing.

"Zelda's not an old man's ride. She's a *smart* man's ride," Hank countered, "especially where road trips are concerned."

Lennie rolled with laughter. "You named your motorcycle *Zelda*? Why?"

"You have to ask Molly that."

"She told me it was her name," Molly said. "I wouldn't come up with something like that on my own."

"Oh no," Lennie said with mock horror. "You're one of those."

"Don't let him get to you, Molly," Chester said. "My motorcycle told me her name is Lucille."

Molly could tell how much Ruth was enjoying the banter. "It's nice seeing you boys so happy, especially you, Hank."

"Comes from being back in the saddle." Lennie turned to Molly. "Every time old Hank came to visit, he'd salivate over our bikes. But he never did go for a ride until last fall, because of that promise you made him make. It was a very hard thing to live with, you know."

Chester leaned forward, eager to say his piece. "I kept telling him it didn't need to be for forever, that he could renegotiate with you once your kids were grown. And I was right, wasn't I?"

"Not by a hundred miles." Molly gave the story of what happened on Hank's birthday the full Finley treatment, and she had her audience hanging on every word.

"You honestly didn't know he was motorcycle shopping?" Helena asked.

Molly laughed at Helena's surprise. "Nope. He never said a word about it."

"Why, Hank. That wasn't gentlemanly of you," Ruth said.

"I agree," Helena said. "I love you dearly, brother, but if I'd been in Molly's shoes, you would have been sleeping in the garage. Indefinitely."

Molly's gratification at having the women in Hank's family take her side lasted as long as it took her to look in Hank's direction. His smile was thin-lipped and the corner of his eye was twitching.

Seemingly oblivious to Hank's shift in mood, the cousins continued joking and laughing. They insisted that Hank go for a ride with them the next morning, and the three of them made plans while Molly helped Helena clear the table. Shortly afterward the guests left, and Hank's parents went to their apartment.

When Hank and Molly retired to the guest room, he shut the door and leaned against it with arms folded and jaw set. "Did you enjoy making me look bad in front of my family?"

"*I* made *you* look bad? You've made me look stubborn and uncaring, like I was making you a prisoner to your promise."

"Weren't you? You nearly flipped out when Wade bought his ATV. Do you really think you would have released me from my promise not to ride if I'd asked you to?"

"I don't know. You never gave me a chance to find out because you never asked. "

"No, I didn't," he admitted after a moment. He sat on a chair and began unlacing one shoe.

Molly had been waiting for the right moment to bring up what he'd said in Brookings. She decided now was as good a time as any.

"Hank? Remember that night when you were telling the Temple Riders about what your father said before he died? You made it sound like life with me and the kids was nothing but drudgery, with Zelda as the reward. Did you really feel that way?"

He glanced up at her. "Keeping a family afloat takes a lot of work. It seemed like I was carrying most of the load."

"Why didn't you tell me how you felt?" She sat on the bed across from him. "We were supposed to be partners. I could have found ways to lighten the load. You didn't give me a chance there, either, because you didn't tell me how you were feeling."

"I gave you a chance in February when you said you wanted to do the finances."

"Yes, you did," she conceded. "But only because I asked."

⌒

Molly took some photos of the Mancuso boys before they set out early the next day for their ride in the San Gabriels. Hank smiled for the pictures, but it was the first time she'd seen him with a pleasant expression since he'd gotten up that morning. *I hope he'll be in a better mood after his ride*, she thought.

"We'll be back in time to help you get ready for dinner," Lennie told Helena before they revved up and left. "Sue made me promise."

"You're hosting a big party again?" Molly asked her when the roar of the engines faded.

"You know the Mancusos. They'll use any excuse to have a party. It's no big deal. I'm going to make spaghetti with meatballs, and the others are bringing salads and desserts."

They went inside to set the table for breakfast. When Ruth and Joseph joined them and Russ in the kitchen, Ruth asked Molly for an update on Wade's children. "I miss getting those newsy letters of yours and pictures of the family. Did you bring some photos of Junie? Babies change so fast, I haven't seen any new ones since February."

"Oh no! That's when Hank and I swapped jobs."

"Swapped jobs?" Ruth asked.

Molly realized Hank hadn't told his family about that, either. In the months since the swap, he'd reduced all the efforts she'd been making to stay in contact with his folks over the years down to an occasional phone call or e-mail. And it didn't seem like he'd given much information even then. He obviously hadn't sent any photos.

"I could show you some photos on Russ's computer now," she said, thinking of her online image storage.

She spent the rest of the morning with Ruth and Joseph, showing them shots of Wade's kids. They spent long minutes with each one. Hungry for details, they wanted to hear all about where it was taken, what the occasion was, and what the kids were doing at that particular moment in time.

Depending on whom you were quoting, either God or the devil was in the details. For Molly, truth was in the details, in the what, where, when, why, and how. In feelings and motivations, in all the things Hank considered superfluous. For him it was "Just the facts, ma'am."

"I've got an idea," she said when they'd had their fill of photos and catch-up stories. "Since you've been enjoying the trip blog, I'll start a family blog and post news and new photos every week."

"Thank you, dear," Ruth said, patting her cheek. "We'd love that."

❧

When guests started to arrive that evening, Molly realized the family phone lines had been humming. All the Mancuso relatives she knew—and some she hadn't met before—came for show-and-tell. Hank showed off Zelda, and she told people about the techniques Nails had used to get her ready to ride.

It took some doing for Helena to get everyone to move inside and take seats at the tables. At the old uncs' insistence, Molly ended up at a table with them, the cousins and Freddy, and all their wives. She saved a seat for Hank, but when he came in, he said, "Thanks, but I'm going to sit with Mom and Joseph."

The uncs had a slew of questions to ask about how she'd overcome her fear. After close to half a century of connecting *Molly* with *hates motorcycles*, they were having a hard time wrapping their minds around "Molly the biker babe," as Chester kept calling her.

Serving bowls were being passed around for seconds when the uncles began telling some of their motorcycle adventures, beginning with World War II. The wizened fellows' delight in having her for an audience touched her.

"Those are such great stories," she said. "How come I've never heard them before?"

"Well, you know . . ." Uncle Leo coughed in embarrassment. "You weren't any fan of motorcycles, so Hank told us to put a lid on it whenever you visited."

"Fortunately, it wasn't often," Uncle Phil said. "It's hard for us not to talk about our rides."

"Phil! You put your foot in it. Again." Rita lavished Molly with apologies. "Don't pay any attention to that old fool. We're always glad when you come. It's too bad you're always so busy with your family theater and your classes."

Embarrassed at how lame her excuses sounded when someone else gave them, Molly said the first thing that came to mind. "It's not like the Mancusos have been burning up the road to come our way."

There was a pained silence. Then Sue said, "We weren't sure you wanted us to come. You seemed ill at ease around us, especially right after you and Hank got married."

Uncle Leo cackled. "Like the first time you saw Phil and me light up at the reception we had at our place. I thought you were going to faint."

"I almost did. I get headaches from cigar and cigarette smoke."

"And you upset her when you kept taking the Lord's name in vain." Thelma swatted Leo's forearm. "I told you not to do that."

She looked to Molly. "He shouldn't have done that. He made you not like us. And we really wanted you to, because we liked you."

Gazing into the anxious faces around the table, Molly realized that all this time Hank's family had been waiting for her to find her place among them, a place they'd been holding open all these years. The way her family had been holding a space for Hank.

"It was never about not liking you," she said slowly. "I was young and inexperienced. I'd never been around people who weren't Latter-day Saints, and I didn't know how to act or what to say."

She was going to leave it at that, but the whole truth pressed to be told. "After that first visit, I took the easy way out and sent Hank to visit you on his own most of the time. I'm sorry I did that."

Sue gave her a hug. "You're here now. And you got here on the back of Hank's bike. I'll tell you, that surprised the lot of us."

"What surprised me is that he wanted you to ride with him," Freddy said. "Chester and Lennie never take their wives riding."

Lennie interlaced his fingers across his belly. "Why do you think we ride in the first place? Being on the road is an escape. It's better than any psychiatrist. Having our women along would ruin that."

"Why do you think we let them go without us?" Sue countered. "It gets them out of our hair so we can go shopping."

"Every trip they take is permission to buy something really nice," Freddy's wife, Angela, said to Molly. "You should remember that."

It felt good to Molly to be included as one of the Mancuso women as they teased their men. "I will," she said.

Later in the evening, Chester called Hank over to their table. "What route are you taking when you leave tomorrow?"

"North to Yosemite, then to Reno, and I-80 home."

Lennie slapped his thigh. "I wouldn't take that route for love nor money."

"Why not?" Molly asked. "It's the safest and easiest way home."

"It's a snorer. If you want bragging rights, take Highway 50 across Nevada."

Chester leaned forward, arms resting on his knees. "You can pick it up west of Reno. It takes you over a bunch of mountain passes and through some old mining towns and crosses into Utah west of Delta."

"This brute and I," Lennie said, pointing a thumb at Chester, "rode it from Carson City to the Utah state line and back on a dare." "We both got that certificate from the Nevada governor's office that says 'I Survived the Loneliest Road in America.'"

Molly's eyes widened. "That's what it's called? 'The Loneliest Road in America?' That's reason enough not to take it."

"Oops." Chester gave Lennie a wry grin. "You probably should have left that part out."

"Don't let the name spook you," Lennie said to Molly. "Some writer called it that in an article he did for *Life Magazine* back in '86, and the Nevada tourist bureau loved it. You know, you can request the certificate if you get this little passport gizzy stamped at all the cities you go through."

"I think we'll stick with our plans," Hank said.

"Oh, come on," Lennie needled. "Don't be a wuss. Where's the challenge in I-80? Where's the adventure? Two-thirds of the old Mancuso Boys trio has ridden Highway 50. You're the only one who hasn't."

"But you and Chester weren't riding two-up with your wives when you did it, were you?" Molly asked him. She pinned Hank with her gaze. "Don't you even think about it."

Chapter 26

As eager as Molly was to get on the road home, it was hard to leave the next morning. The graciousness with which the old uncs and their families had accepted her apologies had awakened in her a new appreciation and affection for them. She also felt closer to Hank's parents and Helena and her family. She wanted nothing more than to spend time in their company.

She was also feeling generous toward Hank. The issues that had been stirred up on their trip weren't anything new, she'd reminded herself as she'd lain awake the night before. They weren't going to be resolved because of a few days riding a motorcycle together.

They might never be resolved, for that matter. But even if that were the case, the good things in their marriage would still far outweigh the bad.

The Mancusos seemed reluctant to see them go. It was like pulling teeth for Hank and Molly to get out to the driveway. Even then, every time the drawn-out good-byes started coming to a close, someone would interject a new topic.

"How far are you going today?" Helena asked.

Hank tucked a map in the fabric saddlebag draped over his gas tank. "To Lee Vining. That's about a six-hour ride, maybe a little more. Definitely our limit for a day."

"I'm glad you're not pushing it," Helena said. "Accidents happen when people are tired."

They were saying yet another round of good-byes when they were interrupted by the sound of motorcycles coming their way. Hank threw back his head and laughed richly as a line of bikes headed by Lennie pulled up in front of Helena's house.

Russ beamed. "Here's your escort. That's why we kept stalling you."

Molly gripped Hank's hand as she scanned the group. After Lennie and one of his sons came Freddy, then Chester, then a son, and grandson. They all looked tremendously pleased with themselves.

Lennie gave them a big wave. "We're riding with you to the 395. Head 'em up; move 'em out."

Molly could have hugged every one of them, especially when Hank fell into formation with the Mancuso honor guard. Once again, they were riding in the outside lane with bikes ahead, behind, and to the left of them. She felt safe and protected in that position, even though they were on freeways all the way to the turnoff for the road they would take north.

The group exited at that intersection and pulled into a station to gas up and say their final farewells.

"I've got something for you, Hank," Lennie said. Grinning, he took a filled quart-size plastic gas container out of his saddlebag and held it out. "Just in case you decide to take the 50."

Molly saw the look in Hank's eyes as he accepted the container. She didn't like it one bit.

The road north took them through wild and beautiful country on the eastern flank of the Sierra Nevadas. Lee Vining, which was close to Yosemite and the otherworldly Mono Lake, had less than three hundred inhabitants. But it had places to stay and places to eat, and that was all they needed.

After checking into their motel room, they had an early supper at a barbeque joint and took a walk to get the kinks out. Then they followed the advice of their waitress and rode a short distance north where they had dramatic views of the lake. The large, shallow expanse of water with strange pinnacles exposed by the falling water level so intrigued Molly that she took photos until darkness fell. It was another good day. The best part of it was that they were one day closer to home. And the next day would bring them closer still.

That's what Molly was thinking when she fell asleep that night.

She hadn't realized that the next day was Sunday. Ever since leaving Salt Lake Valley, the days had been running into each other, with no date or time stamps, only place markers.

"I can't believe I spaced that," Molly said when Hank reminded her in the morning. She pushed herself upright against the headboard.

"You aren't the only one. I only found out when I went to the lobby early to check our e-mails. Comes from days of not reading the paper or watching the news."

"What now?"

"We either pack up and put some miles behind us or we spend the day here. Your choice."

Molly chewed the inside of her lip, considering.

On one hand, she ached to be inside her own four walls. She was eager to show her photography teacher the photos she'd taken. And she was more bothered about missing practices for the Fourth of July program than she'd thought she would be.

On the other hand, she was keenly aware of the blessing of safety they'd enjoyed throughout the trip. It seemed to her they should show their gratitude by honoring the Sabbath day.

"I'd rather not travel on Sunday, Hank."

There wasn't much to do in Lee Vining, Sabbath or no. They read scriptures together, went for a walk, and napped. After warming up their leftover ribs for lunch, they rode a ways along Tioga Pass, which offered spectacular views of the eastern part of Yosemite.

That evening while Molly did some hand wash and repacked her duffel, Hank pored over the Nevada map.

"I've been checking out various routes," he said. "I've found one that would allow us to bypass Reno."

"Will it save us time?"

"I think so. And we'll be on red or blue roads. That means less traffic."

"Sounds good to me."

The sun was shining when they left Lee Vining the next morning, but clouds had begun rolling in by the time they turned onto the road that took them east onto the high plains of Nevada. Two hours later they stopped for lunch at McDonald's in Silver Springs. Molly shivered as a gust of wind blew dust across the parking lot.

"Did you watch the weather report this morning, Hank?"

"Yeah. There's a big cold front moving in from the northwest. It's supposed to bring rain later in the day or tomorrow. I'm hoping we'll be able to stay ahead of it."

She watched the scudding clouds out the window as they ate, not liking what she saw. She was finishing her drink when Hank said, "Well?"

"Well, what?"

"It's decision time. I-80 or The Loneliest Road in America."

"But we already decided. I-80."

"I think we ought to reconsider, Molly. Taking Highway 50 across Nevada would be a great way to end the trip. It's something not many people can say they've done. Think of the fun you'd have telling people we survived The Loneliest Road in America."

"Nobody would be impressed but Lennie and Chester." Molly glared at him. "I can't believe you're asking me to reconsider."

"It's not as bad as Lennie made it sound. I found a site on the Net that says it's not so lonely after all. And it's much more interesting than I-80. It retraces part of the Pony Express Trail and goes through ghost towns and mining towns—"

"And in between there's a whole lot of nothing, right? Lennie didn't give us that quart of extra gas for no reason." Her eyes narrowed as something occurred to her. "That rat. He gave it to you because he knew you wouldn't refuse his challenge. But there's nothing you need to prove, Hank."

"Maybe there is. To me."

He spread a Nevada map out on the table between them and pointed to Silver Springs. "Here's where we are." Then he ran his finger west to Fallon. "Here's where we get on Highway 50. See these little towns? They're all about a gas tank apart. If we hunker down, we can get all the way to Ely before we stop for the night. In the morning, we'll cross into Utah, and once we're on I-15, it's a straight shot home."

The confident way he drew the route gave him away. She felt a flash of anger. "You set me up. You didn't take this road to bypass Reno. You took it so we'd be almost at the 50 when you talked me into it."

He gave her his most charming smile. "Am I having any success?"

"If we weren't in a public place I'd throttle you!" She was so furious it took some time for her to calm down enough so she could speak in a reasonable voice.

"You're dead set on doing this, aren't you?"

"Unless you absolutely refuse."

She wanted to refuse, but she was afraid that if she did, he would hold it against her—*You kept me from doing what I wanted to do. Again.*

"If it means that much to you, okay." She jabbed the air between them with her index finger. "But you'll have to take the heat for anything that goes wrong."

When they left the restaurant, the sky had changed from partly cloudy to cloudy and the wind had picked up. Molly fished a long-sleeved T-shirt from her duffel and pulled it over the short-sleeved one she was wearing. Then she put her jacket back on and tied a scarf around her neck.

West of Fallon, she got her first look at Highway 50. The empty road stretched into the distance, crossing a desert basin and disappearing into a distant mountain range whose peaks still showed traces of snow. There was a certain bleak beauty about the scene, which lay under a windblown sky.

No wonder they call it The Loneliest Road in America, she thought.

But they weren't completely alone. Every so often vehicles coming from the opposite direction passed them. Partway to Austin, Nevada, they saw a bicycle rider in their lane, loaded down for the long haul.

"There's a brave soul," Hank said over the intercom as they passed the cyclist.

"Brave or crazy. Definitely cold." The wind was becoming sharper and the temperatures brisker as the road took them higher.

When they stopped for gas at the historic mining town of Austin, Molly checked the temperature gauge on the front of the convenience store. It was fifty-eight. *No wonder I'm cold. That's a drop of twenty* degrees from yesterday, and the wind makes it seem even colder. She added a fleece jacket to her layering.

The two hours it took to get from Austin to Eureka, another small mining town, were hard going. Hank had to strain to keep the motorcycle going straight in the buffeting wind that threatened to push them off the road. She could smell moisture in the air. Somewhere rain was falling.

They ordered bowls of chili at a fast-food restaurant attached to a gas station off the highway in Eureka. Sitting across from Hank, Molly could see the lines of exhaustion on his face.

"Are you doing okay?" she asked.

"I'm a little tired. This kind of riding is hard work."

"Why don't we stay here for the night? We've been on the road a long time, and we have to go at least another two hours to make Ely."

"Yes, but we'd be two hours closer to home." He finished his bowl of chili and slouched down in the booth, closing his eyes.

She watched him a moment and then said, "Listen, I'm bushed, and you're in no shape to go any farther. I saw a Best Western when we came off the highway. I'm getting us a room." She stood without giving him a chance to argue. "We'll still get home tomorrow."

She knew she'd made the right decision when he conked out the moment he hit the bed. Before getting ready for bed herself, she stepped into the hallway where she could call Wade and Laurel without disturbing him.

Wade reacted with peals of laughter when she told him where they were. "The Loneliest Road in America? What's gotten into Dad?" Wade said. "He's, like, turning into—"

"One of the Mancuso boys," Molly finished. "Those cousins of his are a bad, bad influence."

"Are you two going to be all right?"

"If we don't get dumped on."

"Ah. You're right in that storm track we've been hearing about, aren't you? Why don't you stay over a day and finish your trip when the weather's better?"

Molly snorted. "How well do you think that suggestion would go over with your dad?"

Laurel also thought they should wait out the storm. "Whatever you do, remind Dad to be extra careful on the last stretch. Most car accidents happen within five miles of home. I imagine the statistic is even grimmer for motorcycles."

It was seven thirty when Hank and Molly woke up the next morning. Unhappy at their late start, Hank was in a mood as he turned the TV to a weather channel and started getting dressed.

The report wasn't what they wanted to hear. The unseasonable cold front had caught up with them. The current temperature was forty degrees and it wasn't going to go higher than the low fifties, with wind gusts of up to thirty-five miles per hour. Rain was likely in the valleys, with snow possible on the highest peaks.

"Lovely," he grunted, turning off the TV.

After eating a hot breakfast in the café next door to their motel, they put on all their layers—heated clothing, padded gear, and rain suits. Then they checked out and loaded Zelda.

An older man sweeping the area in front of the motel door stopped working to watch them. "You've got some miserable riding ahead of you."

"We didn't expect it to be so cold this time of year," Molly said, securing the bungee net.

"It can be cold up here anytime of year. Where are you headed?"

"Home to Salt Lake City."

"Well, I hope you make it over Connors Pass before you get dumped on. It can get downright nasty up there in weather like this."

All the way to Ely, Molly was aware of the storm front dogging them. Dark pockets of rain to the northwest were a warning that they needed to push onward, so they only stopped long enough in Ely to fill Zelda's tank and take care of necessities.

The moment they were back on the highway a gust of wind hit them like a freight train. When Hank leaned steeply into it to keep the bike from shooting off the road, she panicked and shifted in the opposite direction.

"Molly!" His voice snapped through the headset, and she quickly corrected her position. Rain pelted them as the road began curving up the mountain to Connors Pass. The higher they went, the colder it was, and right before they reached the summit—a sign proclaimed it to be 7,722 feet—Molly felt the rain turn to slush. She was plugging in her wired clothing when Hank said, "These rain suits and cold-weather gear are going to be worth every penny we paid for them."

They were both in desperate need of a break when they dropped down the other side of the pass and found a restaurant and gas station at a blip on the road called Major's Place. They warmed their hands holding cups of hot chocolate. Molly sipped hers slowly, not wanting to hurry the moment when they'd have to leave the shelter of the building.

"We should stay here until the storm passes," she said, looking through the rain-blurred window.

"Who knows how long that will be? We need to get back on the road."

"Not until I've had another cup of hot chocolate."

She nursed her second cup as long as she could. It paid off. The rain had almost stopped and the sky was lighter by the time they paid their bill. They made good time on the stretch between Major's Place and the Utah border. Molly couldn't hold back a "Hallelujah!" when they crossed over the state line. "We're almost home!"

Hank made a slow turn in the empty road and pulled off to the side facing back west. "We need proof for Lennie we did this. Can you get a shot of me and Zelda in front of that Welcome to Nevada sign?"

"Sure."

She gave him a happy thumbs-up after taking the photo. *I'm going home, I'm going home,* she sang to herself as she got back on the cycle.

They weren't far into Utah when the sky turned dark again and rain came at them horizontally, blown by a fierce wind. Hank immediately slowed down and switched the headlight to high.

"I don't suppose there's any chance of an overpass out here," Molly said.

"Funny, funny."

A movement to the right caught Molly's attention. "There's

something—" She yelped and gripped her armrests as Hank swerved to miss the low form that ran across the road directly in front of the cycle. A nanosecond of relief was followed by sheer panic as the front wheel hit something with a bang.

Chapter 27

The motorcycle bucked wildly, but somehow Hank managed to keep it upright and get it to the side of the highway. "Are you all right?"

"I think so." Her voice was quaking and her heart threatened to jump out of her chest. "What was that?"

"A coyote, I think. We better get off. I need to check the damage."

She stood with her back to the cold rain as he checked the front wheel.

He swore under his breath. "We hit a big pothole when I swerved. The rim's shot. We're not going anywhere, at least not on this bike."

"What do we do?"

"Wait for a tow truck. Assuming I can get cell service out here and make a phone call."

Shivering, she watched Hank push the Gold Wing forward a little, turn the bent front wheel to the right, and lock it. She'd hoped he'd exaggerated the fix they were in, but now she knew he hadn't—that was how you kept someone from stealing a bike stranded alongside the road.

Turning his back to the rain, he got out his cell phone. Another muttered epithet. "No signal. I'm going to see if I can raise somebody on the CB radio."

No luck there, either.

Molly looked to the west, hoping to see the lights of a car coming toward them. Nothing. No lights coming from the east, either. She scanned behind her, hoping to see something, anything, that would give them some protection. The unfriendly landscape was flat with a few scrubby bushes.

"Are we going to just stand here?"

"What do you suggest?" he asked. "That we walk to Delta?"

"Hey, don't get snippy with me. This was your idea."

She shivered and started bouncing in place, hoping to generate some heat. "Couldn't we at least turn on the motorcycle and plug ourselves in?"

He shook his head. "That would drain the battery in no time flat."

"Who cares, if we're stranded anyway."

He dug a tarp out of the trunk and draped it over their shoulders. "Does that help?"

"Some."

She huddled next to him, shivering with cold and shock. It wasn't supposed to go like this—she'd assumed that resting on the Sabbath had extended their "travel insurance." But God had blown away neither the clouds nor the impulse that brought the coyote out into the rain. She could think of a dozen people in her ward who'd told of times when the hand of God had diverted what would otherwise have been disaster. Why hadn't he done the same for them?

She was immediately ashamed of her thoughts. They could have been badly hurt but weren't. That was a blessing. Feeling chastened, she asked Hank to say a prayer for them.

They held gloved hands while Hank asked for protection and help. Then they waited.

And waited some more.

During Hank's prayer, Molly had had the feeling that all would be well, but it faded as the wind rose, the temperature dropped, and the cold began working its way into her joints. She did a two-step in place and rubbed her hands together. It didn't help much, but moving was better than standing still.

"Sure feels like the loneliest highway now, doesn't it?" she said. "We should have taken I-80."

"Something could have gone wrong there as well."

"At least there's traffic on that road. Someone would have stopped to help us by now."

"Someone will come. Eventually."

Another squall hit. Hard rain pelted them and poured over the edges of the tarp they held away from their faces. With each minute that passed, Molly's frustration and anger grew. Their situation wasn't God's fault, but there were others she could justifiably blame.

"I wonder if Lennie would call this an adventure? If he hadn't been such a braggart, and you hadn't been so stubborn, we'd be almost home right now."

"Think of the story you'll have to tell next Bean Night."

"More like a cautionary tale," she sneered. "Don't do anything stupid, or you'll regret it."

She felt him stiffen. "Are you saying I'm stupid?"

"Taking this road was stupid. We wouldn't be here if you'd been thinking of something besides yourself and your motorcycle and proving to Lennie you were a real Mancuso man."

"I hardly *ever* think of myself," he said angrily, shifting away from her. "In fact, I've spent my whole life thinking of other people."

"You didn't this time."

"Well, maybe I figured it was finally my turn."

"So you *do* feel like life with me and the kids has been drudgery."

Hank made a dismissive gesture. "We plowed this field at Helena's. Do we need to do it again? In the rain? In the middle of nowhere?"

"We wouldn't *be* in the rain in the middle of nowhere if you'd listened to me."

"Don't talk to me about not listening. You're the one who didn't listen when I told you I wanted a motorcycle."

"Excuse me? You never once said, 'Molly, I really miss riding a motorcycle and I'd like to buy one.' I'm not a mind reader, you know."

"That's right, I didn't tell you straight out. Because I knew how you would react, and I didn't want to have to deal with your histrionics."

Molly eyebrows flew upward. "*Histrionics?* Are you saying my fear of motorcycles is nothing but drama to get attention?"

"The accident in Murray happened a long time ago. You've had plenty of time to get over it."

"And when I didn't, you chalked it up to me being an irrational woman. That's just great." Molly stomped out from underneath the tarp and stood shivering in the spit and drizzle.

"Don't be childish, Molly. Come back under here before you get sick."

The way he said it made her furious, but she knew he was right. She stepped under the tarp and stood so she was facing him.

"I am not a child, Hank. And I'm not a helpless woman, either. It's time you stopped acting as if I were one. Like when you told Helena I wouldn't be able to make it to Cucamonga. Why did you do that?"

"You were a wreck that night in Portland. When I talked to Helena I was thinking out loud, making contingency plans. That's what I do."

"Because you didn't think I had it in me to make it through," Molly said angrily.

"You don't have a track record for sticking to things, Molly. Look at the way you've jumped from one hobby to another."

"Well, shame on me!" Molly said. "So I like to try new things. That's no reason for you to think I couldn't go the distance. I had two babies without any anesthetic. I walked the floor with sick kids while you got your eight hours. I made sure Wade got his homework done when he was in danger of failing. And I went to PTA meetings and teacher conferences by myself because you were working late. That's what I call going the distance, buster. You only showed up for parties and private talks with Laurel in your office."

"That's all I did?" Hank's eyes flashed. "Nice to know that's how you see it."

"I guess it depends on where you're standing, doesn't it?"

Hank turned away from her. The silence grew. The only reason Molly broke it was that her teeth were chattering and her toes and fingers were beginning to tingle.

"Give me Zelda's key," she said, tugging on his sleeve. "I'm freezing. I don't care if we burn up all our gas, I'm going to plug myself in."

"I'll start her up if it's really necessary."

Hank ran the engine until they both felt warm, but it didn't last long in the cutting wind. Molly tucked her gloved hands under her armpits. "Did you know you can get hypothermia at fifty degrees Fahrenheit if it's windy and rainy?"

"What class did you learn that in?" Hank said in a snide tone.

"Don't talk about my classes that way. They're important. There was a reason I started taking them, and it wasn't just for me."

"For who then? Not for me."

She felt her jaw drop. "What planet have you been living on? I *have* been taking them for you—so you wouldn't be embarrassed by your uneducated wife, and your children wouldn't have a mother who couldn't help them with their homework. I had the silly idea you would be proud of me."

"If you're trying to make me mad, you're doing a great job, Molly. Is there anything I've done right in the past forty years? Because all I've heard since we broke down is what a big jerk I am, and I don't like it."

"Well, I don't like the way you trivialize everything I've done to make a good life for us," she retaliated. "Or the way you blame me for the responsibilities you chose to carry. You *wanted* to be the one making the decisions, controlling the finances, saving the day. Admit it; you liked being on the pedestal with your little wife gazing adoringly upward."

She saw her words hit Hank like a slap, but she was on a roll and there was no stopping now. "I bet you were like that at work, too. No wonder you haven't known what to do with yourself since your retirement. You found out you weren't so indispensable after all, didn't you?"

Hank's face went white, and he stared at her as if she were a stranger. Then he walked away, dragging the tarp with him.

Molly was almost as stunned at what she'd said as he was. She didn't recognize herself in the woman who had spewed such vitriol. She stood where Hank had left her, not caring that she was exposed to the elements. *It would serve me right if I froze into a solid block,* she thought.

"Molly?" Hank's voice was without inflection. "Come over here and plug in your jacket. I'm going to run the motor for a few minutes to warm you up."

"Thank you," she said humbly.

The rain slowed and stopped, but it remained eerily dark, even though it was early afternoon. Molly's teeth clanked uncontrollably. Her toes burned with cold, and her nose was a lump of ice. She'd given up hope they would be rescued before nightfall when she saw the glimmer of lights coming toward them from the west.

"Look, look!" she cried. "Someone's coming!"

Hank turned on the flashlight and began moving it back and forth to catch the driver's attention. She jumped up and down and waved her hands, not daring to hope. When the pickup slowed down and stopped, Molly closed her eyes and murmured a silent prayer of thanks.

The bewhiskered driver rolled down the passenger window. "Looks like you two could use a lift into Delta. But you'll have to squash up some."

"Do you mind if we bring our bags?" Hank asked.

"There's plenty of room in the back."

When Hank had unloaded Zelda, Molly took a photo of her leaning forlornly on her kickstand. Then they climbed into the cab. It had bucket seats, so Molly had to sit on Hank's lap. He put his arm around her, but there was no mistaking how stiff and unyielding it was.

When Hank told their rescuer, LaVerle Mangus, about the critter that had dashed in front of him chuckled. "You probably had a run-in with the Trickster. He should have been in his den, and you should have been under a roof."

LaVerle recommended a towing company in Delta and told Hank he could find a phone book in the glove box.

The minute his cell phone had a signal, Hank shifted Molly a little to the left and started making calls. By the time they'd reached Delta, he had contacted the towing company, his insurance company, and a Honda dealership and repair shop in Orem that Ronald had recommended.

LaVerle dropped Molly and Hank off at the towing company office, refusing to take any money for his service. "Had to haul myself into town anyways."

Hank hadn't said a word to Molly on the ride in, and he continued to act as if she weren't there as he arranged for Zelda's transport to the repair shop. They ate a late lunch in a Mexican restaurant and then headed north on I-15, not triumphant aboard the motorcycle, but in a rented car. It was a miserable and silent end to what had been a trip filled with delight and discovery.

Heart aching, Molly got as close to the heat vent as her seat belt would allow. She shuddered now and then, as if her body were releasing the memory of being so cold. Or perhaps it was in response to the coldness that had settled between her and Hank. She wasn't sure which.

Because Hank wouldn't talk to her, Molly began to pray.

We're in an awful place. I said some terrible things to Hank. And what he said to me . . . It breaks my heart. Help me to know what to do and say so I don't make things worse before they get better.

She felt a sweet comfort wash over her and a prompting: *The soft word.*

"Hank?" She touched his arm tentatively.

He shook off her hand. "Not now, Molly. I need some time to think."

Chapter 28

Molly's thoughts whirled on the silent ride home. She replayed the accusations and counter-accusations, trying to sort out the truth from the anger that had colored every word. *Did I really say all that? I didn't mean it.*

Yes, I did. But I never should have used it as a weapon.

At that thought a new fear surfaced, one that made her anxiety about motorcycles seem small potatoes. Had she irrevocably damaged her relationship with him? Had she ruined her marriage and their future together?

Round and round she went, searching for certainties amid her confusion. By the time Hank pulled into the garage she had discovered four.

She loved Hank. She loved the life they'd led with all its quirks and stumbling blocks. She loved the life she knew they could have together, assuming they could resolve the conflicts revealed in the last twenty-four hours. She promised herself she'd do whatever was necessary to make that happen. But she knew she could do only so much because—and this was the fourth certainty—after his last statement in the car, the ball was in Hank's court.

It was six that evening when they finally arrived home. Molly was so grateful she would have hugged her house if she'd been able to. She opened doors and windows to air it out while Hank brought in all their luggage and the carry-out they'd picked up for supper.

They ate in virtual silence. Then they each emptied their own bags, and Hank took down a basket of laundry to put in the washing machine. He did that and other tasks necessary after a long absence from home with unsmiling efficiency, speaking only to convey necessary information. Molly responded in ways that invited him to converse with her, but he didn't.

So she retreated to her office to download the last photos of the trip and put them in the West Coast Loop folder in her online storage. She was still in front of her computer when she heard Hank call Wade and then Laurel. "We're home safe," he said, but gave no details and hung up soon each time. Then he called Ronald to tell him the same thing and thank him for recommending the repair shop.

When the phone rang a little later Molly saw from the caller ID that it was Micheline, but she didn't pick up. She wasn't in the mood for chitchat. It rang several more times with neither she nor Hank answering, so she finally unplugged it.

She'd been cold all day, and being home hadn't warmed her up. She took a long shower, standing under the stinging spray until it went from steaming to hot to tepid. Then she put on a pair of fleece sweats and some thick, fuzzy socks and crept under her covers. She wondered when—and then if—Hank would join her.

We've become strangers, she thought. *We've both seen parts of ourselves and each other that aren't very nice. Where do we go from here?*

"Molly?"

Hank had come quietly into the bedroom. He stood leaning against his dresser, arms crossed.

She pushed herself into a sitting position. "Yes?"

"I was really hurt by that comment you made about me liking to be on the pedestal. All I've ever tried to do was be the man I thought I needed to be."

Molly saw her chance for a soft word. "You were. You are. But being on that pedestal, you thought you had to do it all. You took on more than you needed to."

"I did what I thought I had to."

"Yes, and by doing that, you made it too easy for me. I liked looking up to you and being taken care of. I didn't take on some of the responsibilities I could have and maybe should have."

Hank seemed to be softened by her acknowledgment of the

mistakes she'd made. "Give yourself the credit that's due, Moll. You did a great job raising Wade and Laurel. And you made our house into a home I was proud of."

His praise warmed her more than the fuzzy socks and fleece. "You never said you thought so."

He smiled a little, looking at her as if waiting for her to get something.

Then it hit her—she hadn't acknowledged him before, either.

They shared a quiet laugh at the absurdity of the situation. Molly was filled with relief that Hank had taken a step in her direction.

"You know," he said, "I'm proud of being a Mancuso man. Chester and Lennie are good guys. And even though the uncs are old curmudgeons who like their cigars and wine, they've been great role models. It's always been a sore spot that you avoided going to Cucamonga because you don't approve of them."

"Too bad you weren't sitting beside me at Helena's dinner. You would have enjoyed the conversation I had with the old uncs and their wives. We worked everything out. I don't just like them, I love them to pieces." She enjoyed his surprise for a moment before saying, "I wish you could feel the same way about my family."

"I do like your family, Molly, but they make me nervous. They don't take life seriously, but everything always seems to work out for them. Your dad is clueless when it comes to business, but he's kept the theater solvent. I don't get how that works. And entertaining comes so easily to you and your relatives. They sing. They tell jokes. They can play any song you ask them to. And they do it at the drop of a hat. I couldn't do any of those things, even if I practiced. I wish I could fit in better, but I don't know how."

"But *we* fit together, the two of us. That's what I wanted to tell you in the car. Even though it might not seem like it after all the nasty things I said, I love you, and I love our life together."

"Thank you for saying that. I needed to hear it." He put her hand up to his cheek a moment and then kissed it. "I love you too, Miss Molly."

The talk with Hank and a good night's sleep in her own bed did wonders for Molly. She woke feeling rested and hopeful. Her world was still intact. It had some cracks, but maybe that was a good thing. Cracks let light in.

And light changes how we see things, she thought. Maybe the cracks in her relationship with Hank would throw light on the parts shadowed by neglect. Maybe even divine light, the kind she'd experienced in the temple when she'd seen things so clearly.

He was working in his office when she got up—she could hear computer keys clicking. She pulled on her slippers and robe and followed the sound to his office.

"You're at it early," she said, leaning against the door frame.

"It's later than you think." He pointed to the clock on his desk.

"It's ten! Why did you let me sleep so late?"

"I was writing something about the breakdown for the blog, and I lost track of time."

"You wrote about what happened yesterday?" she said, surprised. "What did you say?"

"Nothing embarrassing. You can read it now if you want to, but I suggest you get dressed first. Micheline called earlier and said she and Jan are coming over this morning."

She'd pulled on capris and a T-shirt and brushed her teeth when she heard Jan yodel and Micheline call, "Molly, are you there?"

They swarmed over her when she met them in the entryway. "I'm so glad to see you're back," Micheline said. "And in one piece."

"Me too," Jan said. "I listened for your motorcycle all afternoon yesterday but didn't hear it. I got worried when I saw a strange car in the driveway. What happened? Where's Zelda?"

Molly gave them a rueful grin. "That's quite a story. Hank posted his version of it this morning."

"Show us what he wrote," Micheline said.

"Uh . . ." If Micheline had come alone Molly wouldn't have hesitated. But she wasn't sure she wanted Jan to be reading what Hank had written at the same time she got her first look at it. Then she realized there was a plus side. *If she reads it here, I'll get to tell my side of the story if I need to.*

"Follow me," she said.

The title Hank had given his post was, "Breakdown on The Loneliest Road in America." Underneath it he'd downloaded the photo Molly had taken of poor broken-down Zelda on the side of the road.

"That doesn't look good," Micheline said.

"It wasn't."

She read the blog aloud with her friends looking over her shoulders.

If something can go wrong, it will, and at the worst possible time. For us, it was in the middle of a rainstorm on a road that a *Life Magazine* article warned shouldn't be traveled without a survival kit.

Technically we weren't on The Loneliest Road in America at the time, because we'd already passed over the Nevada state line into Utah. But it was still Highway 50, so I'm saying it counts.

What happened was, I swerved to miss a coyote and hit a big pothole that knocked us off balance and bent the rim of the front tire. One look at it, and I knew we weren't going anywhere. Being stranded was bad enough, but the rain and wind and cold made it even worse.

The conversation we had on the side of the road wasn't very pleasant. I'll just say we weren't at our best and leave it at that. Lucky for us, an old fossil hunter going into Delta picked us up. I had Zelda trucked to a repair place in Orem. (She'll be fixed and back home soon.) Then we rented a car and drove home.

A cousin of mine says that a motorcycle ride is always an adventure. If it goes exactly as planned, that's an adventure. If you have a breakdown, that's an adventure, too. It's all a matter of how you look at things.

Micheline caught Molly's arm when they finished reading. "There's a whole lot more to this than Hank wrote, Molly. Come on, tell us the. Paul Harvey version."

Molly shook her head. "I'm not sure you need to hear it."

"'Discretion is the better part of valor,' and all that?" Jan said.

Molly looked at her with surprise. She'd never heard Jan make a literary reference before.

Jan grinned. "I'm taking a class."

Hearing her signature phrase coming out of Jan's mouth surprised Molly into laughter. "Tell me all about it."

Jan answered all of Molly's questions and then started for the door. "I hate to leave, but I've got dogs to groom. Tomorrow at eight, Micheline?"

"I'll be there."

"You're walking with her these days?" Molly asked after they'd seen Jan off.

"Oh, you know me," Micheline said. "If I don't have someone to walk with, I end up staying home eating potato chips."

"But *Jan?*"

Micheline looked thoughtful. "She's a good companion when you get past the gossip. It's just her way of trying to connect. Lately I've been thinking that if we'd been more welcoming, she wouldn't have had to try so hard."

Molly remembered the shy pleasure with which Jan had accepted the invitation to stay for frosty dogs the day Hank took the grand-kids for a ride. "I've not paid very good attention to Jan, have I? Or to you, either, ever since Hank and I connected with the TRA. I have been pretty wrapped up in myself lately, and you've been a true friend through it all. I'm sorry I ruined our trip together, but thank you again for helping me surprise Hank."

"My pleasure. Why, Molly, you're crying."

Molly wiped her cheeks and tried to smile. "I learned something on this trip about seeing the world with my whole self—heart, head, and spirit. I guess it's time I start seeing all my friends and family that way."

Chapter 29

It was almost noon when Molly went into the kitchen, stomach rumbling. She found Hank standing in front of the open pantry, looking at the empty cereal shelf.

"Are you as hungry as I am?" she asked.

"Starving. Do we have anything to eat in this house?"

She opened the fridge and did a quick check. "The milk we left has gone bad, but I think the eggs and bacon are fine. There's juice in the freezer."

He shook his head and said with mock solemnity, "There's no help for it, Miss Molly. I'll have to make Saturday breakfast on a Wednesday."

Hank left shortly after they'd finished eating, saying he was going to pick up the mail. "I'll get milk and a few basics at the grocery store on the way back."

"And I'll clean the fridge while you're gone."

The first of the phone calls from TRA members came just as Molly started clearing out the questionable items. After that, it was one call after the other, and not only from those who'd been with them on the West Coast Loop ride.

When Nails called, she didn't bother with pleasantries. "I just read Hank's post, Molly. Why didn't you tell me that you and Hank were going to ride Highway 50? I would have met up with you in Reno or Fallon and gone with you."

"I didn't know until the last minute. Believe me, you didn't miss out on anything but a lot of misery."

"But you're all right now?"

"Working on it," Molly said. "How about yourself? I'm been dying to know how things went with you and the Odd Couple after we left."

"That Walker. He has a way of getting to me."

Molly heard a smile in her voice. "What about Howard?"

"He and I had quite the talk. After we got through the hard part, he conceded that he and I never had the spark that Walker and I have. I told him he could have that for himself—it was just a matter of finding the right woman."

"I hope he does," Molly said.

"So do I."

Molly had gone back to cleaning the refrigerator when Hank returned with a white plastic box full of mail, some groceries, and a sober expression.

"A lot of this is junk," he said, handing her the mail, "but I kept it because I know you like to look at the ads."

"I bet there are some bills in there. Do I need to get at them right away?"

"No hurry, but if you want to, you can look through them while I mow the lawn."

What's changed since he left? she wondered, watching him go out the back door. *He has that thinking look.*

A second later, he was back inside. "Molly, why didn't you tell me about working with Nails and Ronald? When I asked you before, you said it was because you wanted to surprise me. But that's not the only reason, is it?"

She hadn't expected such a query from him. It showed thought and insight and a desire to understand her. She'd given him the easy answer when he'd first asked, but now greater honesty was required.

"I was afraid you'd take charge of the process and expect me to get over my fear when and how *you* thought I should. I needed to be in charge of whatever happened myself."

"Hmm. Doesn't sound like you trusted me much. It's that pedestal thing again, isn't it? Me being in charge."

Before she could respond, he went out again. A few moments later she heard the lawn mower start up.

She watched as he began to mow the perimeter of their backyard, unsettled by their exchange. Hank was right. She'd basically said she didn't trust how he would respond if she'd told him the truth. And that sounded like what he'd said when she asked him why he hadn't been up front about wanting a motorcycle. *He didn't trust the way I might respond, either.*

Unable to concentrate on mundane things, Molly went into her office and brought up *Hank and Molly on the Road.* On top of everything else, something in Hank's post was nagging at her.

She read it again and then sat thinking about it, especially the last paragraph. She knew the definitions of the word *adventure*—a series of exciting events, an undertaking involving uncertainty and risk. What she didn't know was which definition Hank had had in mind while he was writing.

When she realized she no longer heard the sound of the lawn mower, she took a pitcher of lemonade and two glasses out to the patio table.

Hank had put the mower into the shed and was getting ready to start the weed whacker. "I've got something cold for you," she called, sitting down at the patio table.

He joined her, took a long swallow from the glass she handed him, and sat back with a sigh. "That was just what the doctor ordered."

"I read your blog again while you were mowing. I like it. Especially the last paragraph about adventure." She paused. "Did you know that word has two definitions? I'm wondering which you were thinking of when you wrote it."

He pursed his lips thoughtfully after she recited them. "The *exciting events* part fits."

"And the *uncertainty and risk* part?"

"I'd say that hits a bit close to home." He refilled his glass from the pitcher. "You know, I spent most of last night lying awake, thinking about you and me and our life together."

Molly gripped her hands together under the table where he wouldn't see. "Good thoughts? Bad thoughts?"

"Uncertain thoughts. About where we're headed from here."

"Not toward a Bruce Aldridge moment, I hope." Molly tried to make it sound like a joke.

Hank let out a bark of surprise. "Why would you think that? It never crossed my mind."

"Then what?"

He took his time before speaking. "It seems to me we have to make a fresh start. Renegotiate the terms of our marriage, this time for the real me and the real you."

Molly was both relieved and intrigued. "According to whom?"

"That's the tricky part, isn't it?" He sighed deeply. "Last night I kept coming back to how I used to complain that Uncle Phil and Uncle Leo put me on a pedestal. I said I hated having to live up to it, but, to be honest, I liked it too. Hank Mancuso, the man in charge." He sounded disgusted with himself. "I don't know if I can stop being that guy."

"I'm not asking you to. That guy has made our life together work all these years." Molly scooted her chair closer to his and took his hand in hers. "All I want is for you to move over and make room for me by your side, where I should have been all along."

He laid his other hand atop hers. "I'd like that."

"You know, I prayed all night long for help in finding our way together again, and God answered my prayer."

He chuckled softly. "Maybe that was what kept me awake, thinking about what kind of husband I've been. The one thing I was sure about was that I didn't want to end up like Bruce. He was unhappy, so he left his wife and family—and he's still unhappy. That's a mistake I won't make. The answers I need are right here. You and me together."

"You and me *talking to each other*," Molly amended. "No more holding back things that could make a difference."

"Agreed. Just don't expect me to do this introspection stuff all the time. I'm still a guy."

"And I'm glad of it," she said with an impish smile.

Later that afternoon the shop called with the message that the motorcycle was ready to be picked up. "I'm going to drive the rental car down right now," he told Molly. "Are you coming with me?"

"Absolutely. I want to ride into Salt Lake Valley behind you on Zelda. It won't be the same as if we'd never had the accident, but we'll be finishing what we started. Together."

Chapter 30

Much changed after Molly and Hank got back from their trip, but much remained the same. She felt it when she had to go to rehearsals every day the last two weeks before the Fourth of July performance. She apologized to Hank for being gone so often, but he told her not to worry about it.

"This tribute to your folks is a big deal," he said. "Spend as much time at the theater as you need to. "

So she did, deeply appreciative of the support Hank was giving her and her family.

Everything was ready the morning of the Fourth. The anniversary scrapbook was complete, including the special section on the Finley Family Theater. Her costume, which looked like a blinged-up square-dance dress, was pressed and ready. She had her violin numbers down cold.

She and Hank weren't expected at the theater until after noon. With nothing left for her to do, she walked from room to room, looking for a task to fill the time.

Oddly, Hank seemed to be as restless as she. "We're quite the pair, aren't we?" she said, laughing. "We should go for a walk, work off some nervous energy."

They were starting down the front steps when Laurel pulled into the driveway. She got out of the car and took something from behind the driver's seat. It was the African violet.

"I thought it was time I brought this back to you," she said, holding the plant out to Hank.

"You didn't have to make a special trip for that," Hank said. He passed the plant on to Molly. "I haven't missed it one bit."

They went into the living room, where Molly put the violet on the plant stand. "Thanks for taking such good care of it. Can you stay and visit?"

"A bit. I want to show you something before it causes a stir at the farm tonight." Laurel held up her left hand to display an engagement ring. "Garrett asked me to marry him, and I said yes. This time we're not going to let anyone get in our way."

Molly shrieked and hugged her daughter, jumping up and down. "I was hoping for this. I'm so happy for you. Hank, come look at her ring."

"Very nice," he said after a brief glance. "Who got in your way before?"

"Do we have to talk about that now?" Molly asked. "We should be celebrating."

Laurel ignored her. "You have to ask?" she said to her father. "You made no secret of the fact that you didn't approve of Garrett. Every time I tried to talk to you about the two of us, you'd say something like, 'He'd make a fine Finley.' It wasn't a compliment."

"I'm sorry I—" Hank began.

"If you weren't saying something like that, you turned the conversation to what it would take to become a successful lawyer. It was like you were telling me I had to choose between Garrett and getting my law degree."

"I'm sure he didn't mean it that way," Molly said. "Did you, Hank?"

"Of course not. I could tell you were distracted, Laurel, and I thought you needed a reminder of what was at stake."

"That's not how it came across to me."

Molly had been following their exchange with increasing distress. "Come on, you two. Let's not ruin a wonderful moment."

"I need to get to the bottom of this, Molly," Hank said. He turned back to Laurel. "Are you saying that's why you broke up with Garrett?"

"I had reasons of my own, but that's what tipped the scales. All my life I've wanted to please you, and I've followed your advice because I trusted your judgment. But I regret following it that time."

Hank shook his head. His shoulders, normally so square and strong, slumped in disbelief. "I'm sorry if what I said ruined things for you. I only wanted you to be happy."

"I *am* happy. And I'm absolutely sure about Garrett and me. That's what I came to tell you."

"Then everything's good," Molly said hopefully. "Right?"

But Laurel wasn't done yet.

"What I'm not sure of is what to expect from you, Dad. When you retired, I thought you'd find the next purposeful thing to dedicate your life to. Instead, it was the adventure-a-day thing. Then the motorcycle. I lived my life looking to you for an example, and all of a sudden, presto chango, there was an alien living in your skin."

That's what has been bothering Laurel since Hank's retirement party! Molly looked at Hank and could almost see his synapses firing as he put together everything he'd just heard.

"You're right," he said slowly. "I'm no more the person I was when you first fell in love with Garrett than you are." His shoulders straightened and his expression cleared. "We've both changed, and I, for one, am glad of it. I want you to know you can still trust me to love you and give the best advice I can, but it's time you trusted yourself and your own instincts first."

Now Laurel was the speechless one. "Huh. That's what I wanted to hear, but I didn't expect I would."

"You might have, if you'd known about the changes your dad and I have gone through since our big trip." Molly put her arm around Hank's waist. She was immensely proud of him.

For the first time since her arrival, Laurel sat down. "I think you'd better tell me."

There was a new feeling of love and openness between the three of them after Molly and Hank had spoken frankly about what they'd learned about themselves and each other and their new commitment.

"Amazing," Laurel said when they'd told her the whole story. "I was angry when I came, but now I'm glad things happened the way they did. I think Garrett will be getting a much better wife." A little smile played on her lips. "And much nicer in-laws."

She was about to leave when she said, "Oh, there's something I wanted to show you." She motioned them over to the African violet. "Look down at the center. See all those tiny buds?"

"My goodness. What have you been doing?" Molly asked.

"Besides making sure it got the right kind of light? I watered it, fed it, talked to it."

"I'll need to keep that up."

"No. I will," Hank said.

"You?" Molly didn't try to cover her surprise.

"Lori gave it to me. Being responsible for it will remind me of what I need to do to take care of all my relationships."

Will wonders never cease? Molly thought. *And it's all because of a motorcycle named Zelda. If I'm not careful, I'll start thinking of her as the family's fairy godmother.*

⌒

The lobby and grounds of the Finley Family Theater had taken on a festive air by the time cars started coming up the lane for the chuck wagon dinner at five. Molly and her sisters had draped the lobby with bunting and created displays featuring the scrapbook and other items of family and theater history. Hank and Hope's husband had affixed flags to every fence post along the Finley property and up the lane.

The family had their own dinner in the great room of Roy and Bess's cabin. Partway through the meal, Bess yelped as she noticed Laurel's ring, and extravagant Finley-style congratulations came from all sides. Molly hated to leave when it was time for the performers to meet in the green room with Heather and Wade to go over last-minute changes.

"We've got a full house," Wade said after a rundown. "And we've got a great program. Let's go out there and have some fun."

The night started with a foot-stomping round of fiddling, accompanied by the piano and a three-piece band. The rest of the program went without a hitch, and before Molly knew it, it was time for the tribute. After a slide show of family and theater history, several groupings of family members young and old performed together, and Roy ended the evening by serenading Bess with, "I Love How You Fiddle, but Don't Fiddle with My Heart."

Molly was flying high when all the performers crowded on stage to take their bows. *What a night,* she thought, waving to Garrett and Laurel, who were in the second row next to Nails and Walker. They all waved happily back.

She was expecting the curtain to fall when Wade stepped in front of the microphone. "I bet you thought the evening was over, didn't you? Well, we have one more song for you."

He motioned to the stagehands, who brought out an electronic keyboard and positioned it on its stand in front of the microphone.

They left without plugging it in. Molly was trying to get someone's attention so that could be rectified when Wade said, "Mom, would you step over here, please?"

She hesitated. "What's going on?"

"It's all cool." Taking her arm, he escorted her to the front left of the stage. "You don't have to do a thing. Just stand right here."

Returning to the microphone, he said, "Ladies and gentlemen. I would like to present my father, Hank Mancuso."

"What?!" Astonished, Molly watched Hank walk across the stage.

He looked terrified as he stood in front of the microphone, tapped it to see if it was on, and then cleared his throat.

"Recently, my wife Molly did something for me that was truly amazing. She overcame her fear so she could take a cross-country trip with me on my motorcycle.

"I wanted to do something to show her how much I appreciated that. I thought of getting flowers, but that seemed a little lame, considering the time and effort she gave. A cruise came to mind, but as nice as that would be, it wouldn't take much effort on my part either.

"So I asked myself, What does Molly love to do that gives me the willies? The answer was simple: sing. So here I am."

Molly clapped her hands, biting her lower lip to keep the welling tears from falling.

He flashed a smile at her. Then he wiped his hands on his pants and laughed nervously. "I have to tell you, I'm sweating bullets up here."

Molly could feel how the audience was rooting for him. She was too. *I can't believe he's doing this!*

Hank motioned to Hayden, who came to stand beside him, holding his own microphone. Then he cleared his throat a couple of times and nodded to the piano player, who began a spirited intro à la Little Richard while Hank pounded on the unplugged keyboard as if he were doing the playing.

Then he pulled the mic toward himself and started singing "Good Golly, Miss Molly," with lyrics specially written for the occasion. Molly smiled when she heard "motorcycle mama with her red nails on" in the rewritten refrain. At the point in the song where Little Richard hit a falsetto high note, Hayden supplied it, to the audience's delight.

Was she laughing or crying or a little of both? Molly didn't know. She'd never loved Hank as much as at that moment. When he belted out the last note and the piano player finished with a flourish, she threw herself into his arms and kissed him full on the lips. That got the biggest round of applause of all.

Laughing, Wade took the microphone from Hayden. "That ends our show, folks. We hope to see you again soon. Good night!"

"I can't believe you did that," Molly said to Hank when the curtain fell. "That's the best, most wonderful, most fantastic gift you've ever given me."

"Are we even now?" he asked, grinning.

"I don't know. If I keep riding, doesn't that mean you have to keep singing?"

She laughed when his face fell. "Don't worry. You don't have to if you don't want to."

Epilogue

The first day in August, Molly and Hank loaded up Zelda to ride to Idaho Falls for that year's national TRA rally. By now, they were old hands at packing for a trip. In between the Loop trip and the six-day August rally, they'd gone on several short rides and a longer temple ride to Denver. Where they'd learned to plug in for heat on Highway 50, they learned how to use their cool vests while on the road to Denver. Every time they took a trip, they discovered a new item that made touring more pleasant and learned something new about each other as well.

Sometimes what they learned made them laugh. Sometimes it required a shift to maintain their new balance. But the acceptance they offered each other made their relationship a safe haven in which they both expanded and flourished.

They weren't aware of how much they'd changed until they arrived at Tautphaus Park in Idaho Falls, just one of a long string of motorcycles coming from all around the country, and found some acquaintances from Oregon among the TRA-ers gathering at the check-in point.

Linda Sanchez gave Molly a warm hug. "You and Hank look like you're on a second honeymoon. What's your secret?"

"No secret. Part motorcycle, part miracle, and a whole lot of hard work."

"Whatever it is, you should bottle it."

The big surprise came as Molly, Hank, and the West Coast Loop group were admiring the cycles parked along the street. There, far down the line, was a cycle with swoopy aqua and teal fenders like Gus's Indian. Dusty's unmistakable Darth Vader machine was parked next to it.

"Look, look!" she cried, grabbing Hank's arm. "Gus and Dusty are here. Those are their Indians!" She pestered Ronald, who stood a head taller than the rest of them, to see if he could spot them.

They were all scanning the crowd when someone called, "Hey, Ronald. Hank." Gus and Dusty had found them.

Molly was delighted when she heard that Annabelle had welcomed Gus with open arms. He was living in a small apartement behind the store and was enjoying spending time with her and Dusty and his family.

"Looks like Dusty got you to join the TRA," Doyle said, pointing to a patch on Gus's vest.

Gus grinned. "I turned out to be more of a group kind of guy than I thought."

"You never know when you'll learn something new about yourself," Hank said.

Molly gave his arm a squeeze. "That's for sure."

She didn't think anything could top that exciting beginning, but she was wrong. The temple session on Saturday had hints of what she'd experienced in Portland, and at the group's testimony meeting on Sunday, the Spirit called her to share what she'd experienced. It was something she hadn't done for a long time.

The days following were filled with activities, rides to Craters of the Moon, Mesa Falls, and Grand Teton National Park, with mandatory ice cream stops, special speakers, and entertainment. Hank and Molly were trying out every game and treat at the carnival when Enid Carter grabbed Molly's arm and pulled her to where Merrill's blue trike was parked next to a gentleman on a white trike.

"That's Frank Reese," Enid said, "the man who started the TRA. Merrill and I want you to take a photograph of us with him and his wife, Catherine."

Molly found out enough to write a book while she shot the two couples in a series of poses. Her favorite was of the women sitting in the passenger seats with the men standing at their sides. When she found Hank again, she said, "That Frank Reese is amazing. He's in his eighties, and he and his wife rode their three-wheel Gold Wing all the way from Oklahoma."

"Maybe we'll be doing the same thing when we're their age," he said.

When Molly wasn't taking photos with her camera, she was storing up images in her heart. She was in a tender mood when she and Hank gathered with their TRA chapter for dinner before the Tuesday night dance.

Jeri Connelly sat next to Molly. "How are things going with Laurel and Garrett's wedding plans?"

"All we know is the date," Molly said. "September twelfth. They're doing all the planning, which is just fine with me. But I did get to go dress shopping with Laurel. We had the most fun, and we found a dress that suits her perfectly. "

"Too bad," Nails said. "Walker and I were considering that date for ourselves."

Exclamations erupted up and down the table.

"But isn't that a CTR ring?" Molly said, pointing at Nails's left hand. It looked to her like the simple silver-tone rings with the acronym for Choose the Right that she'd given to each of her kids when they were little. Then Nails extended her hand closer, and Molly gasped. The ring was nothing like the ones her children had worn—it was a custom version in platinum with sparkling baguettes on either side of the CTR shield.

"I was ready to buy a diamond of ridiculous size, but this is what she wanted," Walker said.

Nails leaned against him, contented and happy. "It's perfect. It's my I-Chose-the-Right-One ring."

Later, Hank led Molly onto the floor of the cultural hall in a local church building. It was full of dancers. "It's good we're getting some practice," Molly said, "since we're going to be dancing at Laurel's reception. She and Garrett are taking lessons in anticipation of the first dance of the evening."

They danced, visited with old and new friends, and danced some more. Then they walked hand in hand out under the starry sky. It was a beautiful night. There was a balmy breeze, and the running sprinklers had filled the cool air with the smell of wet concrete and grass.

"Do you realize it's been almost a year since you retired?" Molly said.

"Hard to believe, isn't it? A lot has happened since then."

"No kidding." She rested her head on his shoulder. "I hope you don't have any surprises up your sleeve for the coming year."

He chuckled. "No. All I want to do is spend more time with my mom and Joseph and the rest of the Cucamonga clan. Get to know Garrett better. Laurel, too, for that matter. I'd like to do more with Wade and Heather's kids. Hayden will be in Scouting soon. I think it would be fun to help him get his badges."

"It sounds like you're going to be busy," she murmured.

"I'm hoping you'll be doing a lot of that with me. Spending time with you comes first."

Everything he'd said was about being with people and building relationships, Molly noticed. It fit right in with what had been on her mind.

"Speaking of your folks, I think we ought to offer to stay with Ruth and Joseph for a couple of weeks, so Helena and Russ can have a real vacation. We should have been doing that all along."

"You're right. If you'd consider it, I'd like us to spend an extended amount of time there once or twice a year as long as Mom and Joseph are still with us."

"I'm not sure how that would work, but I'm willing."

"I really appreciate that, Miss Molly. And if I haven't told you yet, I'm grateful for every letter you wrote and every phone call you ever made to them since we got married. I really dropped that ball when you handed it off to me."

He bent to kiss her, and they stood in each other's arms a long time. Then Molly asked, "Anything else?"

Hank smiled slightly. "I wouldn't say this to just anyone, but I'd like to live the way I ride my bike. Being alert and aware of what's around me. Experiencing life as it comes at me. Leaning into the curves."

Molly clasped her arms around his waist, resting in the warmth and security of his embrace. "There'll be plenty of curves on the road ahead, no doubt. We can lean into them together."

About the Authors

Real life sisters Nancy Anderson and Caroll Hofeling Morris first collaborated on the popular series *The Company of Good Women*. Carroll is also the author of *The Broken Covenant* and *The Merry Go Round*. She and her husband, Gary, have four children. They enjoy life in the retirement community of Green Valley, Arizona. Nancy and her husband, Jim, have five children and eleven delightful grandchildren. They are residents of Sandy, Utah.

To contact Nancy and Carroll go to www.virtualsisters.net or crustyoldbroads.blogspot.com.